The wife is always the last to know?

Ryan held a smiling baby in his arms, the pink-frocked tot waving plump arms and cooing charmingly.

"And who is this?" Amanda asked, surprised but enchanted by the baby grabbing her fingers. "Is she your niece?"

Ryan didn't return her smile. "This is Brianna. My daughter."

Amanda stared at him.

He met her gaze challengingly. "Lost in your thoughts?"

"Don't you think I have a right to be?" She couldn't believe this guy! "How could you just forget to mention that you have a daughter?"

"Hey, I'm sure you didn't tell me everything about yourself." Ryan glared at her over the baby's curly brown hair.

"No, I concealed the fact that I'm an escaped transvestite homicidal maniac." Amanda slapped her hands on her hips. "But I didn't leave out something as important as a child!"

ABOUT THE AUTHOR

A hopeless romantic, Bonnie K. Winn naturally turned to romance writing. This seasoned author of historical and contemporary romance has won numerous awards, including having been voted one of the Top Ten Romance Authors in America, according to *Affaire de Coeur*.

Living in the foothills of the Rockies gives Bonnie plenty of inspiration and a touch of whimsy, as well. She shares her life with her husband, son and spunky Westie terrier, who lent his characteristics to Mackie in *The Daddy Factor*.

Bonnie welcomes mail from her readers. You can write to her c/o Harlequin, 300 E. 42nd St., New York, NY 10017.

Books by Bonnie K. Winn

HARLEQUIN AMERICAN ROMANCE
624—THE NEWLYWED GAME
646—WHEN A MAN LOVES A WOMAN

THE DADDY FACTOR

Bonnie K. Winn

Harlequin Books

TORONTO • NEW YORK • LONDON
AMSTERDAM • PARIS • SYDNEY • HAMBURG
STOCKHOLM • ATHENS • TOKYO • MILAN
MADRID • WARSAW • BUDAPEST • AUCKLAND

For my mother, who made me believe wishes
can come true and who, along with my father,
made me believe in myself.

ISBN 0-373-16680-X

THE DADDY FACTOR

Printed in U.S.A.

Prologue

Stanton, California

Amanda Thorne regarded her circle of friends with affection...and a bit of exasperation. They had been inseparable all through high school. Even though their lives had led them in different directions, when they got together, they instantly felt a timeless bond. This reunion, their fifth, had been one of their best so far. Until the subject of husbands had come up.

"So, is it a pact?" Madcap Suzy Burns was relentless. Tossing her blond curls, she turned on her friends with a vengeance, her signature laughter spilling into the hotel corridor. "No matter what Gloria Steinem says?"

Amanda laughed, thinking they were all still joking about Suzy's dare. It had begun as a jest as they all clowned around about the importance of husbands in their single, independent life-styles.

Linda Danvers pirouetted on the plush mauve carpet, the movement more the result of champagne than talent. "I'm game. If I can't find a husband before our fifteen-year reunion, I'll hang up my license."

Candy Johnson arched one perfectly formed brow. Always the acknowledged beauty of the group, she also possessed an acerbic wit. "I didn't know you had to have a license to hunt for a husband."

"It's big game, *dahlin*," Linda chirped, her smile more than a tad on the sloshy side.

Amanda rolled her expressive green eyes, a smile tipping her lips upward, unknowingly transforming her seemingly plain features into something striking, remarkable. "I think this would qualify as the hunt of the century."

"So we're in agreement," Suzy insisted again.

Amanda glanced at her in surprise. "You're not serious?"

"Deadly, my dear. We have ten years to snag world-class husbands. Frankly, if the bet goes on any longer than that we'll be waving goodbye to our early thirties and the prospects will be...shall we say...dim?"

World-class husbands. The notion sent an unexpected ripple of apprehension through Amanda, but she shook it away. After all, Suzy was talking ten years from now. That was practically an eternity. Look how much had changed in the previous five years since they had graduated together from Stanton High. College, entry into the business world, the transformation from girls to women, her own move to the big city.

Amanda swallowed any objection since the others were all in smiling agreement. She glanced up at the Welcome Graduates banner that graced the arched doorway of the hotel ballroom. In ten years another banner would be welcoming them. And by then they would all be married women. Amanda glanced at the dear, familiar faces of her friends. And wondered suddenly about the men they all would choose, thankfully remembering that the time to find her own husband stretched out endlessly.

Chapter One

Ten Years Later, San Francisco

Amanda Thorne crossed her legs at the ankle, resting them on the steamer trunk that served as her coffee table. Staring at the invitation in her hand, she wondered how it could possibly be time for another reunion. *The* reunion. The one that would decide the winners *and losers* in their wager.

MacDougall, an energetic West Highland terrier and her constant companion, stood pleadingly by her feet, waiting for permission to join her on the sofa.

"Okay, MacDougall. You know I'm a pushover. Jump up."

The dog obeyed quickly, settling next to her side.

"I'm not sure what the point of teaching you to stay off the furniture is. You spend as much time up here as I do."

MacDougall stretched out lazily in response.

Amanda stared again at the invitation to her class reunion. She'd received the invitation more than a month earlier, but being somewhat forgetful she'd stashed it in the rolltop desk. It had remained there until tonight when she'd being looking for some inventory sheets and stumbled on the invitation. "Where have ten years gone to?" she wondered aloud.

Since MacDougall didn't answer, Amanda sighed in reply to her own query. What had seemed close to a millennium at the time was now at hand. And she remained disgustingly single.

"This is going to be some fun reunion," she muttered. Amanda could just imagine the looks of speculation, and no doubt pity, on her friends' faces. Because each one of them had married. The years had brought their wedding invitations, one by one.

Even though building her business in antiques and collectibles had been rewarding, Amanda knew it had had its costs. There hadn't been time to develop relationships. In truth, there had scarcely been time for even casual dating. Which left her no one to accompany her to the reunion. Groaning, she slid deeper into the couch. How had she gotten into this fix?

Closing her eyes, Amanda did something she seldom indulged in. She made a wish.

She wished for a husband.

Her eyes flew open as she heard a distinctive thud. Rising from the couch, a curious MacDougall beside her, she stepped over to the bookcase and stared in surprise at the hardwood floor. A book she'd recently purchased lay sprawled on the oak planks.

She stifled amusement and surprise as she stooped over to retrieve it. *How to Find Your Perfect Mate* rested in her hands. It had been a stupid impulse buy. When she'd received the reunion invitation, she had bought the book in a desperate moment. It was an idiotic notion, thinking she could produce a husband, a world-class one at that, in a few weeks. It wasn't as though she had a boyfriend she was hoping would surprise her with an engagement ring. Realizing she would never have the time or courage to implement the book's suggestions, she'd shoved it into the back of the shelves.

Turning the book over quizzically, she wondered how it had managed to fall. She glanced at the other books still sitting where they had been placed, all neatly aligned. Perhaps there had been a small tremor. After all, this was San

Francisco. But why would just one book fall? Glancing around, she saw that everything else was in place. And she hadn't felt anything. Still...

Suddenly remembering her wish, she felt the hair on her neck rise. Maybe this was what she'd gotten in response to her wish—a manual on how to track down Mr. Right.

MacDougall whined and Amanda bent down to pet him. "I just wasted one of my wishes, Mackie. And all I got for my trouble was this stupid book."

Amanda had always believed a person had so many wishes in a lifetime. She also believed that most people wasted them on foolish things like wishing a traffic light would change, or that an elevator would arrive quickly. Feeling that way, she'd carefully guarded her own wishes. Until now.

Standing up, Amanda reshelved the book. "Since Prince Charming isn't going to burst through my doorway tonight, I guess it's safe to drag out my fuzzy bathrobe and make a pot of tea."

MacDougall cocked his head in a beguiling manner.

"And Milk-Bones for you, of course."

SUNLIGHT PUSHED insistently through the drapes, but Amanda didn't even stir. Since she'd rediscovered the reunion invitation, she'd spent several restless nights dreaming about weddings and mythical grooms.

Through the deep fog that always accompanied Amanda's mornings, she heard a distinct ringing. Fumbling, eyes still closed, she whacked repeatedly at the alarm clock, but the ringing continued. She groped across the nightstand, picking up the telephone, ending the annoying sound.

Her friend Suzy's voice rippled into her ear. "Morning, Sunshine! It's Suzy. I already called your shop and the assistant said you'd be home, and I wanted to catch you before I left."

"Uh-huh," Amanda mumbled, not yet even beginning

to focus. Mornings were her biggest weakness—or rather the fog she spent them in.

"I thought maybe you were avoiding me. I haven't heard anything from you since the reunion invitations were mailed. You *did* get your invitation, didn't you?"

Amanda mumbled another sound of agreement.

"Good!" Suzy chirped. "Then I'm sure you haven't forgotten what reunion this is—the one where we all show up with our world-class husbands!"

The mumbled response on Amanda's end was scarcely intelligible.

Suzy didn't seem to mind, nonchalantly interpreting the mutter. "So, you *know* we're all bringing our husbands...."

"That's right," Amanda murmured as she reached for her pillow.

Suzy's voice suddenly filled with a knowing, thready excitement. "You got married on us, didn't you?"

Burrowing deeper into the warmth of the covers, Amanda's reply was something between an inaudible nod and grunt.

"I knew it!" Suzy exclaimed. "I figured you were just holding out on us. You've known when we all got married because of the wedding invitations we sent you." The volume of Suzy's voice escalated. "That's it! You eloped, you little devil. No invitation, no warning! I gotta hand it to you, Amanda. Pretty clever. You've met our husbands and yours will be a complete mystery."

Amanda's grip on the phone loosened as she pulled the quilt up farther.

But Suzy didn't seem to notice. "Even though you were a sensible girl, you always did have an impulsive streak. I love it! Well, I can't wait to see you again *and* meet your husband. I do enjoy a man of mystery. Well, Sunshine, I have to go. Early appointment at the stylist. Great talking to you."

The buzzing as she disconnected didn't get through to Amanda any more than the conversation had. Instead, the phone slipped off the side of the bed as Amanda nestled into the comfortable mound of quilts, her sleep still undisturbed.

Three hours later, Amanda emerged from her fog, saw the time on the digital alarm clock and vented her displeasure. As she crawled from the nest of rumpled linens in her bed she saw the disconnected phone on the floor. So that was why her assistant hadn't called to wake her. Of course, Amanda knew that once asleep she was nearly impossible to waken. And even once awake, she was pretty useless for the first part of the morning.

Amanda stood, heading toward the shower and coffee pot, not necessarily in that order. As she spooned coffee into the basket she'd forgotten to line with a filter, she had a strange nagging feeling. More like a vague recollection. It seemed that she'd talked to her high school friend Suzy; someone she spoke with only once every few months. Had she called? Or had Amanda dreamed the conversation? With all her disturbing dreams this week, it was more likely a dream, not a real call.

Fitting the basket into the coffee maker, she pushed the start button, having forgotten to add any water. Nodding her head, Amanda headed for the shower. She was sure of it. It had all been a dream.

A WEEK LATER, Amanda stared at the note from Suzy, a sick feeling settling in her stomach. Suzy's note replayed their conversation, ending with her excitement at seeing Amanda soon *and meeting her husband.*

Apprehension filled her as she shakily dialed Suzy's number. She almost wished her friend wouldn't answer. But Suzy's bubbly tone vibrated across the lines.

Screwing up her concentration, Amanda began to plunge into her explanation, but Suzy cut her off.

"I'm so glad you called. Since I talked to you, I've gotten in touch with all the others—told them you had an ace up your sleeve, that you weren't giving up on the wager.

Now we've got a second bet going—over who's most likely to win!''

"But—"

"I told Linda and Candy about your elopement, and they agreed with me that it's just like you—and so romantic! This must be some guy if you've waited to surprise us."

Amanda tried desperately to get a word in to the nonstop flow. "I really didn't—"

"I know. You're being modest about him—that's so like you, but it just ups the tension that much more. After all, we'll be meeting him this weekend—but I have to admit I admire your technique. This guy must be something. You must really want to win the world-class husband competition. Candy's ready to pop—you know how she is. She just *assumed* she'd won. Not that Linda and I were ready to concede—"

"Suzy, you've got to listen—"

"And I told all our friends, too. Sorry to scoop your surprise, but I couldn't resist. Everybody from school is thrilled for you—and they can't wait to meet Mr. Right."

"You told everybody?" Amanda managed to ask in a strangled voice.

"Sure—practically the whole senior class. It's the best part of being on the reunion committee. I get to catch up with all our old friends. And you know me...I never could keep a secret. Now, I'd better ring off...."

"But—"

"We'll have all the time in the world to talk next weekend at the reunion. We're all about to bust with anticipation."

"Suzy, I have to tell—"

"Save it for the reunion, Sunshine. I'll see you then."

Left with only the dim buzzing of a disconnected line, Amanda stared at the blasted telephone. The darned things shouldn't be allowed to ring before noon. Then she wouldn't be in all this trouble. What in the world was she going to do? And, more to the point, how was she going to produce Mr. World Class in less than two weeks?

AMANDA PUSHED THE DOOR to her apartment shut with a booted foot, bending over to greet an enthusiastic Mac-Dougall. Every evening the dog burst with lightning speed through the pet door that opened in from the garden. But today even MacDougall's enthusiasm wasn't contagious.

Finding no solution to Suzy's warped version of the truth, and suffering through days filled with frustrating mishaps and bungled deliveries, Amanda was tired and out of sorts. Mostly because the reunion loomed on the horizon. Precious days had ticked away, with no changes, no brilliant ideas, and no way out. Short of a miracle, this weekend she would have to attend the reunion alone and endure her friends' speculation.

The doorbell rang suddenly and insistently. Amanda considered ignoring it, but MacDougall, eager to protect his territory, was already barking madly.

Glancing out the peephole, all she could see was some wild, longish dark hair and a pair of broad shoulders. If this was the new maintenance man, he would just have to find another time to fix her dishwasher.

Opening her door, preparing to tell him just that, she was cut off as he whirled around and then barked out, "Amanda Thorne?"

"Y—yes," she stuttered, astonished at the anger on the man's face. Nervously she glanced behind her, glad of MacDougall's defensive posture, despite his small, compact size.

"I'm Ryan West," he bit out in a challenging tone.

"Yes?" she questioned, debating whether to slam the door and throw the lock.

"Is that all you have to say?" he taunted.

She pushed the door a few inches in his direction. "I'm not sure what you're expecting me to say, Mr.... Is it West?"

"You know it is, lady. Pretty hard to put yourself on my bank records without knowing my full name."

Pure astonishment froze her in place. "I'm sorry, Mr. West. You're obviously mistaken. Now, if you'll excuse me…"

"There's no excuse for what you've done, *Miss* Thorne."

Convinced he was a nut case, she made a gesture toward closing the door, but the man deflected her move, instead stalking past her and into her living room.

Her mind filled immediately with visions of assailants, psychos and every bogeyman she'd ever conjured up in her years of living alone. Trying to remember if she was taking the right tack with the intruder, she forced her voice to sound commanding, although she knew she hadn't a prayer of controlling over six feet of barely contained male rage. "Look here, Mr. West—"

"You've found the wrong mark this time, lady. You may have gotten away with this before." His dark, forbidding gaze swept over her expensively decorated apartment, full of pieces that would eventually find their way to her shop. "Apparently you've been very successful at this scam. But not this time."

"I don't know anything about your bank records and—"

"Then how did you go about having yourself placed on them as Mrs. Ryan West?"

Amanda discarded the notion of making it past the man and out her front door. His quick movements assured her she would never make it. "You're making a big mistake, Mr.—"

"No. You're the one who's made the mistake. But you're going to rectify it."

"I can assure you that I've never called myself Mrs. West," she replied in exasperation. "Since I've never been married, I haven't called myself Mrs. Anybody."

"And it's not your information that's now polluting my bank records?" he challenged again.

"Of course not. I don't know where you got this crazy idea, but you're wrong!" Anger added volume to her voice, still, the sound of the doorbell startled them both.

Releasing an exasperated sigh, she flung open the door.

A bored-looking young man in his late teens greeted her. "Delivery for Mrs. Ryan West."

Amanda couldn't help it. Her mouth fell open with disbelief as Ryan swore beneath his breath and then turned to her triumphantly.

"What a surprise, *Mrs.* West." Ryan threw the words at her, not bothering to hide his disgust.

"This isn't what it seems," she began, then glanced more closely at the package the young man handed her. It was labeled Mrs. Ryan West, with Amanda's address typed clearly beneath the name. She knew she was forgetful, but not this forgetful.

Amanda looked up at the deliveryman. "I'm not signing for this."

The young man consulted the clipboard, then shrugged. "Doesn't require a signature. See ya."

Before she could protest, the deliveryman spun around and disappeared.

Which left her with the forbidding Mr. West. Strange how he dominated the apartment, a place that always seemed more than spacious. His body was lean, yet it seemed to fill the living room.

Those darkly condemning eyes had summed her up and apparently found her lacking. And ridiculously, now Amanda felt *she* was on the defensive.

"So you don't know anything about how your name appeared on my bank records?" he asked caustically, everything in his tense stance demanding an answer. "If you wanted to pull this off, you shouldn't have listed Thorne on the line marked maiden name."

She thought quickly. "Where do you bank?"

He issued another muffled curse. "As though you don't know."

She stared pointedly at him, her silence effectively repeating her request.

"Merchants Bank," he snapped.

A light dawned. "I just opened a new account there." Relief started to filter through her. "Apparently my information has gotten mixed up with your wife's. Clearly it's a case of crossed wires."

His expression remained cold, as chilled as his voice. "I don't *have* a wife."

She scrabbled in her mind for something, anything, that made sense and came up empty. "Then I guess you'll have to contact the bank and ask *them* how they've messed up our account information."

"You're cool, I'll grant you that." His rugged features continued to show his contempt as he studied her face.

Beginning to feel like a mugshot on a police blotter, Amanda squirmed. "Apparently we're victims of the computer age," she argued. Glancing at the package still resting in her hands, she tried to thrust it at him. "This must be yours." His hands remained firmly at his sides, and she was left awkwardly holding the box.

"Aren't you going to open it?" he asked, watching her carefully.

She didn't want to, but she hadn't missed the challenging note in his voice. Reluctantly she tore open the brown wrapping paper. A small inner box distinctly labeled "Checks" rested inside. Her stomach churned uneasily as she lifted the lid. Personalized checks reading Mrs. Ryan West along with her address were inside. Uneasily, she cleared her throat. "As I said, you'd better ask the bank."

The dark slash of his brows rose as he took in the contents of the package. "I've already done that, Miss Thorne. Or whatever your name is. I had a complicated bank loan in process. The more I protested that there was no Mrs. West, the closer I came to having to scrap the loan and start over." He gestured to the checks she held. "Because of whatever con game you're playing, I have only one choice.''

Amanda tried to look nonchalant, even though she was compelled by his overwhelming presence and the command in his voice. ''And that is?''

''You have to sign the papers, Miss Thorne.''

''What papers?''

''My loan agreement.''

Amanda blinked, then shook back her thick mane of golden strawberry curls. ''You're not serious? You waltz in here, a total stranger, accuse me of pretending to be your wife, and you think I'm fool enough to sign bank papers? What, and then you run off to Acapulco with the proceeds and I'm on the hook for the money? I don't think so, Mr. West. Being a businesswoman, I'm not quite as gullible as you think. You had me going at first, but no, I'm not *that* stupid.''

''Signing papers as Mrs. Ryan West hardly makes you liable,'' he pointed out coolly. ''Since you're not Mrs. West.''

Good point. But she didn't want to admit that to him. ''At any rate, the only sensible plan is to drop your current loan and initiate a new one.''

''At almost any other time I would agree. However, at the moment, I have a highly leveraged deal in progress. By the time I restart and complete the loan process, the deal will collapse. And right now I can't afford to let that happen.''

Amanda realized with sudden insight that it galled the man to have to deal with her when he considered her to be a con artist. An untenable position for someone so arrogant.

MacDougall nudged her knee and she glanced down at him absently, petting his head. As her glance swept upward, it flickered past the hall table. *How to Find Your Perfect Mate* was angled on the table, staring back at her. Her eyes continued traveling back toward her guest when it registered. She jerked her gaze back to the manual. How had the book gotten on the table? She was certain she'd re-shelved it the previous evening.

A disturbing notion was sidling through her thoughts. This man needed her to sign the loan papers. She needed a husband for the weekend. A curious weakness curled her insides. Could her wish have been granted?

Ryan West certainly wasn't the sort of man she would wish for. He was too formidable. Too blatantly male.

She would never choose someone like him as husband material. She wanted a gentle, kind man, one who would be her friend as well as her lover. Certainly not this restless, rugged sort who showed little patience, certainly no gentleness. But then, she only had a few days left to find Mr. Right.

And, with his dark, good looks Ryan West *would* impress her friends. Most of them would see his demeanor as sexy and compelling. All were assets, especially when you had blown your ten-year deadline to find your soul mate.

"So, it's crucial that you have these papers signed," she mused aloud.

He shoved one hand through his longish hair, the gesture making him seem even more dangerous. "Here it comes."

"What?" she asked absently, still rubbing MacDougall's ears.

"The shakedown. What's it going to cost me?"

"A weekend."

His brows pulled together over that hawkish nose, and his face reminded her of the turbulence before a storm blew in, shaking the rafters and ripping the limbs from the trees. "What did you say?"

Amanda gathered her bravado, realizing what she was asking, deciding at the same time it was worth the risk. It meant not having to endure the coming weekend as the only one in her group who had failed to live up to the pact. "I'll sign your papers, but I want a favor in return."

"One that'll cost me?"

"Only your time. Like I said, I need one weekend."

"Doing what?"

"Being my husband."

She'd finally succeeded in surprising him, she noted with satisfaction. In fact, she'd wiped that knowing smirk completely off his face. Quickly Amanda relayed the pact she'd made with her friends and the reunion planned for the coming weekend. "And so you see, you'll have to pose as my husband."

He stared at her, his voice flat. "You're crazy."

"Crazy enough to know that if you want my signature on your loan papers, you'll play the role."

"And if I refuse?"

Amanda shrugged her shoulders negligently, her reputation as a merciless bargainer standing her in good stead. That ability had been a major part of her business success. "I imagine it will be easier for me to find someone to pretend to be my husband for the weekend than it will be for you to get a new bank loan."

From the corner of her eye, she could see the struggle on his face. Purposely she pretended to study the design on the tapestry chair her fingers rested on.

"One weekend?" he asked, obviously hating to give even that much.

"As I explained, it's just for the reunion." Having held the trump card, now she pulled it out and played it for all its worth. "But if you don't convincingly portray the loving husband, I won't sign the papers."

Anger flashed in his eyes, accompanied by a tic in his jaw as he clenched it. "That's blackmail."

Amanda covered her sudden spurt of nervous uncertainty with another shrug. "Call it what you like. But if the bank loan means as much as you've said it does, then perhaps you can think of it as a negotiating point."

His eyes swept over her, and she felt a heat that had nothing to do with the artificial warmth that seeped through the heating ducts.

"Negotiate this, Amanda Thorne. A weekend as Mr. and

Mrs. West means we'll have to share a hotel room.'' His eyes darkened until they were obsidian chips in the growing twilight. "I hope the price of getting a husband is worth it.''

Apprehension bloomed, and she opened her mouth to protest. Meeting the challenge in his gaze, she let the words die, swallowing her thoughts of retreat, wondering if she'd bargained or blundered.

Chapter Two

Ryan West closed the last page of the investigator's report. It appeared that Thorne's Treasures, Amanda's shop, couldn't be completely pegged. To most appearances, her business seemed successful and aboveboard. But Ryan seldom believed in appearances. He turned his gaze on Barry Daniels, a rumpled, low-key detective who resembled an absentminded professor in search of his missing pipe. But, falling in with Ryan's theory, Barry's looks were deceiving. The man happened to be the best in the business.

Ryan rested both hands on the report cover. The report was disgustingly insufficient. While it didn't paint a precise picture of a con artist, it also didn't clear Amanda. "What's *not* written in your notes?"

Not taking offense, Barry stretched out his legs, resting one foot negligently on the claw foot of Ryan's oversized desk. "I didn't comment on this monstrosity of a desk," he retorted mildly. "Or the fact that I pulled off two men working on your new deal to chase after a harmless-looking babe."

Ryan lifted an eyebrow. "Babe?"

Barry snorted as he crossed his feet at the ankle. "You go blind recently? I don't know what she's doing buried in that shop, but from the pictures I saw she's definitely one of the best assets in Thorne's Treasures."

Ryan wasn't surprised by Barry's unconventional observations. They had been friends long before West Enterprises had grown large enough to require the security division that Barry now headed. And Barry didn't stand on ceremony. Technically they might be boss and employer, but their friendship superseded and blurred those lines. And the bottom line was that Ryan trusted Barry implicitly.

"You were supposed to be checking out her business assets," Ryan pointed out.

Barry shrugged. "I checked those out, too. No need wasting the scenery while I was working, though. And my men were the ones in the shop. I got my vicarious thrills through the photos they took."

"It's not like you to be swayed by a great-looking pair of legs."

"It's not like *you* to miss them," Barry shot back. Then his grin broadened. "Oh, I see. There's the hitch. You *didn't* miss them."

Maybe not, but he wasn't admitting that to Barry. His friend would gnaw on that tidbit like a dog with a month-old bone, just hoping for another bit of gristle. Sure, Ryan had noticed the Thorne woman's legs, but he wouldn't exactly call her a babe. Right now he had a lot more to worry about than her physical attributes.

Ryan leveled a glance at his friend. "As you pointed out, I had good reason to pull you off the new deal, and that reason doesn't include an assessment of the woman's legs. I want to know everything about Amanda Thorne. Is she using that shop as a cover-up, a place to run smuggled goods? It wouldn't be the first time a small-time operator cashed in on their import-export license in a less than legal manner."

Barry shrugged. "It's possible, but not too likely. The majority of her business focuses on collectibles, and those aren't imported or exported. Most of them come from rural America, which isn't exactly a hotbed of the drug cartel. So, James Bond, she's not up to her elbows in international intrigue." Still, he frowned. "Some of her purchases are costlier than I'd expect for the volume of business, but she may have may have acquired them for a customer who consigned the purchase. Certain parties might consider her inventory transactions suspicious.... But we're still checking things out. We should know more as soon as we see the rest of her records.''

Ryan lifted his eyebrows, not questioning just how his security chief would get his hands on the records, simply trusting it would be done. ''Smuggling may be old hat—but it's still done. And quite possibly by Amanda Thorne. Don't dismiss the possibility just because you considered it too obvious.''

Barry slid farther down into the chair, managing to shrug at the same time. ''The biggest mystery about Thorne's Treasures is how she squeezes all that merchandise into her shop. Take a look at the pictures. Shopping there would be an adventure—kind of a rabbit's warren with stuff crammed into every available inch. But her customers don't seem to be complaining.''

''What about her cash flow?'' Ryan asked abruptly.

''About what you'd expect. She's been in business for seven years, and she's plowed the profits back into the shop for most of that time. Still, she's in respectable shape. A little inventory-heavy, but that goes with the nature of the business. I haven't figured out why she does the importing and exporting, but so far, the most remarkable thing I could dig up about her was the lack of a man in her life.''

''Oh?'' Ryan tapped down his unexpected interest in that information.

''Doesn't figure.''

''Maybe you didn't dig deep enough.''

Barry pushed the shapeless cap back on his thick, crumpled hair. ''Nope. She's unattached, all right. Maybe the other guys she's been meeting lately are blind, too.''

''Corral your hormones. This is business. Strictly business.'' Briefly, Ryan outlined Amanda's involvement in his bank records. "You know what an effect this could have on the new deal."

Barry let out a low whistle. "I'll get on the bank angle right away. Try to get a look at some of her other records. Some reason you didn't give me the whole picture to begin with?"

"I didn't want it to influence your opinion of Ms. Thorne," Ryan admitted. "It's easier to look through a clear lens than one that's been smeared."

"And you're going to have her sign the loan papers?"

Ryan couldn't prevent the downward twist of his lips or the grimness in his voice. "I don't have much choice, do I?"

AMANDA ABSENTLY SEARCHED for her reading glasses as she pulled a pencil from its resting place behind her ear.

"On your head," Karen Summers pointed out with affectionate amusement as she arranged the pink depression glass on the shelf.

Amanda smiled at her assistant, and also at herself as she pulled her glasses from the riot of strawberry curls she could seldom keep contained. "Perhaps I should have my glasses glued to my face," she replied ruefully.

"It's part of your charm," Karen said, not taking her eyes from the arrangement of glassware. "Forgetfulness and femininity go well together." She stepped back, critically surveying the arrangement. "Does this stand out?"

Laughter bubbled, deep and throaty. "I thought *I* was the absentminded one here." Amanda gestured to the brimming shelves, the floor space covered so thoroughly that narrow paths wound through the shop like a maze. The only clear space was the corner Amanda had supplied with toys, which was reserved for customers' children.

Karen returned the smile. "Okay, let me rephrase that. How's it look?"

"Great. Ready to tackle another project?"

Karen took one more fond glance at the glassware as she

sighed wistfully. A true romantic, Karen was always looking for her white knight to ride in, fill her empty life and shower her with baubles, beads and affection. Amanda also knew that Karen pictured most of the shop's items as they would look in her hope chest, and ultimately in her dream house. "I don't suppose it's diamonds and rubies."

"Not this time. But almost as good. Spode Blue Willow. Entire set from the Emerson estate. She took better care of those dishes than most people do their children. Not one crack or chip."

Karen's eyes lit up in anticipation. Her enthusiasm made her an excellent assistant; she was nearly as possessive about Thorne's Treasures as Amanda. "Thinking of a private sale?"

Their list of specialized collectors included an impressive number of people interested in Spode, especially a stamped, dated set like this one. "Perhaps we'll hold a tea," Amanda mused. "A very formal tea."

"Served on the Spode?" Karen guessed gleefully. "Brilliant. They'll be fighting over who gets to take it home."

Amanda grinned. "The thought had occurred to me."

"Can we set up the tea party for the weekend?"

Amanda's smile faded. "I have my reunion this weekend."

"That's right. Oh, well, a weekday might be better, anyway. Fewer commitments to distract the customers."

Amanda wished for a few more distractions of her own. The prospect of spending the weekend with the formidable Mr. West was making her more nervous by the moment.

"Geez, you look like they're going to line you up in front of a firing squad. If you're dreading it so much, don't go."

Amanda's laugh lacked humor. "It's not like I have a choice, is it?"

"You *could* meet Mr. Right there." Karen practically sighed as she reverted to her favorite theme.

Fat chance, Amanda thought. Not with Ryan West on

her arm. "I'm not going there to meet someone. I'm going to see my oldest friends."

Karen issued an unladylike snort. "Lot of good that'll do you. What about the single, unattached males? Reunions bring out the predator in most men."

An immediate picture of Ryan West popped into Amanda's head. It was too easy to see him as a determined predator, stalking his prey. And far too disturbing.

Shaking her head, Amanda tried to dislodge that mental flash. "Not every occasion is designed to be a male-hunting ground."

Karen rolled her expressive brown eyes. "Talk like that's probably why you're the only one who didn't catch a husband before the reunion."

Amanda kept her eyes on the display, not wanting Karen to see that the words stung a bit.

"It's just that when a good-looking man comes in here, you act like he's invisible," Karen continued earnestly.

Ryan West certainly wasn't invisible, Amanda thought with a start.

"And if you keep wearing blinders, you'll wind up alone." Karen's voice quieted, her own loneliness seeping through. "I should know."

Amanda flinched slightly as she searched for her pencil. Had she been pushing men away?

Instantly contrite, Karen reached for the pencil that Amanda had absently stuck behind one ear and placed it in her hand. "I didn't intend for that to come out sounding mean. It's just that you've got a golden opportunity here and I'd hate to see you blow it."

Was Karen right? A golden opportunity. The possibilities of that expression swirled around her as she thought of the upcoming weekend...and Ryan's words to her.

"Negotiate this, Amanda Thorne. A weekend as Mr. and Mrs. West means we'll have to share a hotel room. I hope the price of getting a husband is worth it."

An unexpected shiver tripped over her body and danced through her veins. What exactly would that price be?

Chapter Three

Punctually, on Friday morning of the reunion weekend, Ryan rang Amanda's doorbell. Wiping suddenly perspiring hands against her shorts, Amanda smiled nervously as she opened the door.

"You're right on time," Amanda began as she gestured him inside. "Punctuality is a great trait—something I admire. I'll just grab my garment bag. Guess you don't have much luggage—I know men pack light. I try to, but I always bring too much...." Her voice trailed off as Ryan stared at her. Realizing she was babbling, Amanda offered a weak smile before fleeing to the bedroom.

Carrying out the bulky garment bag, makeup case and tote bag, Amanda started for the door, but Ryan stopped her, lifting the heavy luggage from her hands, treating it as though it weighed nothing. "I'll put this in the car."

"That'd be great." She took a deep breath. "And I'll just grab Mackie's stuff."

Ryan's brows drew together as he stared down at her. "Who's Mackie?"

Amanda sensed her smile was bordering on desperate. "He's my dog. His real name is MacDougall. You saw him the other night. Usually my neighbor Lorraine takes care of him when I'm out of town. She's crazy about animals...has three dogs of her own. She'd have more but the landlord told her one more dog and she was out. Our limit is supposed to be one pet, but she talked him into letting her have the other two. And she loves taking care of MacDougall, since the landlord doesn't object,'' Amanda finished, speaking so rapidly that she hadn't even paused for a breath.

"So you're taking the dog to her apartment?"

Amanda twisted her hands, then quickly stuffed them into the pockets of her shorts so Ryan wouldn't see the agitated gesture. "Uh…not exactly."

"Spill it," he ordered, easily shifting her densely packed luggage.

"I'm sure the suitcases are getting heavy—"

He ignored her lame attempt to sidetrack the conversation. "What *exactly* do you mean?"

"Lorraine's out of town herself this weekend. She and the dogs are camping. She takes them everywhere… otherwise I'd have been pet-sitting for—"

"Then, where are you taking the dog?"

What Amanda intended to sound like a laugh came out more like a high-pitched squeal that trailed into silence. "Well…with us."

Exasperation covered those hawkishly handsome features. "You never heard of a kennel?"

"I don't leave MacDougall in places like that. He could catch kennel cough or all kinds of diseases. Besides, he hates being left with strangers…he'd think I'd abandoned him. And it's not like I have family here to take care of him—they all live in Stanton—my family, I mean. Besides, he's a little dog, doesn't take up much room." Amanda leaned forward earnestly, still speaking rapidly, cramming far too many words in her explanation. "And he's used to riding in cars—loves it, in fact. All I have to do is say 'car' and he's out the door. If he could drive, I don't think he'd wait for me…." Amanda finally allowed her voice to trail off as she stared at Ryan's disbelieving face.

"You intend to take that dog to your high school reunion?"

Amanda stiffened her shoulders. "Look, it's not what I'd planned, either. But I didn't think I was going to the reunion, so I didn't make any arrangements for him. I'll take care of him, and you'll hardly know he's along. He's more like a big dog in a small package—Westies don't get all hyper like other small breeds. He really won't be any trouble."

Ryan stared skeptically at the dog who stood close to his mistress. "Look, I don't want dog hair all over my car...."

MacDougall chose that moment to cock his head in a particularly beguiling manner, his stance a pleading one. With his long, silky white hair and huge brown button eyes and black nose, the dog was appealing under any circumstances. But when he turned on the charm... Then, surprising even Amanda, Mackie sat back on his haunches, holding up his front paws in a begging position. Aware that she was prejudiced, Amanda still knew the pup was hard to resist.

Ryan started to shake his head, then blew out an exasperated sigh. MacDougall took this as acceptance. He jumped up on Ryan, his head barely reaching Ryan's knee. Mackie's tail wagged madly as he barked and then raced around in circles.

A suspicion of a smile hovered around Ryan's lips, and Amanda suspected he was having difficulty containing a full-fledged grin. "All right, enough. We'd better hit the road." Ryan's gaze flicked to meet Amanda's. "I hope you don't have any other surprises."

"Like what?"

"That's why they're called surprises," he pointed out dryly as he moved to the front door. "And don't bring every toy the dog has. We're going to be cramped for space as it is."

Amanda again regretted that her own roomy Jeep Cherokee was in the shop. But Ryan was probably exaggerating. His car couldn't be that small.

BUT IT WAS. Well onto the highway, Amanda shifted gingerly, hoping the tightly packed luggage wouldn't move and fall forward. He hadn't exaggerated. The low-slung sports car barely contained them and all the paraphernalia.

As MacDougall slept contently on the floor at her feet, ecstatic under the cooling rush of the air conditioner, Amanda shifted her purse for the dozenth time, wishing she could quench her still raging case of nerves. "Thanks for agreeing to take Mackie. I just couldn't leave him."

"I'm surprised you didn't think about making arrangements."

"I *told* you, I didn't know until the last minute that I was going to the reunion."

His gaze flicked away from the road for a moment, but it was long enough for Amanda to see the skepticism. "You didn't get yourself on my bank records in only a few days...not to mention ordering checks, waiting for them to be printed. That's hardly an overnight process."

Exasperated, Amanda blew at her bangs, fluffing out the golden strands. "I told you that was all a mix-up. True, it worked out to my advantage, but a weekend in Stanton will hardly kill you. It's a quiet little town, no big-city problems. The pace is slow, progress even slower."

"Sounds exciting."

Amanda couldn't suppress a defensive tone. "It's not New York or San Francisco, but it's a great place. My parents and brother still live there—it was a great place to grow up."

"Then, why did you leave?"

Despite her nerves, Amanda warmed to a subject close to her heart. "I wanted more choices, a broader panorama. I love everything about San Francisco...it has drawn me since I was a child." She couldn't prevent a breathy sigh of recollection. "I knew the first time I saw it, I'd come home."

"Everyone's second hometown?"

She wrinkled her nose. "Not exactly. It's something

more to me. Something I can't really explain. But the sounds, the smells, they're part of my memory…part of my today. I know it sounds crazy, but I come alive in San Francisco.''

Unexpectedly, a look of understanding crossed his face. ''It's that way for a lot of us.''

Surprised, but pleased, she relaxed her death grip on her purse and angled toward Ryan, curling her legs upward on the seat, tucking them beneath her as far as the seat belt allowed, careful not to start an avalanche of luggage. ''As a kid I always felt it. But then, after college, I knew it the first time I saw the sun setting on the Golden Gate Bridge. I was at Pier 47 on the Wharf near Scouma's.'' Momentarily forgetting her nerves, she grew nearly poetic. ''I was surrounded by boats, watching the masts dance as the wind played with the rigging. I glanced toward the bridge just as the sun struck it and I realized why the bridge was named Golden Gate. Until then I thought the bridge was painted pink and someone just fancied the name.'' She laughed softly. ''No doubt thinking it sounded better than the Big Pink Bridge. But when I saw the sun setting on the bridge and watched it turn absolutely gold, it all came together for me.''

She turned to find Ryan's thoughtful gaze on her. A light in his eyes nearly chased away the intimidating look he'd worn since she'd met him. ''You go to Scouma's much?'' he asked, referring to the landmark restaurant.

''When I can…''

''For the martinis,'' they finished simultaneously as his voice chimed in with hers.

Looking at each other first in surprise, then in a moment of fleeting understanding, they quickly broke the gaze. Ryan glanced back at the road, and Amanda pretended to study the towering trees dotting the landscape.

It was strangely disconcerting to learn they shared even that one interest, to know that perhaps they had sat within touching distance of each other at the bar in Scouma's waiting for a table. She preferred to think of him only as a necessary stranger, one to help carry out her charade at the reunion.

Sneaking a glance back at him, she realized that she wouldn't have forgotten this man even in a casual encounter. Arrogant, darkly handsome, he was as compelling as he was attractive. Not the kind of man she could have bumped into and ignored, especially if he allowed that grin of his to completely surface.

Absently, Amanda toyed with the buckle of her sandal. "Funny, isn't it? How people live in the same city, share the same interests, yet in most cases never meet. Not unless they're thrown together..." Sitting up straighter, Amanda cleared her throat. "Of course, this is just for the weekend—and we'll both get what we want."

"Considering we're sharing a hotel room tonight, that's an attractive offer."

Amanda puffed up, righteous indignation ready to spill out. Then she caught the unexpected twinkle in his eyes. The man was teasing her!

"If you think that's an offer—" deliberately, Amanda drew out her words, rewarded by a spurt of interest in Ryan's expression "—wait until you see the sleeping arrangements." She allowed a few moments for the provocative words to linger in the air, watching the subtle signs that told her Ryan was hanging on to each syllable. "You'll be in for a quite a surprise." Using every remembered feminine wile, she adopted a sultry, knowing expression, her voice nearly a purr. "Mackie makes a great bed partner."

Ryan blinked, briefly tightened his hands around the steering wheel, but kept his voice even despite the grin tugging at his lips. "Then, I guess I'm lucky you don't prefer potbellied pigs for pets."

This time Amanda didn't have to strain to make her laugh genuine. "I bet you can't say that again—what a tongue twister."

Shrugging, Ryan slowed down as they approached the

turn. "I have a very talented mouth…at least that's what the women who've kissed me say."

"And modest, too. Any more wonderful attributes I should know about?"

"I won't bore you with a long list."

Amanda made a sound of disbelief. "Are you going to be this charming all weekend?"

This time the grin turned up his lips. "Just might."

Amanda narrowed her gaze. "You're not planning to deliberately sabotage things, are you?"

He managed to look wounded. "Now, why would I do that?"

"I can think of at least one good reason," she muttered under her breath.

"Oh? Because you're blackmailing me? Holding my loan as a hostage?"

"I told you several times—"

"And it's no more convincing now. Guess you'll have to trust me." Ryan glanced away from the road long enough to see apprehension bloom in her expression. If he wasn't so damned mad that she'd bested him with her con game, he could almost feel sorry for her. She probably would have preferred a more willing escort. As Barry had pointed out, Amanda was quite a babe. Which left a big question. Why didn't she have a man in her life, one who would have been her date for the reunion?

He nearly laughed aloud at himself. Hell, *he* was alone and wouldn't have had anyone to invite to a reunion. And he planned to keep it that way. Trusting once before had taught him that women were like full-blown roses, beautiful to look at, but not to be counted on. Like the flower's fragile petals, women quickly turned, withered, then disappeared. Despite these dark thoughts, Ryan couldn't resist taking one more long, leisurely look at his companion.

She'd propped her legs against the glove compartment, affording him a great view, one he sensed wasn't planned. Long and tanned, her shapely legs were as sexy as the rest of her. Her nervousness could be a well-played act, or for some reason the cool logic behind her fraud had somehow come unwound.

As long as she didn't unwind him as well, Ryan knew he could play her game and walk away the winner. And spending the weekend with a beautiful woman wasn't exactly punishment. There'd been a time when he would have welcomed the diversion, enjoyed the challenge of learning what made this woman tick, why she'd chosen fraud for her occupation. But he no longer had time for frivolity. Heavy responsibilities had killed impulsive fun, not to mention impulsive weekends.

Once more he glanced aside, studying her profile. Elegant, fine-boned features were at odds with his image of a criminal. But that's probably what made her so good. No one would suspect her.

Amanda shifted just then, meeting his gaze. "Well, this is some drive, isn't it?" The thready quality of her voice didn't fit the cheerful tone she forced into it. "When I was a kid, I loved driving with my parents to San Francisco—and always hated to leave. But on the drive home to Stanton, I'd get excited, too."

"I didn't realize there was that much excitement in Hooterville."

Amanda cut her eyes toward him. "After we slopped the pigs, milked the cows and forked the manure, we got to play horseshoes or bingo. Between that and bobbing for apples, it was hard to beat the excitement, especially on days when we didn't have to get to bed until seven o'clock."

His lip curled upward again. "And to think, I guessed it would be a boring town."

Amanda sniffed delicately. "I doubt you'll be bored the *entire* time."

"Not sharing a hotel room with you."

Nerves that had begun to rescind a bit now clamored to

attention. "That's not the kind of excitement I had in mind."

"Do I look like the kind of man who'd spend his time at church socials and picnics?"

No, most definitely not. Amanda reluctantly studied his classic profile, that air of confidence that bordered on cockiness. If asked to sum him up in one word, Amanda would have chosen "dangerous." Her throat dried up at the thought, and she deliberately wrenched the conversation in another direction, her voice unnaturally high, her speech rapid.

"I don't think I told you much about my friends. Suzy, Linda, Candy and I were like sisters during high school. And going to college didn't change that. It just made us closer. Three Musketeers and a spare—that's what everyone called us. But then, after college, we scattered in all four directions. I guess that's why this reunion is so important to me. I don't want to disappoint them."

"Or yourself?"

That slowed her down for a moment. Then her rush of words returned. "First, there's Suzy Burns-Meriweather. She's the one who called me before I was awake and got the nutty idea that I was married."

"You talked to her before you woke up? I hate to tell you, Amanda, but you're the one who sounds nutty."

"Did I mention that I'm not exactly a morning person?"

"I'm guessing this is one of the greatest understatements of the twentieth-century."

Amanda ignored his perceptive comment. "Back to Suzy. She's blond, kind of crazy, great fun. And she'll be relentlessly inquisitive."

Ryan slanted his face toward her for a moment. "What did you tell them about me?"

Amanda took a deep breath. "I haven't. Yet. They think we eloped."

"And why did you keep our 'marriage' a secret?"

Good question. She thought for a moment. Inspiration

struck. "I'll tell them that we just met recently and I wanted to surprise them."

"Sort of a whirlwind romance?" he responded dryly.

She gritted her teeth. "You could call it that."

"I'm not the one lying to her friends."

Oh, it was going to be a *very* long drive. "I told you why all this is necessary."

His voice held a suspicious tinge of amusement. "Sure. Your friends all managed to snag husbands and you didn't, so you're blackmailing me."

"*You're* the one who needs papers signed."

"And you're the one who needs a husband for the weekend."

Amanda sucked in her breath, knowing he was right on target. "You were convenient."

He tsked under his breath. "A good-looking woman like you shouldn't need to resort to blackmail."

Watching for hidden traps in his words, she focused on his carefully bland expression. She didn't trust his sudden compliance. "I believe we were talking about my friends."

Amanda pushed back her unruly curls. "Let's see. I told you about Suzy...there's Linda Danvers, she was always the clown of our group."

"I suppose she's a career woman with Ringling Brothers," Ryan commented, slowing down as he approached a stop sign.

Amanda refused to be amused at the analogy, although she suspected Linda would appreciate its humor. "Close. She's in the state legislature with her eyes on a national spot. She met her husband in politics."

"Truly strange bedfellows," he muttered, watching the road.

Amanda decided to ignore him. "She's bright, ambitious, and she won't be easy to fool."

"Then you'll have to watch that waspish tongue of yours," he pointed out as he navigated the turns of the twisting road.

Amanda silently counted to ten, trying not to show her temper.

"Is that everyone?" he asked with a note of impatience.

She hesitated, then chose her words carefully. "I think you'll enjoy meeting Candy Johnson."

He was quiet for a brief moment. "She must be the looker."

Amanda twisted in her seat to stare at him. "What makes you say that?"

"Am I right?"

"Well…"

"She's the looker."

"But how could you know that?"

"The hesitation in your voice, the careful phrasing. It doesn't matter if you're interested in me or not, you don't want me paying more attention to the beauty in the group than to you."

Amanda resented his quick perception. "If you pay more attention to Candy than to me, no one will buy the whirl-wind romance story."

He lifted the left side of his mouth in a knowing quirk. "That, too. Don't worry, Miss Thorne, by the end of the weekend they'll wonder how we get anything else done with our hands all over each other."

Amanda blanched even as a curious fluttering feeling clutched her. Sitting up primly, she hoped the warmth in her cheeks wasn't a telling shade of red. "We don't want to overplay our parts."

His laugh was rich, full and throaty as he threw his head back. "Oh, but there's no such thing as being *too* much in love."

That fluttery feeling was growing deeper, warmer.

Trying to displace it, she searched for something, anything, to grab on to. "You probably need to know something about me."

A curious look flickered across his face before it resumed its previous noncommittal expression. "Uh-huh."

Amanda was hardly encouraged by his lack of interest, but nonetheless she thought about the essentials of her life, the things he needed to know to convince her friends. "I run a collectible and antiques business. It's called Thorne's Treasures."

"What sort of collectibles?"

She laughed softly, thinking of her maze of items, some so dear she hated to part with them, some so eccentric and far removed from her own taste they begged for homes of their own. "Primarily late-nineteenth, early-twentieth century. But I have some stock that dates back to the mid-1700s, and with the newest craze in collecting, I have items from the 1950s and sixties."

"What's collectible from the fifties and sixties?"

"You name it. Aluminum glasses, Mickey Mouse Club things, metal lunch boxes since they don't make them anymore, even plastic Kool-Aid pitchers. And, of course, lava lamps and rock 'n' roll posters."

"In other words, garage sale material."

Slightly insulted, she huffed a bit. "Not necessarily. I was just telling you what was *considered* collectible. That doesn't mean I specialize in Kool-Aid pitchers. In fact, I don't carry that kind of merchandise. The only stock I have from the fifties and sixties are some rare, truly remarkable pieces. I have too many serious collectors who want higher-quality items. Besides, I don't have room to carry everything."

He glanced at her again, that funny sort of look covering his face. "You have a small shop?"

"Not really. It's in an old two-story Victorian house, which gives me lots of nooks and crannies."

"You need them to hide something?"

Puzzled, she glanced at him. "No, I don't keep most of the loot in the store." Her attempt at levity fell flat as he scowled first at her, then back at the road. Geez, he was acting like a pompous prison warden. Deciding to accommodate his suspicions, Amanda couldn't resist one more jab. "But I do carry a hatchet in my luggage—comes in handy when the scary music starts to play. Never know when the urge to go ax murdering will strike me."

"Breaking the law isn't particularly funny."

"That's amazing," she commented, studying him intently.

Distracted, he glanced at her. "What is?"

"How you went from...what...thirty-five years old...to at least eighty in under five seconds. If you could reverse the process, you'd make a fortune selling your fountain of youth."

His lips definitely twitched. Maybe there was hope for him, after all. "And what about Amanda Thorne, the person. Who is she? Her best qualities, her worst...perhaps even a deep, dark secret."

"Sorry to disappoint you, but there aren't any juicy secrets. My best qualities...loyalty, I suppose...enough business sense to keep my shop in the black. I can spot the most valuable collectible at an auction in less than ten minutes, and I can outbargain the best wheeler-dealers in the business. As for my worst qualities...I guess I am a bit forgetful."

Ryan stared pointedly at the pencil still stuck absently behind her ear, but she didn't notice. "Go on, surely you haven't run out of bad qualities already?"

"Perhaps we shouldn't have started with forgetfulness," she admitted.

Ryan rolled his eyes. "Okay. Is there anything else I need to know about your friends?"

"I don't think so," she mused. Then, struck with a thought, she bolted upright, nearly unsettling the precarious load in the car. Even Mackie opened one eye to shoot her an annoyed look. "But they will want to know how we met. Since they believe we eloped, we won't have to dream up wedding details, but how we met is nearly as important."

Baffled, Ryan stared at her, unable to keep from noticing

how attractive she was with a perky expression lighting her face and sparkling eyes. "Why?"

"Hmm? Oh, about how we met. I guess it's a woman thing. And from what I've heard, the chase is a lot more romantic than the actual catch."

"You can say that again," he muttered.

"What?"

"So, what's the story?"

Amanda crinkled her face into a mask of concentration. "This has to be good or my friends will never buy it." She fell silent, thinking, then nearly shouted as a fragmented idea formed. "It must be something logical," she declared.

"It *must?*"

Amanda ignored him, and Ryan guessed she hadn't even heard him. "My friends might believe we eloped—a very impulsive gesture for me—but initially deciding to go out with you—now, that's a different matter. They all have my profile of the perfect man." She met his gaze briefly as her voice went flat. "And he doesn't bear even the slightest resemblance to you."

Ryan wondered if he should be insulted, flattered or amused. He chose the latter. "Tell them you got lucky— after you'd upped your standards."

"Don't flatter yourself."

He shrugged. "Suit yourself. I can be charming or obnoxious to your friends. You decide."

To his satisfaction, she hastily changed her tactics. "Why don't we concentrate on filling in the background? Now, as I see it, we met at...the grocery store."

"Fulfilling every sitcom's premise of dating in the nineties? Confirming that men shopping for melons aren't looking in the produce section?"

"Okay, so maybe not the grocery store," Amanda muttered. Then she brightened. "Of course, I'll tell them we met doing business."

"And what business would that be?"

Blankly, she stared at him. "I just realized I have no idea what you do for a living."

"Taxidermist. You can tell your friends I mount all the animal trophies in your shop."

"I seriously doubt you're a taxidermist. Not to mention I have only *one* animal trophy, a collectible from the early nineteenth century. I doubt even you could have managed to pull that off."

"Don't underestimate me, Amanda. I have quite a few hidden talents."

Amanda sucked in a deep breath, hoping to stave off the rush of reaction. Maybe she was getting too worked up about sharing a hotel room with him. It seemed every word the man uttered was a double entendre. She forced disinterest into her tone. "I doubt one of those talents is taxidermy...or time travel. My friends are going to want to know everything about you. What do you *really* do?"

"I'm a commercial real estate developer. I put package deals together—attract the investors, scout the property, prepare the presentations for the lenders."

She thought of his problem with the loan papers. "Then, it seems like you'd have a good relationship with the bank."

"I deal with more than one financial institution. In today's speculative market, they tend to be very careful. Trust is at a high premium these days." Ryan glanced at her, and for a moment she thought she saw something flash in his eyes. But the change was so fleeting that it was gone before she could analyze it.

"The doomed Savings and Loan debacle of the eighties hasn't been forgotten," he explained. "No one wants to repeat that mistake. They're more cautious about the money they lend—especially when it concerns real estate. No one wants to be left holding an empty bag again."

This was not exactly the background she'd been going for. Amanda felt as though she were reading an article in *Newsweek.* "I need to know more about you than how your business works. My friends will hardly believe I was swept away by the charm of your real estate expertise.''

He lifted his eyes from the road to meet her gaze. She was struck again by his forceful good looks, and she realized something unexpected was sweeping over her now. Could the wish have delivered someone more compelling than she was prepared to handle? Despite what she'd said, Ryan had more charm than should have been legal. Her case of nerves hadn't been caused just by her concern over telling him about Mackie. No, the nonstop thoughts she had about him since their first encounter had provided those nerves. Not to mention the unsettling reaction he continued to cause.

But he broke the spell, his voice somewhat wry. ''As you know, I'm single.''

Amanda wondered if there was someone important in his life, a significant other, but she didn't dare speak the thought aloud.

''I went to school in the East and I moved to San Francisco eleven years ago. I'm thirty-six years old—you were close.'' His gaze swept over her again, almost intimately this time. ''And you can see the vital statistics for yourself.''

That was the understatement of the century. He'd look great on her arm at the reunion. She managed to sound noncommittal. ''Uh-huh.''

''And I normally don't spend my weekends with beautiful con women.''

Amanda blinked, thought of a thousand things to say, then stifled all of them. She needed a logical story about how they met. His war of the wits was starting to wear on her. ''Now, back to how we met…oh, yes, in business. Actually, real estate is great.''

''Don't you think—''

''Look, the reunion is my territory. I think I know more about how women are going to react to the story of how we met than you do.'' Amanda waited a moment, then, satisfied when he didn't comment, continued in an authoritative tone. "And this is going to be our story. I met you while investigating a land deal I thought about investing in. One of your clients knew us both, invited us to dinner. One thing led to another, we dated, then eventually eloped."

"And did I make any money out of your investment?" he asked wryly.

Amanda frowned at him. "Just stick to the basic facts. Too many details will only get us all bogged down. Don't improvise. I'll be making the explanation—just let me handle it. This is a nice, bland, uncomplicated story. What could be better?"

He shook his head sadly. "If you don't know, Amanda Thorne, I can see why you resorted to kidnapping a husband."

Amanda opened her mouth, then closed it without speaking.

"Don't worry. I'll try to make it sound like we at least enjoyed holding hands—when we weren't poring over the statistics for my latest land deal."

"I know you think this is very amusing," Amanda began stiffly.

But the twinkle in his eye was back. Taking one hand from the steering wheel, he reached for the forgotten pencil tucked behind her ear, pulling it gently from the tumble of her hair. "Don't worry. By the end of the weekend you'll be flinging yourself into my arms with gratitude." He ignored her gasp of protest. "And it won't have anything to do with statistics."

Chapter Four

The hotel was exceptional. A historic building that had once been the home of the local gentry, it had been redecorated into a luxury hotel that catered to travelers who appreciated the finer values of northern California. But luxury hadn't taken away the intimate nature of the hotel.

As they walked inside, Amanda sensed the romantic mood of the establishment, from the fresh flowers decorating each antique pie table, curio and marble-topped dresser, to the tucked-away tables for two in the cozy dining room hung with rose-patterned swag draperies and lacy sheers. Original oil paintings were part of the fine art collection that formed a passageway between the lobby and the dining room.

Suzy, as head of the reunion committee, had done an excellent job procuring the site. Amanda noted wryly that as the graduating class aged, each reunion grew markedly more elegant. They had come a long way from the Holiday Inn.

Ryan casually draped an arm around her waist as they stood at the front desk prepared to register. Amanda glanced at him in surprise, then noticed a few of her classmates, already wearing badges, heading in their direction.

Ryan leaned toward her, his warm breath tickling her neck as he bent close to whisper, "Don't act like I'm about to bite you. You'll blow it before the reunion even starts."

Closing widened eyes, she forced a smile, making it both intimate and slightly sultry. She kept her voice equally low. "Thanks for the reminder." She tilted her head in a deliberately provocative gesture, hearing her classmates coming closer. Purposely, she raised her voice as she leaned into his hold. "You're such a darling."

Even though Ryan knew her act was for the benefit of others, he was caught suddenly by the fire in her expression. During the drive, he'd purposely ignored the sprinkle of freckles that danced across her nose and the startling transformation of her face when she smiled. He'd also ignored the way the sun glinted on that outrageous riot of strawberry blond curls. But it was more difficult to ignore all those attributes when she stood in the curve of his arm, her face tilted toward his in blatant invitation. The invitation might be fake, but the answering reaction he felt was completely genuine.

Luckily, the hotel was agreeable about accommodating Mackie—as long as they agreed to a hefty deposit. Disregarding the surprise on her face, he pulled out his wallet and laid a credit card on the desk when the clerk asked for the method of payment. Scribbling his signature on the register, Ryan accepted the room key and draped his arm around Amanda again. Unable to keep from provoking her, he leaned close. "Don't worry. I'll bill you."

Her mouth was a soft "oh" of surprised confusion at his sudden urgency. But she soon picked up his cues as they quickly followed the bellhop with their luggage. Ryan wanted to escape before he was forced into his first confrontation with her friends. Even Mackie's short legs were moving fast as they crossed the lobby.

They were quiet as they entered the elevator, and the bellhop glanced at them as though wondering about their silence. One of Amanda's hands clutched Mackie's leash as though it were a lifeline. Ryan moved closer and picked up her other hand. It was soft within his, and he couldn't help note the contrast. Her eyes questioned him, and he glanced casually at the bellhop. Understanding dawned, and she leaned into him slightly.

The bellhop glanced their way again and then smiled. When the elevator slid open, Ryan let the man proceed them down the hall. Lowering his voice, Ryan bent close to her ear. "You should know everyone in a small town talks. If you want to make this look good, we're on all the time."

Ryan was surprised he was having to take the lead. He'd expected Amanda, as the spirited woman she'd shown herself to be, to be at ease when they strolled inside the hotel, to play her part to the hilt. An experienced con woman shouldn't have any problems taking on another role. He was surprised to see her hesitate. From the moment they'd met, crashed head-on, so to speak, he hadn't seen the least bit of indecision on her part. Until now.

Glancing over at Amanda, he saw even now that her footsteps were lagging. MacDougall was too well trained to pull on the lead, but it was apparent he, too, wanted Amanda to walk faster. It was clear she wasn't enjoying the Aubusson tapestry rug covering a good portion of the hardwood floor, or appreciating the valuable antiques lining the corridor. No, she was definitely dragging her feet. Ryan wondered why.

The bellhop had opened the door to their room and was carrying in their luggage. Ryan turned to Amanda and watched as she tugged at her lower lip with her teeth. When she realized he was observing the nervous habit, she stopped, offering him a cheerless smile.

Lord, she was acting as if she were stepping into a jail cell. But then, remembering the words...and threats...that had passed between them when she had demanded that he come on this weekend masquerade, Ryan suddenly realized why. He'd only insisted on the shared room because he'd been so angry at her manipulations—ones that had threatened the very foundations of his business, a business that was shakily supporting the most important thing in his life.

And even though his demanding the shared room was to torture Amanda, if she could get beyond feeling like a martyred victim, she'd realize it would be hard to explain newlyweds staying in separate rooms. But in the meantime, he could make her sweat. And maybe he could find out just what her con game was.

Ryan gestured for her to proceed him through the doorway, but Amanda stopped in front of him, seemingly frozen in place. Gently he prodded her forward. The bellhop was opening the drapes, so Ryan took advantage of his distraction to whisper to Amanda, "Perk up. Even a doomed man gets a last meal."

Amanda raised startled eyes that quickly showed a glint of humor. She tossed her head back in a motion that was becoming familiar, her voice shaky yet silky. "It wasn't food I had on my mind."

Ryan sucked in his gut, unexpectedly affected by her humor, sharpness and innuendo.

The bellhop spoke, pointing to the French doors. "These lead to a private terrace. Temperature controls are next to the window, and room service menus are on the desk." He gestured toward the fireplace. "Be sure to open the flue before lighting the fire. When you need more logs, just call the desk. Will that be all, sir?"

Ryan nodded and handed him a generous tip.

"Thank you, sir. Call if you need anything else." The bellhop closed the door as he left.

The tension and silence escalated simultaneously.

Ryan met Amanda's gaze, and he watched the pupils in her eyes dilate, then she cast her eyes away before glancing around the room. Bending over, she unfastened Mackie's leash. Then crossing to the window, Amanda looked out on a town he assumed she'd seen countless times in her youth; yet she managed to look fascinated. It should have been amusing; instead, his eyes softened as he watched her. He had to remind himself that she was a slick operator. This was no doubt part of her act.

Amanda loosened her grip on the lace panel at the window. She'd tried to rid herself of the ridiculous nervousness that had gone into overdrive once they'd arrived at the hotel, but it was only multiplying. She'd told herself this was only for one weekend, that the threats he'd issued had been nothing more than that, but she had been unprepared for the first thrust of intimacy.

The hotel catered to romance, and this charming room with its four-postered double bed, tub for two and bouquets of sweet-smelling flowers closed around her like a choking fist. How in the world was she going to spend an entire weekend with this man, closeted in this room for two nights?

"What about your family?"

Distracted from her wandering thoughts, she jerked her head up in surprise when he spoke. Then *what* he said penetrated. *Her family!* Why hadn't she thought of them when she'd cooked up this scheme? Groaning aloud, she clapped one hand to her forehead. It was one thing to fool her friends. It was another to put on a charade for her family. Yet she couldn't come to town and not see them. Nor could they get wind of her "marriage" from anyone else. "I...didn't exactly think about that aspect of my plan."

His dark brows rose in disbelief. She didn't blame him. "How'd you manage to put your entire family out of your thoughts?"

She shrugged, realizing there was a lot to this plan she hadn't thought out. Most especially sharing a room with a stranger. Without volition her eyes traveled to the bed. Feeling the warmth of his gaze on her, she reluctantly lifted her eyes. She cleared her throat, but her voice was still husky. "I'm sure I'll work out something with my family."

His expression told her he was no longer thinking of her family, either.

Tension cloaked them both, and she made a halfhearted gesture toward the pile of luggage. "Tonight's the welcoming cocktail party. I guess we should work out bathroom arrangements.''

He didn't answer immediately, and she felt her own senses blur as her head began to buzz. What was it about this romantic chalet of a hotel, with its intimate rooms and sense of whimsy that had stolen her confidence…made her think there was more to this agreement than simple business?

''Whatever you say,'' he answered.

The buzzing increased. ''About what?''

''The bathroom,'' he replied, an amused light in his eyes.

Feeling stupid, she tried to sound brisk. ''Right. The bathroom.'' *Oh, this was going well. The reunion hadn't even officially begun and she was already blathering mindlessly.* She moved toward the luggage. ''I'll just…ah…unpack.'' Amanda knew she had to get a grip on herself. It was just a hotel room, after all, and she needed to regain control of the situation. She wasn't going to give Ryan West the satisfaction of knowing she'd been unnerved, even temporarily. ''You go ahead.''

''I'm going down to the bar for a while. The bathroom's all yours,'' Ryan announced, his manner easy, his tone careless, unconcerned.

She nodded her head. When the door closed behind him, she pushed her fingers through her hair and exhaled in relief. Not wanting to be caught in the shower when he returned, she grabbed her overnight case and hurried into the bathroom.

Though her nerves screamed for a long, relaxing soak in a hot tub, Amanda made her shower quick. Wrapped in a thick terry robe, she reentered the bedroom, grateful to find it still empty. But as she finished the thought, the door opened.

Amanda purposely kept still, refusing to clutch at the lapels of her robe and look like a quivering virgin being delivered to the sacrificial altar. With some effort she made her voice as nonchalant as his had been. "The bathroom's yours now."

He grunted and grabbed one of the cases, disappearing into the bathroom.

Wishing she was already dressed and could flee to the hotel bar as he had, she began to unpack. Glancing around, she realized there was only one closet. It seemed far too personal to hang their clothes together. Shaking aside the notion, she quickly hung her dresses inside.

She smoothed the material in place just as the bathroom door opened. Glancing up, she immediately saw that Ryan had ignored the robe provided by the hotel and had instead chosen to wrap a towel around his lower body. Amanda deliberately tried to keep her expression neutral, which wasn't easy considering how he looked draped only in a towel. Broad shoulders, only hinted at beneath the well-cut jackets he wore, topped a well muscled torso that tapered to a lean waist and hips. A light sheen of moisture still clung to him, shimmering in the glow of the lamps.

"How formal is tonight's party?" he asked, shaking back freshly washed hair. Droplets of water slid down the muscled curvature of his chest.

Amanda yanked her gaze away. "Just suit and tie."

He picked up his garment bag. "Fine, then I'll get out of your way."

Surprised that he wasn't holding her to his threat, she was at the same time grateful. He retreated into the bathroom, and it didn't take him long to dress. When he reappeared, it was hard to say whether he looked better in the crisp white shirt and charcoal suit or the towel. Both were impressive.

"How long will it take you to get ready?" he asked, glancing at his watch.

She thought quickly. "Thirty minutes."

"I'll be back then."

Amanda hesitated. "I could dress in the bathroom...you don't have to go."

His eyes rested on her face, then traveled over her terry-clad body. "I'll be in the bar."

He left, and she stared at the closed door for a moment. It almost seemed as though he was doing the gentlemanly thing, but that didn't fit with the man who had stormed into her apartment, then questioned her honesty ever since.

Another thought struck her. *God, what if he has a drinking problem? Was that why he kept going to the bar? Wouldn't that be embarrassing? Sloshed in front of her friends!* It seemed there were countless things she hadn't taken into consideration in planning this weekend.

Collecting herself, she realized that time was passing. She quickly applied her makeup, then piled her strawberry curls on her head in a style that was elegant, yet at the same time uncontrived. She chose a simple black dress, one that set off her pale skin and vivid hair coloring. The short-ish, swingy skirt whirled around her thighs, and she opted for high, delicate heels. Diamond earrings she'd inherited from her grandmother were the final touch.

Glancing in the mirror, she saw that the scooped neck and spaghetti straps called for a necklace, as well. She dug into her small jewel case and brought out a golden heart suspended on a fine chain. She struggled with the fastening just as a knock echoed at the door.

"Come in," she called out absently.

"You've put the time to good use, I see." Ryan's voice resembled warm whiskey and Amanda glanced at him, wondering if whiskey had indeed put the warmth in his tone. She was glad to see that he held his liquor well. At least he didn't show any effects of drinking.

In a smooth motion, he was at her side. He gestured to the fastening. "Allow me."

His hands lingered for a moment, brushing the tendrils of hair near her neck. Then he let his hands drop after the clasp was secured. She turned to face him, saw an unsettled expression on his face and offered him a tentative smile.

His eyes roved over her. "Perfect."

Amanda's hands strayed toward the necklace. "Thank you."

Ryan reached into his pocket, withdrawing a small jeweler's box. "Perhaps I should have said 'almost' perfect."

She stared curiously at the box as he opened the lid and withdrew a gold ring. A wedding band. Her startled gaze flew to meet his.

"You did say you would only sign my loan papers if we convinced everyone?" His questioning gaze met hers. "You want this to work, don't you?"

She nodded, unable to speak.

"Then, you'll need a wedding ring." Picking up her left hand, he slid the ring on her finger, holding her hand longer than necessary before releasing it.

"Thank you. I...I didn't think about a ring."

"That's what the groom is for." It looked as though he were about to say more, but he turned away abruptly. "Ready to face the firing squad?"

She drew in a reinforcing breath, knowing his words weren't far from the truth. After patting Mackie and giving instructions for him to behave, Amanda knew she couldn't stall any longer. Picking up her evening bag, she turned to Ryan with a forced smile. "As ready as I'll ever be."

Once downstairs, they were soon swept into the crowd gathering in a room that formerly had been a parlor in the grand old house. Aware of numerous admiring looks directed at Ryan from the women, Amanda was glad to have him on her arm.

He guided them toward the bar and she stiffened, wondering again if he had a drinking problem. Maybe he was the type who took advantage of every open bar like a kid set loose in Disneyland with no lineups, no admission fees.

"What would you like, Amanda?"

She withheld a sigh. "Red wine."

He turned to the bartender. "One glass of red wine and a club soda with lime."

She wondered if her feeling ridiculous showed.

Ryan placed a tip in the bartender's glass. "I don't like to drink on the days I travel—by plane or car. Dulls my reactions." He lifted their drinks and held out her red wine.

Accepting the glass, she glanced around the room, rather than at Ryan, suspecting that her absurd thoughts must be written across her face. But by avoiding him to glance around the room she found herself in the direct path of her oldest and dearest friends, all with their husbands at their sides.

Linking her arm through Ryan's, she turned to him. "This is it."

He glanced up, saw the group gaining on them and nodded, a devilish glint in his eyes. "Good. The looker's here, too."

Amanda shot him an exasperated glare, before turning back to her friends. Not liking that gleam in his eyes, she hoped it didn't mean he planned to sabotage her plan before it began.

She visualized introducing him as her groom while he put the moves on Candy Johnson.

The gushing and round of introductions filled any awkward pauses. Each of her friends proudly presented their handsome, successful husbands. And then it was Amanda's turn.

Suzy Burns might be Burns-Meriweather now—but she clearly hadn't changed her relentless ways. Her eyes remained fixed on Ryan, and she spoke as though she knew a delicious secret. "And this handsome mystery man must be yours, Amanda."

She took a deep breath and placed her fate in Ryan's hands. "This is Ryan West...my husband."

Chapter Five

Babbling, squeals and feminine shrieks of excitement filled their corner of the room as the musketeers converged on Ryan.

Suzy combined her cheerleader grin with a knowing smile. "Amanda, your husband's everything I thought he'd be…and more. No wonder you kept this one hidden—why take a chance at having him stolen?"

"This is your husband?" chimed in Candy Johnson and Linda Danvers at the same time, crowding around Amanda much as they had done as teenagers. The years fell away. Once again they were standing in the halls of Stanton High with incredible good news to be shared.

Amanda took another deep breath. "We eloped, and I wanted it to be a surprise. I knew the reunion was coming up and I wanted to tell all of you at the same time, but I guess Suzy beat me to the punch."

"A mystery whirlwind romance?" Candy questioned, looking skeptical.

Ryan put his arm around Amanda. "She swept me off my feet."

They all laughed at his quick wit.

Encouraged, Ryan pulled Amanda closer into his embrace. "And we're still on our honeymoon."

Amanda couldn't prevent a gasp at his statement. She

tried to cover her gaffe. "You don't have to advertise, Ryan."

"They'd have noticed, anyway, dear," he replied smoothly, before leaning over to nuzzle her neck.

"It's hard to hide that much happiness," she responded, managing not to blow their cover by gritting her teeth.

Ryan moved one hand to rest on the exposed flesh of her shoulders covered only with the narrow straps, and she repressed an unexpected shiver. The electricity of his touch had her eyes jerking upward to meet his intent gaze.

His voice was rich. "Aren't I one lucky guy?"

Amanda's friends nodded easily in agreement while she tried to breathe past the sudden obstruction in her chest.

Candy Johnson latched a possessive grip on her husband, while arching a coy brow. "So, you didn't break our little pact, Amanda. And we thought you'd be the only one."

"But that's just because we didn't know about your surprise," Suzy put in loyally. "It's not that we didn't think you'd find a husband." The words were barely out of her mouth when it apparently occurred to her how they might be interpreted. She smiled lamely at Ryan. "Sorry. I didn't mean for that to come out the way it sounded."

Ryan's smile oozed charm as he glanced down in apparent affection at Amanda. "No offense taken." One hand cupped her chin. "Never underestimate a determined hunter."

"Goodness, now we're really going to think *she* chased *you*," Suzy added with a gleam of humor.

"You know how stubborn I am," Amanda retorted as she considered strangling him.

"I never had a chance," Ryan chimed in helpfully, with a shrug of his brawny shoulders. He looked about as helpless as a Dallas Cowboys linebacker.

"I *am* persuasive," Amanda muttered.

"But she did make an honest man of me," Ryan replied.

John Meriweather, Suzy's husband, roared with laughter.

"We're glad she caught you. You'll liven up the weekend."

Suzy held up her glass for a toast. "I agree. To the newlyweds!"

"To the newlyweds!" the others chimed in.

Amanda forced an answering grin. She hadn't dreamed Ryan possessed such a glib side to his personality. If he wasn't using it to needle her, she could appreciate his considerable charm.

Ryan linked his arm through hers as they raised their glasses to the toast, forcing her face next to his, his lips dangerously close.

The others applauded the romantic gesture, and for an instant Amanda wondered how it would feel to truly share such an intimate gesture with this handsome, charming stranger. Then the moment was broken as music crashed down around them.

While the band bombarded the room with songs from the seventies and eighties, their small group filled one another in on the time they'd been apart.

John Meriweather spoke to Ryan with more than polite interest, after learning that he was a real estate developer. "I'd like to hear more about the deal you're putting together. Maybe tomorrow at the picnic, when we don't have a band blasting around us."

Amanda watched Ryan nod his agreement as the small band that had been hired for the reunion segued into music more suited for dancing. Slow strains of a romantic song popular when Amanda was in high school began to play.

"Oh, this one's for the newlyweds!" Suzy exclaimed.

"Yes, yes!" Linda chimed in, clapping her hands. "You two look so romantic together. This dance must be meant for you."

Even Candy's possessive smile seemed to have melted. "They're right. Give us old married people a thrill."

Amanda glanced skeptically at Candy. If anything, she resembled a fashion model, certainly not a harried housewife. But the others were also urging them toward the center of the floor where a few couples had begun dancing.

Ryan held out his hand. Hesitantly, Amanda accepted his grasp, unnerved again by his touch. Thinking she'd gotten too serious in playing her role, she tried to ignore the thrill that swept through her as Ryan pulled her into his arms, fitting his body close to hers.

Ryan glanced down at the tumble of fiery curls that strayed toward that long, lovely neck and wondered if he was crazy. If they got any more convincing, he would have to meet her family.

Still, he pulled her close. "We need to look realistic, like true newlyweds," he murmured, taking an opportunity to breathe in that unique scent of hers, an intriguing combination of flowers and spice, innocence and fire. It had clung to the shower and the towels she'd neatly folded in the bathroom. It had followed him down to the bar, then back to the room again.

For a slick operator, she wasn't too smooth. In fact, he was fairly certain that if he hadn't stepped in, she would have blown their cover. It didn't fit the profile of the woman who had navigated through complicated bank records to commit fraud. Still, it was no misunderstanding that her name *had* appeared on his loan papers.

But her scent still tantalized him, and her softness made him long to keep on dancing, holding her close. Realizing just how close he *was* holding her, he forced himself to put some distance between them.

Amanda glanced at him as he subtly separated them. "Isn't our admiring audience still watching?"

"I'm sure they're still there."

She tilted her head back. "You're doing a great job."

Ryan stiffened, but she apparently didn't notice.

"You've got them all convinced. I wasn't sure it was possible, but you did it," she continued.

"Does this mean I get a bonus in my pay envelope?" he asked dryly.

Her brows drew together in a frown. "Is something wrong?"

Ryan wasn't sure why it rankled him that she was treating him like an employee who had performed exceptionally well. "Nothing that taking your name off my bank records won't fix."

"I told you—"

"I know. Computer imps had their way with my loan papers. You're going to have to do better than that."

Her steps slowed. "Funny way you have with this charm business. It turns on and off like a light switch."

"Don't you want to fool your friends?"

He heard her suck in her breath. But the song was ending.

Keeping his hand at her back, he walked Amanda back to the rest of her musketeers. They'd found a place to sit, a round table that had been meant to accommodate six people, but her friends had crowded eight chairs in that same space. It was a cozy setup, forcing Ryan and Amanda to sit shoulder to shoulder.

Candy Johnson leaned across the table. "Okay. How did you two meet? I want details!"

Amanda smiled at Ryan, then opened her mouth to speak, but Ryan started talking first. "You all know how wild and crazy our Amanda is."

"Only on rare occasions," Suzy replied, her face lighting up.

"But when she does go crazy, she *really* goes crazy." Ryan's eyelid dropped in that all-knowing male wink. "But I digress."

Amanda, already pinkening in embarrassment, leveled him a telling glare. Ryan smiled in return. Thinking he'd taken her broad hint, she opened her mouth to speak, but he beat her again.

"She had her vacation to Cleveland all planned..."

Amanda's jaw slackened as she mouthed "Cleveland?"

"The day of her flight, she got to the airport, had a wild

idea, changed her ticket and flew to a beach in the south of Britain.''

"Just like that?" Linda breathed.

Ryan snapped his fingers together. "Just like that. Turned out to be the best thing that ever happened to me." He glanced down lovingly at Amanda. From the wattage of anger reflected in her eyes, he suspected she was transmitting more volts than the local electric company. "Wasn't it, doll face?"

"Right, pumpkin...head."

Ryan laughed at the word play. "She knows I love all her little pet names for me. She even has one that she calls me when—"

Amanda's sharply rising voice cut in. "Weren't you telling them about how we met?"

"Right, sweet cheeks. It was a big British holiday and the beaches were packed. I'd managed to find my own square foot of beach, but I couldn't help noticing Amanda—" his eyes flicked knowingly at the other husbands "—just like every other man on the beach had. She was wearing the smallest bikini...I have handkerchiefs that are bigger than that suit." He paused, obviously enjoying being swept into the memory. "You can guess how great she looked."

A mottled flush crept up Amanda's neck, especially as the others hooted in agreement.

Ryan accepted their admiration as his due, acting as though they'd just commented on a prize horse he owned. "Amanda hadn't found her piece of the beach, but you know how stubborn she is."

The other three musketeers all nodded in agreement.

Traitors, Amanda fumed silently. They were supposed to be *her* friends!

"Luckily, she put her sandals and towel close to the spot I'd staked out—gave me an excuse to keep staring at her even when she'd swum out in the water, especially since she ignored the warning flag about currents, heading straight for the most dangerous area. I was enjoying the view, when I noticed something was wrong. She had a look of pure panic on her face.''

Amanda had a sudden overwhelming urge to bury her head in her hands, dreading what Ryan might say next.

''I thought she'd been caught in an undertow, or was wrapped up with a jellyfish. Since I'd been watching only Amanda, I saw her before the lifeguard did and went out after her.''

''Was it the undertow?'' Suzy asked breathlessly.

''Yes and no.''

Now caught up in the story, his rapt audience looked puzzled, but insatiably curious.

''The undertow caught something. It wasn't Amanda... but it *was* the top of her bathing suit. And right about the time I reached her, a good-sized wave crested, then broke, carrying her right into my arms. I took one look at...Amanda...and scooped her up. Since I'd saved her modesty, the next logical step was to save her reputation.''

''Her reputation?'' Candy echoed in delight. ''Oh, this must be good!''

Amanda glared at Ryan, willing him to stop, but obviously he was an accomplished liar. *Real estate developer, my eye, she thought. More likely he was a used-car salesman. He was spouting fast, slick lies as though he did it every day.*

Ryan chose that moment to wink at her deliberately as he answered Candy's question. ''When we got back to my spot of the beach, both of our towels were gone. There was literally nothing standing between Amanda and thousands of gawking tourists.'' Ryan judged their reactions, pausing for effect. ''Except for me.'' He was rewarded with a gasp, not to mention a mounting glare from Amanda. ''And you know how stuffy and disapproving the British can be.''

Murmurs of horrified agreement met this statement.

Ryan shook his head at the ''memory.'' Then he continued his story. ''And since she'd taken a local bus to the beach, Amanda didn't have her own car to hide in. Unfortunately mine was parked several blocks away. Amanda really had only one choice since she couldn't ride the bus...without getting arrested. So I carried her to my car." Ryan paused again, stretching out the moment. "Unfortunately a press photographer was getting into his own car, just one length down from ours. And the next morning, Amanda's...face...was splashed on the front page."

"Why did they care about one American tourist?" Linda asked, her eyes wide, obviously caught up in the drama of the story.

"Normally they wouldn't, but Amanda had made a generous donation the day before. It was a rare collectible she'd uncovered while antiquing in the countryside. Realizing its value and the hopelessness of tracing the original owner, Amanda donated the piece...to the local order of Benedictine monks."

Gasps punctuated this morsel as Ryan moved in for the kill. "The headlines had a great time with the whole thing..."

He paused as Amanda made a strangled sound.

"The headline read From Monks to Monkey Business." They all broke into laughter.

"Oh, Amanda, how awful for you!" Linda exclaimed.

"She didn't come out so bad," Candy drawled, gesturing to Ryan. "Look what a little fishing in the ocean netted her."

Suzy's face was all mischief. "It sounds terrific! What an adventure! And think of the fun you'll have telling this story to your children."

Amanda glanced at the overladen buffet, wondering what her friends would think if she poured the entire bowl of sherbet-laced red punch on Ryan's head.

But he was smiling again. "Since I was the man in the picture, I released a press statement saying that Amanda and I were engaged, and that she'd only swum in the treacherous current because I'd dared her to."

Ryan purposely met Amanda's answering glare with a tender, if amused, smile. "In the course of pretending to be madly in love, we found out that we actually were."

Three of the musketeers sighed in romantic envy while the object of that envy sent lethal missives of anger from her flashing green eyes. Enjoying every moment, Ryan returned her glare with a slow, lazy and promising look. Then he turned back to the others. "A little bizarre, but far less boring than meeting at the grocery store, on a blind date...or even while doing business."

Amanda wished she could slide bonelessly beneath the chair and out of sight. But first she wanted to kill Ryan West. It would certainly be a crime of passion—rage in the first degree. Too bad there were so many witnesses around.

Suzy turned to Amanda, puzzlement replacing the mischief on her face. "But you never did much swimming when we were in school. You didn't even like it. We had to drag you out in the sun because of that delicate, white skin. And you went to the beach for a vacation?"

Ryan reached out to pull Amanda close, then squeezed her affectionately, keeping his arm around her shoulders as he poured insinuation into his deep voice. "She enjoys a lot of things now that she never used to. Isn't that right, angel?"

"Yes, pumpkin head, I'm not nearly as discriminating as I once was."

Suzy laughed and the others joined in mere seconds later.

"Lucky for me her bark's worse than her bite," Ryan replied, clearly relishing this payback. "But then, her bite's not half bad, either."

"So you honeymooned in Britain?" Candy asked.

"No, we were back in the States by then," Ryan supplied. "So we decided to keep it simple, stay in California and fly somewhere close."

"Where did you go?" Linda asked.

"Carmel..." Amanda answered.

"Napa Valley..." Ryan said simultaneously.

"That was some plane ride," Candy remarked, her glance markedly roving from Ryan to Amanda.

"Actually, I love Carmel and we thought about going there, but there was a wine-tasting in Napa Valley that Ryan had planned for us, along with a darling bed and breakfast for us to stay in," Amanda replied, realizing that even though Ryan had made her look ridiculous, he had handled the explanation better on his own. "And we decided to save Carmel for another time."

"You're already planning a second honeymoon?" Suzy asked. "Oh, this must be true love."

Ryan laid his hand over Amanda's. "Every day is another honeymoon."

Amanda stared for a moment at his large, tanned hand covering her smaller, paler one. She had a disconcerting flash of premonition, something resembling déjà vu, only in reverse. There was familiarity coupled with an exciting newness. And for a moment she was tempted to blurt out the truth, to tell her friends about their charade before the wheels she'd set in motion were too irreversible.

Linda Danvers broke through those thoughts, and the moment of truth was gone. "Amanda, I'm so glad for you both. And since you waited till we were all together to tell us, it's like we're all part of the celebration *now*. And this weekend will be great. It'll be better than if we'd been at the actual wedding."

Amanda and Ryan's eyes met and held. Hers promised retribution, his guaranteed more of the same treatment.

"She's right," Candy admitted. Then a grin covered her exquisite features. "We'll roll your bachelorette party, shower and reception into one great big bash!"

Suzy leaned forward. "Great idea." She held up her cocktail glass and glanced at the others. "Agreed?"

Amanda swallowed as the others chimed in their agreement. She'd thought she had Ryan over a barrel in this bargain. But it was becoming rapidly clear that she was rushing down Niagara Falls without even a sliver from that barrel.

Chapter Six

Amanda entered their hotel room in silent fury. She knew that Ryan followed her, then shut the door, but she refused to acknowledge his presence. Absently, she bent to pet Mackie, who bounded around them in circles, ecstatic at their return.

Crossing the room, she stood by the French doors, staring out at the darkness. She was glad that only one lamp was lit in the room. She didn't need another spotlight. What she needed was a way to vent her anger—but she didn't think the quiet hotel would appreciate a brawl.

She considering squandering another wish on having Ryan appear in the lobby of the hotel clad in the male version of the teeny bikini he'd dreamed up. But somehow she suspected that instead of embarrassing him, he'd be the center of attention for some very appreciative ladies.

"You still steaming?" Ryan asked, taking a paper napkin from his pocket. Unfolding it, he whistled for Mac-Dougall and offered the dog a present—a slice of the succulent roast beef that had been served on miniature rolls at the buffet. Gratefully, Mackie chomped down the treat, then propped his paws on Ryan's knees in appreciation. Ryan ruffled the long hair on the dog's head, then rose.

Amanda stared at him a moment, some of her anger deflated. It was hard to maintain her cold mask of fury when the man had thought to bring her dog a goody, something she hadn't remembered. And Mackie, normally very persnickety about strangers, was accepting him completely.

Amanda suspected that Ryan's elaborate story to her friends was a payback for forcing him into coming this weekend. Another portion of her anger leaked away. Reluctantly, Amanda realized she could give him this one point. She knew that in his place, she wouldn't have complacently accepted the weekend, either.

And realistically, she knew that if they had a huge blowout, it would be difficult to convince her friends they were a loving couple for the remainder of the weekend.

Ryan's voice shook her from her reverie. "You didn't answer. Are you still mad?"

"I'm not too thrilled at the moment," she conceded. "But I'll probably get over it. How did you come up with that story, anyway?"

"Don't see yourself romping topless on the British coast?" He unloosened his tie. "I could have made it the French Riviera."

Something other than anger was weaving its way inside. It was too easy to imagine them both frolicking in the ocean with nothing but the sun-kissed waves between them. Alarmed, she tried to put the brakes on her overactive imagination. "I'm not really the bikini-romping type."

His gaze took a leisurely survey down the length of her body. "Don't sell yourself short."

Suddenly flustered, Amanda turned away. On exhibition for the entire evening, she had been relieved to get offstage, but now she felt back on display with the evening to face. In one room.

With one bed.

To busy herself, Amanda stepped toward the window. Abandoning caution, she flung open the old-fashioned sash windows. A blush of nighttime air tinged with sweet-smelling flowers greeted her. She took a deep breath, hoping to cleanse away some of the tension that even now was increasing.

"The fresh air feels good," Ryan commented from behind her.

"It's been a claustrophobic evening. I think I'll open the doors to the terrace, too."

Amanda darted back toward the center of the room, putting some distance between them. "Um, yes, it has been. More air would be good."

"Are you going to stay dressed up all night?"

Glancing down at her forgotten evening wear, Amanda realized she was still wearing her cocktail dress and killer heels. Ryan, meanwhile, had removed his jacket and tie. "I guess not."

Ryan's raised eyebrows pointedly reminded her that all she'd shed was her evening purse.

Reaching up, she slid the pins from her hair and gingerly shook her curls to her shoulders as she stepped out of her heels.

Ryan's voice was coated with pure amusement. "Ready to let your hair down?"

Damn him, the man was laughing at her! Amanda knew she could get prim and huffy, no doubt what he was expecting, or simply ignore him. Doing just that, she ran her fingers through her hair, finger-combing the wild mane.

In a moment, he broke the silence. "Not speaking to me again?"

She glanced at him calmly. "What's the point? If you insist on behaving like a hormonal teenager on his first date, I'd have a better conversation with Mackie."

This just seemed to amuse him more. In fact, his smile escalated into a full-fledged grin. "I'm assuming he's passed the hormonal stage."

"Which is more than I can say about you."

Some of his good humor faded. "You don't know enough about me to make any kind of judgment."

"That didn't seem to stop you in judging me," she retorted.

"*I'm* not the one who orchestrated this weekend."

Some unfathomable desire to needle him until he blew his cool was gripping her. Amanda turned, her chin lifted high, poised for a fight. "Intending to make good your threats?"

His eyes darkened, then roved over her. She kept her posture defiant, guessing that she was going to use a year's worth of adrenaline this weekend.

But his voice remained even, if clipped, containing neither anger nor apology as he refused to rise to the bait. "It's been a long day. I suggest we don't make the night the same. We both need some sleep."

Her gaze skipped pointedly toward the bed.

"I suppose you expect me to say that I'm going to be a gentleman and let you have the bed..." Ryan met her gaze, and the force of his personality was as visible as a red warning flag. "Well, I'm not. I don't plan to spend the night sleeping on the floor."

Amanda couldn't prevent a glance downward at the shiny, well-polished hardwood floor. Not an appealing prospect. Yet she lifted her chin upward again. "What do you suggest?"

"That's a loaded question. But for now I suggest we act like reasonable adults." As he spoke, he loosened the tails of his shirt at his slim, belted waist. Next came the first few buttons.

Reasonable. She could be reasonable under most circumstances, but these circumstances might change depending on just how much of his clothing he planned to take off. "Do I have your word on that?"

"Disappointed?" As she sputtered, his brow furrowed, and she saw a return of his forceful side. "Look, lady. I'll do what it takes to get through this weekend because I need your signature on my loan papers, but don't expect any promises. I'm not here to make you feel good." His expression changed, that trace of humor lurking in his eyes. "Unless that's what you really want."

Realizing that he had effectively turned the tables and

was goading her, Amanda refused his challenge, wishing she'd not started this stupid game of wills. *Great, another valuable wish down the tubes.* Her color climbing high, Amanda spoke stiffly. "As you said, we can act like reasonable adults."

Ryan finished unbuttoning his shirt, pulled out the tails, then slipped it off. "At least *I* can."

Amanda refused to react, though she itched to wipe the smirk from his face. She suspected he would enjoy her discomfort if she tossed down the gauntlet again. Grudgingly she admitted that he was a formidable adversary. With a start, she wondered if she'd lost her mind, baiting him on this crucial first day of the reunion.

And although she needed Ryan to carry out her plan, she was now having serious doubts about that plan. These were her friends she was deceiving. Was pride more important than friendship? Not to mention the fact that she still had her family to deal with.

But thoughts of both family and friends fled as she watched Ryan step out of his pants. Clad only in brief silk boxers, he casually strolled across the room. She tried not to notice the ripple of abundant muscles, the length of bared, tanned skin. And she was supposed to climb into a bed next to him and get a good night's sleep? She *was* crazy.

Deciding not to duplicate his casual striptease, she picked up her overnight case and marched into the bathroom. Once inside she slipped on her baby doll pajamas. Glancing in the full-length mirror on the back of the door, she frowned. At home these had seemed like the most practical nightwear she owned. Right now, she wished they had a few more yards of material. Had the scoop neck seemed this low at home? Had the shortie bottoms been this skimpy?

Digging through her suitcase, she searched for the long bottoms she'd packed as an alternative. After a few minutes, she gave up the search, realizing it was futile. Apparently, she was once again a victim of her own forgetfulness. It was a nuisance at times. She glanced down at her bare legs. Especially now.

And he was brash enough to notice every detail. Why couldn't Ryan West be the kind, gentle sort of man she'd always envisioned as a husband? A man who would be a friend as well as a soul mate. Even if he was only a pretend husband.

She wished Ryan was the kind of man who would behave as a perfect gentleman, who would not make her so intensely aware of the length of bare legs her pajamas exposed. Amanda clapped one hand to her forehead. There went one more wasted wish. Ryan was more likely to turn into a snake oil salesman than a perfect gentleman.

A thoughtful, sensitive man wouldn't have casually stripped down to his boxers while announcing he had no intention of sleeping on the floor. And a different sort of man wouldn't have made her so intensely aware of their enforced intimacy.

Perhaps when she'd made her initial wish, she should have specified the kind of husband she'd always wanted—a considerate helpmate who would walk hand in hand through their years together, one who would be a partner, a steady rock. Never once in those dreams had a man of Ryan's rugged features with wild, longish hair and intimidating manners appeared. Maybe she'd gotten someone *else's* wish.

Shaking back her unruly riot of curls, Amanda braced herself to return to the bedroom. She could hardly hide all night in the bathroom, although she longed to. But hiding would simply be grist for mockery.

She eased the door open and padded quietly back into the bedroom.

"If you're trying to be inconspicuous, you shouldn't flaunt those legs."

Amanda froze as his voice rose from the near darkness. Uncertain whether to take his words as a compliment or simply a come-on, she shook back her hair and acted as though the words meant nothing to her. "Look, Mr. West—"

"Isn't that a bit formal, *Mrs.* West?" His mocking laugh rolled over her. "Or is that *Miss* Thorne? I could call you Thorny for short. Fits your personality."

"Suit yourself. I'm too tired to argue with you. I, for one, am going to get some sleep." Concentrating on ignoring him, she walked to the side of the bed, took a bracing breath and slid into the bed and beneath the plump down comforter.

Ryan's body weighted the mattress, forming a groove that made a natural incline that sloped toward him. She fought gravity as well as the overwhelming sensation of sharing the bed with him. The springs squeaked as he shifted, and she stiffened into a rigid line. The musky tang of his after-shave drifted over her, along with tendrils of warmth from his body.

Knowing she faced an even more harrowing day ahead, Amanda tried to relax, releasing a death grip on her side of the bed. Ryan turned toward her at the same time, and she instantly realized there would be no sleep for her that night.

Ryan watched Amanda for several minutes, aware of her agitation, delighting in escalating it. But the day was catching up with him, and he decided to give both of them a break. Turning his back to the center of the bed, he tried to relax and forget the flash of her long legs. And although that particular vision wouldn't even dim, much less disappear, pure exhaustion began to overwhelm him. Several days and nights of working endless hours, coupled with Amanda's glitch on his bank papers, the drive and tonight's performance were taking their toll. Despite Amanda's allure, he found his eyelids drooping.

On the edge of sleep, Ryan stirred as he felt a hesitant touch, then a nuzzle on his earlobe. Cracking open his eyelids, Ryan mentally reassessed his sleeping partner. The weekend could have untold promise, after all. Unable to repress a sleepily satisfied grin, Ryan turned to face Amanda in the center of the bed.

And met Mackie's muzzle as the dog happily retrieved the rawhide bone on Ryan's pillow. Satisfied, the dog settled into the curve of Amanda's back, cradling his bone.

Ryan allowed himself one leisurely look at those sweet curves before returning to his own side of the bed, a self-mocking, yet amused grin tugging at his lips. Oh, yes, this was going to be *some* weekend.

Chapter Seven

Sunshine streamed through the opened windows, along with a gentle breeze carrying the scent of pine and honeysuckle and the melody of songbirds. Amanda stirred, burrowing deeper beneath the comforter.

"You going to sleep all day?"

Amanda squinted, then glanced around, trying to remember where she was, finally focusing on Ryan. Dressed in jeans and a casual shirt, he looked as though he'd been up for hours. Never a morning person, she struggled to recall the night, realizing she couldn't even remember falling asleep. She did remember thinking she couldn't possibly sleep next to Ryan. Apparently she had, though.

Pushing herself to a sitting position, she longed for some privacy and at least a gallon of coffee. It always took her forever to wake up. She began her days semicomatose, and most of her mornings were a complete blur. She wanted her coffee so badly, Amanda could swear she was smelling some wickedly fragrant wake-up brew.

She shook back tousled curls. "I'll get ready and we can go have breakfast." She forced reluctant eyelids to open wider, managing nearly invisible slits. "Just give me a few minutes."

Ryan tossed her the terry robe from the bathroom. "I ordered breakfast in."

"Then that's really coffee I'm smelling?"

Humor laced his voice. "Just follow the yellow brick road to the terrace."

Glancing past him, she saw that he'd opened the French doors to their private terrace. Morning cobwebs made her forget how uncomfortable their bedroom situation was as she pulled on the robe and padded outside. It wasn't a cruel joke. There *was* coffee. Pouring a cup, she reverently inhaled the much-needed caffeine.

He didn't bother hiding his amusement. It was clear she was oblivious. "You want some company or is this a private religious moment?"

She waved indulgently to the other chair. "Anyone who orders coffee before I wake up can't be all bad."

"I thought you might want to have breakfast away from prying eyes."

In the process of pushing her hair off her forehead, Amanda paused. Although not completely focused, she realized how considerate he'd been. She was *not* looking forward to another session of pretense. "Any special reason for thinking about this?"

"I figured facing your family this morning would be bad enough. I didn't particularly want to start the day with two performances."

Her family. She nearly groaned the thought aloud. She'd called them the previous evening from the reception, and they were expecting her for coffee and cake around mid-morning.

She wasn't even fully awake yet, and sometime between now and then she was going to have to think of an explanation for her family. It occurred to her that maybe Ryan West was right. This *was* an idiotic idea.

THE THORNE FAMILY HOUSE was an unexpected pleasure. Ryan hadn't been sure what to expect, but this charming replica of a French château wouldn't have been his first guess. Nor his dozenth. Ivy and bougainvillea softened the aged brick and leaded glass pane windows. Terrazzo flagstones formed a welcoming path amid the greenery and blooming flowers. Architectural assets aside, it was the warmth of the family inside that made the home so welcoming.

Dan and Marjorie Thorne had greeted him with no reservations. It was clear that friends of Amanda's were always welcome. And apparently no explanation of their relationship was required. Amanda took MacDougall off his lead and the happy dog dove into the brush, his stiffly upright white tail a fast-moving flag as he disappeared.

Marjorie fussed over them both, offering coffee, homemade pastries and a wicked-looking chocolate cake. It was obvious that Amanda took after her fiery-haired mother, who was still a striking woman. It was also obvious that Amanda was dreading the explanation she needed to offer her parents.

"Beautiful gardens, Mr. Thorne," Ryan said as he looked at the peaceful setting. Lush greenery surrounded a graceful fountain. Twined amid the paths and a reflecting pool were curved benches meant for introspection—or perhaps a tryst for two.

"Marjorie deserves all the credit. She worked with a landscape designer, but the inspiration was all hers. She has an artistic streak a mile wide," Dan Thorne said with pride, smiling affectionately at his wife, who returned his look with a loving glance almost intimate in nature. Obviously, this was a happy marriage.

"Dad, why don't you show Ryan around the gardens? I know he won't want to miss them," Amanda suggested, a touch of strain evident in her voice.

Dan Thorne glanced between his wife, daughter and the man she'd brought to their home. Clearly he wondered what was going on, but was too polite to ask. Instead, he guided Ryan through the extensive grounds.

"Ah, stables," Ryan said with pleasure as they left the garden and walked toward the riding area, barn and stables.

"You like horses, then?"

"Very much. Unfortunately, now that I live in the city I don't get a chance to ride much."

"From what I understand, this reunion business will take up most of this weekend, but the next time you and Amanda visit, we'll be sure to get some riding in."

This was tricky ground to navigate. Uncertain what Amanda was telling her mother, Ryan hesitated. "I'm not sure how busy our schedules are going to be."

Dan Thorne snorted. "My daughter thinks there are thirty hours in every day. Don't worry, she'll be able to squeeze in a visit. She has a way with schedules."

Among other things. A picture of Amanda's long legs and fiery curls flashed in his mind. Looking at the kind, sincere man who had openly offered his hospitality, Ryan realized that there was far more to this weekend than he'd realized. He deserved an Oscar if they pulled this off.

"ALL RIGHT, AMANDA. Spill it."

"Do you suppose *Leave It to Beaver*'s mom talked like that?" Amanda asked her mother, an impudent grin lurking on her lips.

"Nope. Which is why she didn't know what was going on most of the time," Marjorie Thorne replied calmly. "Now, who is Ryan West and why haven't we heard about him?"

Amanda debated her choices and regretfully realized that the truth was her only option. She explained everything, including the previous evening. "So," she concluded, "when everyone congratulates you on our marriage, you'll be prepared."

Marjorie Thorne lifted delicate eyebrows. "For what? If we accept their congratulations, how do we explain our missing son-in-law in the future?"

"Well, I haven't exactly thought that out," Amanda admitted. "But I guessed...knew...I ought to warn you," she finished lamely.

"About what, hot stuff?" Larry Thorne, Amanda's

brother, strolled onto the patio, squeezed her shoulder affectionately, then reached immediately for one of the pastries.

"About pastry-snatching marauders," Amanda replied with equal affection. Her eyes signaled to her mother that she didn't want to discuss her fake marriage with Larry.

Marjorie's answering expression told her she would have to deal with the problem eventually.

Just then, Ryan and her father returned from their tour.

"Glad to see that your young man appreciates good horseflesh," Dan Thorne told his daughter.

Amanda cocked an inquiring eyebrow at Ryan.

Dan Thorne glanced between them and drew his own brows together in confusion. "Don't tell me you didn't know he liked horses, Mandy."

She flushed and tried to change the subject by introducing her brother to Ryan. During introductions, Larry and Ryan sized each other up. As the older brother, Larry had always been protective. And he hadn't changed.

"Good to meet you, Ryan. So you're Amanda's date for the reunion?"

Ryan met Amanda's pleading eyes. "Someone had to do it."

Larry laughed, a deep, hearty sound. "Spoken like someone who knows our Amanda and has a healthy respect for the gathering of old friends."

Amanda's smile spelled relief as she relaxed, surrounded by her family. Although Ryan kept up his end of the conversation with the other Thornes, he concentrated on watching Amanda, discovering this side of her. There was more to this woman than he'd initially suspected. Why would someone who came from this obvious prosperity need to scheme to include herself on his bank records? Even more so, why had she needed to scheme to secure a date?

As Ryan watched her, sunlight danced over the freckles sprinkled across the bridge of her nose and lit that incredible mass of hair into a flame. Those extraordinary green eyes of hers flashed like stolen emeralds.

As she smiled at her family, her features softened, and Ryan realized just how beautiful she was. Last night, he'd found it difficult to focus on anything other than her fabulous legs, legs that had begun somewhere near the equator and stretched clear to Antarctica. And, of course, on the soft curves her ridiculously scanty sleepwear hadn't disguised.

Watching her sleep this morning had been a form of torture. One he'd had to end before he awakened her to discover if her passion matched her fiery coloring. He had to remind himself this was strictly a business deal, one he'd entered reluctantly.

Perhaps she was a smoother operator than he realized. One who could fool family and friends. It was a sobering thought. Maybe even her reluctance was a well-orchestrated act to lend believability to her performance.

Just then, she laughed at something Larry said, then punched her brother smartly in the arm. If there was artifice in that wide grin of hers, Ryan couldn't see it.

"I don't know how you stand this brat," Larry told him, rubbing his arm in feigned injury.

"She has a way with words," Ryan replied, catching Amanda's glance. "It's hard to say no to her."

"Yeah, she's a pain, all right," Larry agreed artlessly.

"Is this some sort of instant male bonding?" Amanda asked, glancing between them. "If so, it's revolting."

"She never has appreciated my many finer qualities," Larry complained, wiggling his eyebrows at his sister.

"That's because they're so well hidden," she retorted in mock anger.

Ryan glanced between them, wondering at their rapport, something he'd never experienced in his own family. An only child, living alone with his father, Ryan had never known anything like the Thornes seemed to share. He'd always suspected this sort of family life didn't exist beyond the confines of television shows like *The Waltons* or the *Brady Bunch*. It wasn't as though he hadn't been to friends' homes, ones that carried their share of laughter and happiness. Still, he always doubted just how much of that happiness remained once behind closed doors.

Yet Marjorie and Dan Thorne seemed to be genuine in their affection. As his gaze shifted, Ryan watched a different Amanda. This was an easy, natural Amanda. Unselfconscious and unconcerned, she glowed. It was a far cry from the calculating image she'd projected when conning him into this weekend.

"As much as I'd like to continue this battle of the wits—" Amanda paused, grinning devilishly at her brother "—especially with the unarmed, we have a picnic to attend." She offered her parents an apologetic look. "I'm sorry the morning's so rushed, but next trip I'm all yours."

"Along with Ryan, of course," her father added.

She smiled uneasily, then glanced at Ryan.

"It's been a pleasure," Ryan told the senior Mr. Thorne, rising and shaking the older man's hand, deflecting the question. It bothered him to deceive these people. He wondered how the deception made Amanda feel. Thinking of her cloudy business practices, Ryan tightened his lips. Maybe this, too, was just business as usual.

Amanda called the dog, and MacDougall appeared in short time, tongue wagging, looking as though he was grinning widely.

After climbing inside the car, they waved goodbye while pulling out of the driveway. As they drove out of view, Amanda slumped back in the seat. "Geez, I feel like slime."

Her words surprised him; still, he wondered if they were strictly for his benefit. "They seemed all right with whatever you told them."

"Yeah—for now." She glanced through the window, away from him. "I knew it would be rough, but I didn't think my family would want to practically adopt you."

Ryan straightened up in the seat, feeling both surprised and slightly insulted. "You were *hoping* they'd find me unacceptable?"

"Of course not!" She blew out an exasperated sigh. "I just hoped it would be easier, less complicated. I don't know...I wish I'd never started this thing." Then she whacked her hand against the armrest as she muttered, "There goes another one."

Ryan glanced at her, wondering how much of the truth she was editing, both to him and to her parents. "I'm guessing you told your mother."

Amanda propped her legs up against the dash. "There's no fooling her." She hesitated, drawing out the next words. "I appreciate the way you handled things. I know it was awkward—"

"They're nice people," he replied shortly, not wanting to delve into why he'd felt compelled to impress them. If they didn't know what their daughter was involved in, it wasn't up to him to point out the truth.

"Still..." She twisted toward him. "Look, I know you didn't want to do this whole weekend thing, but I appreciate your not hanging me out to dry with my family."

Ryan grunted an unintelligible reply and glanced away from her, not wanting to see how captivating she looked in the morning light, her face appealing in its earnestness.

Amanda twisted around again, her expression an illuminating canvas of her thoughts. "Time to change gears again. Ready to face my fearsome friends?"

Ryan let out a short laugh. "I thought you were rethinking the weekend idea."

"Don't think you're getting out of this. We still have the rest of today and tomorrow to get through."

"That would be pretty hard to forget...Mandy."

PEOPLE SPILLED THROUGH the picnic grounds, old friends latching onto one another, couples relaxing beneath the canopy of huge trees. Decorated with gigantic bouquets of helium-filled balloons, the park resembled a country fair. Some people brought their children, allowing them to run free over the grass carpeting the area. Their happy shrieks combined with the adult chatter.

Amanda was glad of Ryan's arm looped casually around her shoulders. It seemed that everyone in her graduating class was paired off. Had she missed out on something important? Sneaking a glance at Ryan, she realized how grateful she was for his cooperation. At the same time, she wondered why he was doing such a good job. A picture of his angry face as he demanded that she sign his loan papers flashed into her mind. There was a reason, she reminded herself.

"Amanda! Ryan!" Several voices shouted from a nearby picnic table.

"It's the gang," Amanda whispered to Ryan.

"And I thought we might be spared," he muttered, raking a hand through his hair.

Glancing at him, she saw him through the eyes of the admiring women even now noticing him. He was lean and dangerous-looking, his wild, dark hair on the long side of conventional, his forbidding gaze as intriguing as his handsome face. His shoulders were broad enough to intimidate, his tapering torso and lean hips an invitation for a second look.

And the women around were definitely looking.

It was Ryan's manner as much as his looks, Amanda realized. Apparently, his in-control, take-no-prisoners attitude appealed to some women. Although, she reminded herself, she personally had always dreamed of a gentler man, one who would appreciate her interests, perhaps share them, not one who stared at her as though he were examining every pore of her skin, every cell in her brain. Strangely, the thought of him studying her skin made her uncomfortably warm.

Her feet stumbled for a moment, and she felt Ryan's

strong grip around her arm. It was disconcerting the way his touch made her nervous system stand on alert.

Trying to ignore those feelings, she waved broadly to her friends. Already in fine form, the group had gathered at a redwood table littered with beer-filled paper cups. The reunion committee had arranged the informal barbecue so that the graduates could bring their families. Tonight's dance was the most formal event of the weekend.

"You'll have to scrunch in," Suzy greeted them, gesturing to the small space left on the bench.

"Won't be hard for you newlyweds," Linda agreed with a knowing grin.

Amanda remembered to smile as she and Ryan were crowded next to each another, legs molded side by side, shoulders crammed together. They were close enough for her to feel the rigid, unyielding length of muscles in his leg, the solid bunching of strength in his shoulders, and the heat that flowed from his body to hers.

Disconcerted, she turned toward Suzy and spoke brightly. Too brightly, gauging from Suzy's expression. "So, is everyone having a great time?"

"Not everyone's on their honeymoon," Suzy replied dryly.

"Not that we wouldn't like to be," Linda chimed in, reaching for her husband's hand.

Candy arched her perfect eyebrows. "Maybe our Amanda will start a trend."

Suzy picked up her paper cup of beer. "Here's to trends." As she raised her glass she bumped into her husband, causing a chain reaction down the crowded table. Amanda swerved to avoid being bumped off the end of the picnic bench. As she moved, Ryan turned at the same time and her breasts grazed his chest. Frozen by awareness, they stared at each other in the small space, made smaller by the bodies jostling one another to regain their seating.

"She's too taken by her new husband to worry about trends," Candy teased.

Ryan and Amanda deliberately moved apart as far as the crowded conditions allowed.

"I think it's sweet," Linda put in. "The first stages of romance are so exciting."

Amanda couldn't prevent her glance from straying back to Ryan. His dark eyes were still unreadable, but there was a new light there, one she couldn't decipher, but one that pulled at her.

Ryan picked up his paper cup and held it toward Amanda in a salute. Sucking in her breath, she saw for an instant what was hidden in his expression. A flare of desire revealed itself and then was masked as quickly. Had it been for the benefit of her friends? Or was this strictly a one-on-one response?

"Amanda, I want to hear about your business," Linda said as they lowered their cups. "I love collecting. It must be wonderful to be able to do it all the time."

Amanda jerked her eyes away from Ryan. "I think so. But then I'm prejudiced because it's what I've always wanted to do."

"Tell us about your shop," Linda encouraged.

Amanda gathered her scattered thoughts and launched into a description of Thorne's Treasures. Despite the distraction of Ryan, it was easy, since she loved her business. "...So I specialize in collectibles, although I do a brisk antiques trade as well," she concluded.

"I'm dying to do my house in art deco," Candy confided. "But I don't know enough about the style not to get ripped off."

"I'd be glad to give you some pointers," Amanda offered.

"What exactly *is* art deco?" Linda asked, picking up a potato chip. "I hear people talking about it, but I'm not really sure."

Ryan's knee nudged hers, and Amanda straightened up, trying to remember what her friend had asked. Oh... yes...deco.

"Please tell us," Suzy urged. "I'm not sure, either."

"You're not alone," Amanda replied, deliberately ignoring Ryan's closeness, trying to concentrate on her expertise rather than the long, muscular thigh wedged against hers. "Especially since art deco actually started as an architectural style. The lobby of Coit Tower on Telegraph Hill is an art deco landmark you've probably seen. And as art deco caught on, the style influenced home decorations, then jewelry."

"I wonder why it caught on so fast," Linda mused.

Amanda moved a notch away from Ryan, still unable to shed the connection of his body seated so close to hers. "Art deco was a protest against the fussiness of art nouveau. I suspect its very disparity made it popular." Glancing to one side, she caught Ryan's gaze, studying her face. The rest of her thought trailed away.

Linda smiled at Amanda, catching her attention. "You really love your business, don't you?"

Amanda couldn't contain a grin. "Guilty. Sometimes I feel like I'm going to get busted for having a job I like so much. It hardly seems like work." She was surprised to see a startled expression flit across Ryan's face.

"Speaking of business, I'd like to talk with you, Ryan." John Meriweather, Suzy's husband, was capturing his attention. "I'd like to hear more details about that development deal you mentioned last night. Why don't we get a few plates of barbecue and discuss it?"

Ryan glanced at Amanda and the others hooted.

"Ah, newlyweds!" Suzy chortled. "Don't worry, you'll bear the separation."

Candy laughingly agreed. "You men go on. We want this to be a girls-only table for a while."

The husbands shrugged collectively and moved off toward the large serving tables.

As soon as they were out of earshot the others pounced on Amanda.

"He's a dream," Linda announced. "So dangerous-looking."

"Is he this sexy all the time?" Suzy demanded.

"And how did you manage to bag such big game?" Candy asked wickedly. "Or did you really net him with a teeny-weeny bikini top?"

Amanda could only laugh. These were, after all, her dearest friends. In moments, they were laughing with her, the years disappearing as their pact was remembered.

"We're kidnapping you," Suzy announced.

The others smiled knowingly at Amanda's surprise.

"And going to your bachelorette party!" Linda said with a whoop.

Amanda glanced at their bubbly faces. "You guys aren't kidding."

Suzy smiled conspiratorially. "There's never any kidding when love's involved."

Chapter Eight

Ryan waited on the terrace, preferring the fresh night air to the confines of the hotel bar. Tonight was the reunion dance, and he was allowing Amanda all the time she needed for primping. Although he'd quit smoking well over a year ago, he had a sharp, piquant need for a cigarette. He could almost taste that first drag, that sweet rush of nicotine. Issuing a muffled curse, he settled for a gulp of cooling coffee. The pot of dark brew, ordered from room service, was nearly empty.

Ryan paced the terrace, picturing Amanda that day. First, with her family. Then, when they had first arrived at the picnic and he'd gone to get their drinks. Unaware that he had returned and was watching her, she'd been completely unselfconscious. Her face, free of tension, was animated as she laughed with her friends. She'd talked, giggled and behaved like a high school girl. Not to mention how she'd reacted when the muskateers had kidnapped her, whisking her back to the hotel. There she'd been surprised by a roomful of friends who had combined a Chippendale dancer with a bridal shower—two very different kinds of gifts to be unwrapped. Amanda's laughter had outshone that of her friends as they'd spilled out of the impromptu party.

And later, when talking again about her business, she'd simply lit up, caught in her enthusiasm. She was either a very accomplished actress or she really loved her kooky business, which made him wonder why she would endanger it with the bank fraud scam. Not to mention a clouded set of books. Was everything about her simply a well-orchestrated act?

He'd known of equally complicated scams when a woman was out to take a man for everything he was worth. Ryan thought of his ex-wife, Danielle. She, too, had been an accomplished actress. He'd believed her sweet, thoughtful, loving persona, but then the pretense had disappeared once she had a wedding ring on her finger. And beneath the pretense the real person was nothing like she'd seemed. Danielle had duped him completely—and he'd been a careful man even then. But now he'd increased that awareness. There wasn't a woman alive who could fool him again.

Was Amanda playing a similar game? Could she be even more accomplished at it than Danielle had been? A flash of the way Amanda had been all afternoon struck him—the unguarded smile and surprising behavior. Even her unconventional features and that wild cap of hair were deceiving, because one of her remarkable smiles turned her face into an ivory-skinned pool of beauty.

It amazed him that he hadn't noticed immediately. His friend, Barry, had seen it at once. What had he called her? A babe? Ryan glanced at the French doors, seeing Amanda's shapely silhouette through the gauzy linen curtains. Barry was right...and if he'd seen her in those pajamas she'd worn the previous evening his friend would have upped his assessment to babe-plus.

Amanda moved across the room, and he watched the grace in her walk, the slight sway of her hips. He remembered their first encounter. Then she had combined bravado with a swagger he'd assumed she used to cover her guilt. Even as he wondered what her swagger disguised, Ryan couldn't move his gaze.

As he completed the thought, Amanda opened the French doors, the light from the room spilling over her. Ryan caught his breath. Disdaining the expected little black dress, instead she'd chosen a sleek-fitting, copper-colored gown. With her vivid strawberry curls spilling over her shoulders, she looked like a flame. Wild and hot.

The only color not resembling fire was the green of her eyes. And they flashed like heated jewels.

"Do I look all right?" she asked, tilting her head and making the diamonds in her ears glitter.

All right... No, she was way beyond all right. Somewhere in the vicinity of fantastic...magnificent.

Ryan cleared his throat. "You look lovely." *Now, where had that come from?* He'd intended to say "fine," but the compliment had slipped out.

Her smile softened. "Thanks. I know I shouldn't be, but I'm kind of nervous about tonight. People who couldn't come last night or today will be at the dance tonight since it's the big event. I just want to look okay."

Which was like saying the ceiling of the Sistine Chapel looked okay. Didn't she have any idea of how fabulous she looked? "You do," he replied shortly.

But it seemed to be enough for her. She nodded her head in approval. "You look pretty okay yourself."

He glanced down at his tux, guessing that she hadn't expected him to care about his appearance. "Thanks."

She opened her tiny evening bag. "Now, if I can just find my earrings."

Despite his suspicions about her, Ryan couldn't resist a chuckle. Then he reached toward her ears where he fingered the diamonds she'd placed there. As his hands lingered, his amusement at her forgetfulness changed to something else.

"Oh," she breathed, noticeably missing a beat. "I'm always misplacing something."

Ryan knew he should take his hands away immediately, yet he hesitated, feeling the softness of her skin, the silky brush of her hair.

He met her eyes, read the question there and wanted to answer it by touching his lips to hers, by pulling her body closer to his....

Abruptly he stepped away, knowing the danger of forgetting she wasn't what she appeared to be. "Well, now you know where your earrings are."

Amanda's laugh was thready. "I'm terribly forgetful. I'm always forgetting where I've put my reading glasses, and my keys, and...but I guess I already said that...." Her voice trailed off.

Their gazes didn't break, and he wondered what he saw flickering across her expression, but then she clutched her small purse. "Are you ready to go to the ball?"

He cleared his throat, chasing away the previous moment, reclaiming his own distance. "Sure, Cinderella. Luckily we don't have to go to all the trouble of turning a pumpkin into a coach. We can ride down in the elevator."

"And, after the ball, you won't have to run all over the countryside with a glass slipper in your hand looking for me."

"I'll know right where to find you," he replied, instantly feeling the tension flare again between them, seeing the light of recognition in her eyes.

Amanda turned abruptly toward the doors leading into their room, apparently eager to flee the intimacy of the terrace. He considered saying more, rattling her composure before the evening began so that she might possibly reveal more to him than she intended. But instead he chose to remain silent as they boarded the elevator and then walked into the ballroom.

Ryan told himself it was because he didn't particularly want to start out on a strained note, either, not that he couldn't find it in himself to crush her before her big evening.

Swept into the crowd, Ryan realized immediately that Amanda was right. There *were* more people here tonight. And the mood was electric. Now that they were old enough to be swamped by responsibilities, children and careers, the graduates relished a chance to relive a time in their lives when their prom dates were their most pressing concern. Voices were excited, gestures loud and demonstrative.

Ryan draped an arm around Amanda's waist. He felt her stiffen slightly, then relax into his hold. Glancing around, he saw speculative looks from some of her classmates, male and female. He suspected many of the men would like to know if she was still available. Unconsciously, he tightened his hold on Amanda and saw her glance at him in surprise.

"Amanda! Ryan!" Suzy hollered from several feet away. Her husband, John, and the rest of the high school quartet weren't far behind.

But Ryan didn't mind as much as he had expected to. Actually, her friends were likable people. He hadn't expected to like anything about this weekend. He glanced down at Amanda, realizing the weekend was full of surprises, ones he was no nearer to deciphering.

She looked up just then, caught his gaze and sent him a tentative smile. He noticed that she had a dimple, a beaut that added sexy charm to her smile. Before, he'd just been struck by the way her smile changed her face. He hadn't noticed this particular detail.

"Hey, you two," Suzy greeted them.

Linda and Candy flanked her like bookends while their husbands trailed behind.

"How are the newlyweds?" Candy asked with a wink. "We weren't sure you'd make it down from your room."

"Luckily it's not far to go at the end of the evening," Ryan replied smoothly, not taking his arm from around Amanda's waist, playing his part so well it looked as though he couldn't keep his hands off his new bride.

"You two are so sweet," Linda gushed. She turned to her own husband with a loving smile. "Let's dance."

"Good idea," Candy agreed, taking her husband's hand.

Suzy and John Meriweather were already heading off to the dance floor. Suzy turned back to them, winked, and then slid into her husband's arms as a slow song began playing.

Ryan glanced down at Amanda, knowing what the others expected. "Would you like to dance?"

She nodded and he held out his hand, leading her to the edge of the dance floor.

The music, subdued and romantic, swirled around them as Amanda slipped close in his arms. Her body, soft and lush, met his. Ryan had to remind himself that this was just a role he was playing, that she was a scam artist, that he should resent her for forcing him into this weekend. But the reminder slid away as her breasts touched his chest, and the spill of her tawny hair brushed the underside of his chin.

It was easy to spin her to the music, to match their steps so closely that their bodies moved in a hypnotic rhythm. The first number ended, seguing immediately into another sentimental song, and they continued dancing, neither stepping apart.

Soft and yielding, Amanda was a surprise in many ways. Ryan knew he didn't need any more surprises. His life had held enough of them already. Surprises that now had a chokehold on everything he held dear. But, for the moment, he disregarded his normal caution, leading her into the next song as it began.

The trio of soft songs ended and a wild rock hit filled the air. Amanda didn't release his hand, and he led them over to the bar.

"Something to drink, Amanda?"

"Red wine, please." Her voice sounded reedy and high, and there was an attractive flush to her cheeks.

"I thought you two were going to stay out there all night," Suzy said from behind them.

"Leave them alone," her husband inserted. "Real life will set in soon enough, and then they'll just be boring married folks like us."

Suzy whacked him playfully, then turned back to Amanda and Ryan. "We have a surprise for you."

Amanda and Ryan exchanged a cautious glance.

"Not just John and me," Suzy continued. "All of your 'pact' buddies have nominated you for a special treat."

Amanda swallowed a sip of her wine and cleared her throat. "I'm not sure I dare ask what that might be."

Suzy positively beamed. "Wait, let me get Linda and Candy over here first." She sped off to gather the others while Amanda and Ryan stared in consternation at each other.

John patted Amanda's arm. "Don't worry. She hasn't got anything terrible up her sleeve. But you know Suz— she loves a drama."

Amanda murmured her agreement, her anxiety escalating as Suzy returned with Candy and Linda in tow. All three were beaming.

"Okay, what's up?" Amanda demanded.

But a drumroll prevented any answer. Dave Matthews, their class president, stood at the mike. Grinning into the glaring light that shone into his eyes, Dave began his talk. Amanda didn't pay much attention until she heard her own name and realized with a sinking sensation that John was right. Suzy was taking her sense of drama to the extreme.

"What?" Amanda asked. "What was that all about?"

Dave's voice answered her. "That's right, our own Amanda Thorne and her brand-new husband will lead the spotlight dance." He paused as another drumroll began. "And...the sweetheart kiss. Come on, everybody, let's give the newlyweds a hand!"

Applause broke out as the light that had been shining on Dave at the podium moved erratically over the crowd, settling on Amanda and Ryan. She stared at him helplessly as her old friends squealed in delight.

"This is perfect," Suzy shouted. "The spotlight dance *and* the sweetheart kiss."

Amanda's stomach plummeted even as her gaze zoned in on Ryan. But he simply held out his hand. The spotlight continued shining on them as the music started. It was an evocative song that spoke of unfulfilled love.

Glancing up at Ryan, she saw the dark hunger in his eyes and wondered if it was for show. Could it possibly be real? He looked especially dangerous tonight in his well-fitted tux and crisp white shirt. Lean, mean and incredibly sexy. There wasn't a shred of thoughtful sensitivity shining from those fathomless dark eyes, and for some reason that made him impossibly exciting.

Stepping into his arms, she had the fleeting notion that she'd stepped past some boundary, as well. At his strong touch, Amanda felt the same electricity she had when he'd offered the first mock gesture for her friends' benefit. But now the voltage had increased, multiplied, grown out of control.

Ryan bent his head close to her ear. "Amanda..."

"Yes," she breathed in return.

"What's this sweetheart kiss?"

Her insides churned at the thought, but it was more anticipation than dread. "When the dance ends, before the next one starts, well...we kiss."

"In the spotlight?" he asked, still guiding her around the dance floor, making their bodies glide in a curiously familiar unison.

"I'm afraid so," she whispered against his shirtfront. She couldn't help noticing the sharp, fresh aroma of his cologne, the woodsy scent of his soap. Beneath her hand, she felt the broad width of his shoulders and remembered just how they had looked when he'd bared them, wearing only a towel after his shower. Her blood heated at the thought, especially when she realized the song was drawing to a close.

And then they were standing still, locked in the hush of the quiet room. Amanda stared upward at Ryan as he tilted his head and bent his lips toward hers. She expected a quick caress, something just for show. She should have known that Ryan West never delivered the expected.

His hand cupped the back of her head, lacing his fingers in her hair, pulling her mouth to his. The unresolved tension between them exploded at that first exploration. His mouth moved over hers, sliding his tongue over the pressed line of her lips. At the thrill of that move, she opened her mouth and felt him search farther, inciting images of other motions.

Her hands curled in the length of his untamed, dark hair, pulling him even closer. Ryan's other arm tightened around her, drawing her body flush with his, setting off a new set of alarms. Feeling the muscled expanse of his thighs against hers, his lean hips aligned with hers, a whipcord of pure desire coiled within her. It struck, then reverberated as he devastated her lips with sensation. Vaguely, she was aware of the strength of his hands, the control he exercised. But everything else fell away under his delicious onslaught.

Then, like swimmers emerging from a drowning cascade of water, they heard the applause. Amanda's classmates were clapping and hooting with approval. The class president had manned the mike again and could be heard as well.

"We'll have to remember not to ask newlyweds to do the sweetheart kiss. They might not give it up until the next reunion!"

Breaking apart, they glanced first at each other, then at the amused spectators. But then their gazes locked back on each other. Desire was stronger than embarrassment.

The light dimmed as the band started to play again and the others took to the dance floor. Ryan held out his hands, and Amanda stepped into his embrace as naturally as though she'd done it for years.

His head bent close to hers, she could feel the whisper of his breath on her neck, the beat of his heart so close to her own. As though a magical spell enveloped them, the crowd, the reason for appearing as newlyweds, fell away. There was only the two of them. There was only now.

The warmth of Ryan's body communicated itself to her, and she felt a responding heat, one she hadn't expected, but one that wasn't entirely unwelcome. Feeling rash,

Amanda let her emotions tangle themselves in the winsome dance, forgetting that she'd blackmailed Ryan into this weekend, that they'd agreed to walk away at the end of the reunion.

She also forgot her friends, their pact and any impression she hoped to make. Right now, her heated blood could only concentrate on the formidable man who held her so strongly. The last cognizant portion of her brain knew that he was not the kind of man she wanted. But every other cell of her body recognized the want for what it was. Neither logical nor well thought out, it was nonetheless stronger than anything she'd ever felt before.

"You're a mystery, Amanda Thorne." Ryan spoke quietly in her ear, his voice ripe with undercurrents she didn't fully understand. "Far more complex than I imagined."

She tilted her head, purposely making her curls cascade over her bare shoulders. "What am I hiding?"

Amanda felt him draw in a deep breath, saw his face tighten. "I think I'm better off not knowing," he replied after a long moment, tracing one curl over the slope of her shoulder, making her tremble. "You hoard dangerous secrets in that delectable head of yours."

Delectable. The word tingled and chased around her mind. He thought she was delectable. Her breath seemed too erratic to contain, and something inexplicable was happening to her bones, making them shaky, uncertain in their ability to support her.

"And you, Ryan West. What secrets are you keeping?"

Something she couldn't fathom flashed in his eyes, then it was gone. "Nothing that concerns this weekend, Amanda. Interludes don't come my way that often."

"Is that what this is?" she asked quietly, "an interlude?"

"One we can grasp or let fly away."

It seemed desperately important that she not let the magic of this moment escape. Like a balloon transported by helium high into the sky, this magic could be fleeting and lost in an instant. She knew with utter certainty that she couldn't allow that to happen. Tracing the curve of his jaw, she recognized the hard set to his handsome face, knew that he could never be part of the comfortable life she wanted for herself, and opened her mind to other possibilities.

Like a magical interlude.

After tomorrow they would part. Their lives would take separate, preordained paths. That wouldn't change. But there was tonight.

And meeting his eyes, she telegraphed that message, saw the quick flare of answering need and allowed herself a joyous moment of triumph.

Ryan's face angled close to hers, his eyes dancing wickedly. "So, how long do we have to stay at the ball, Cinderella? I'm dying to take off your glass slippers."

MOONLIGHT SPILLED THROUGH the open French doors, and the fire Ryan lit now danced, gaining brilliance. Lush rugs softened the thuds as Amanda kicked off her high heels, immediately forgotten as she walked across the wooden floor in her stocking feet.

Ryan watched the curve of her long legs, exposed by the thigh-high split in her gown, something that had been difficult to keep his eyes off all night. Then she turned and faced him. The sweep of her wild hair, her bare shoulders and that flame of a dress, backlit by the light of a full, generous moon hit him like a fist to the gut. Had he been so busy investigating her schemes that he'd missed her incredible beauty?

The dimple in Amanda's cheek deepened as her smile curved into a sultry invitation. "I was ready to get rid of my glass slippers, too."

He crossed the room in a few impatient strides. Curling his fingers over the enticing skin of her shoulders, he pulled her close, cradling her body next to his, wanting to forget her con game, the bank fraud. "You may regret this, Amanda Thorne," he warned her, the only warning he planned to issue. "I'm not the kind of man you're looking for."

"It's only a weekend."

Ryan made his words purposely blunt. "I have other commitments that come first…that will always come first."

A hesitant note crept into her voice. "You're not married? When I met you, you said there was no Mrs. West."

"And there never will be," he assured her in a cryptic tone.

"Then, as I said, it's just a weekend."

In spite of her assurance, he could feel the erratic thumping of her heart caged against his own. An answering shudder of need swept through him, despite all he suspected about her.

As their lips met, his hands skimmed over hips that curved into an impossibly tiny waist, then traveled up her torso, resting on the bare skin of her shoulders. It was suddenly incredibly easy to forget Amanda's deception.

Scooping her into his arms, he carried her to the rug that flanked the fireplace. Nestling her within his embrace, he bent to inhale her scent, then pulled the pins from her hair, allowing it to fall to her shoulders.

Amanda's hands stretched out to trace his features, then journeyed over his chest. Shrugging his jacket off, he reached for her again. The heat rose between them as her fingers wound insidiously between the opening of his shirt.

Ryan's lips moved slowly over her neck, her fragile collarbones, then the hollow of her throat, where he could feel the uneven rhythm of her pulse.

Ivory skin beckoned, and Ryan slipped the delicate straps of her dress away, pulling the bodice down, exposing the first thrill of her breasts. He sucked in a jagged breath. Firm and full, their rosy peaks hardened as his mouth lavished them with attention.

Amanda couldn't stifle a cry of pleasure. Each touch, each movement was sending her slipping toward an edge she couldn't control. Then his hands were exploring beneath the high slit in her skirt, cupping the source of her heat, making her long for more. She knew she was reaching the point of no return. Was this what she wanted? A quick tumble with a stranger? They didn't even know each other, and tomorrow they planned to walk away forever.

As the thought formed, she felt him reach for the zipper of her dress. She knew once past that barrier, there was no turning back. Shakily she pulled away.

"Ryan?"

His breathing was rapid, harsh with desire. "Amanda."

The words stumbled, nearly freezing in her throat. "I...I thought this was what I wanted...but..."

He pulled back slowly, the flush of passion still clouding his eyes. She stared back at him as he searched her eyes. Then he reached for the bodice of her dress. For a moment she wondered if he would ignore her protest.

But then he gently slipped her bodice back in place, lifting the slim straps of her dress onto her shoulders. "Too much, too fast."

"I...yes. I didn't mean to lead you on. I thought I—"

He raised two fingers to her lips, stopping the flow of jumbled words, knowing she was right...it was safer for them to remain uninvolved. "This way we'll have kept our bargain. With no regrets."

Chapter Nine

Sunshine replaced the moonlight, but Ryan decided it suited Amanda. She was a golden girl, from the flaming golden strawberry curls to the sooty eyelashes shadowing her ivory skin. Watching her sleep was even more torturous now that he could guess how special she could have made the night.

Still, he let her continue sleeping. Despite his own words and continuing suspicions, regret struck him, hard and fast. He wished they had more time, that they didn't have to part, but he knew there weren't any options. Once, he had disregarded common sense and his usual caution because of a woman's appeal. And look what happened then—he was still recovering from his ex-wife's manipulations.

From the day in his childhood when his mother had walked out on him and his father, Ryan had been on alert, aware that women weren't to be trusted. Danielle had slipped past his defenses, but it wouldn't happen again.

And if Amanda discovered that he was on to her game, investigating her business, she'd be running away as fast as those glorious legs of hers would take her. It was best that they say goodbye now.

Yet Ryan continued to watch as she stirred in her sleep, her mouth curving as though remembering a shared smile. The pink tip of one breast peeked at him, escaping the low neck of her pajamas.

Repressing a groan, he fisted a handful of her silky hair. He had never expected such a wild riot of curls to be so soft. So much of Amanda had been a surprise. And glancing at her now, vividly remembering the previous evening, he felt his arousal.

Amanda's eyes opened, her lashes fluttering over those incredible emeralds. Surprise flared, then disappeared as longing curled in her eyes, sending a corresponding heat through his body.

"Did you order in this morning?" she asked huskily.

Ryan's brows lifted. "I ordered in." His eyes roved purposely over her. "And I got exactly what I wanted."

Her arms reached up to loop around his neck, causing the quilt to fall away to her waist. "Gives a new meaning to room service, doesn't it?"

He swept away the remaining covers, pulling Amanda's warm body into the curve of his own. Shadows plied over the hollows of her throat, and he sought out each one before kissing her eyelids and then moving to nibble on her lips. Knowing their time was quickly running out, he deepened the kiss.

Then she pulled away, a replica of his regret lacing her expression. "I don't think we'd better continue this."

Knowing she was right, Ryan brushed his fingers once more over her hair. "You're right." He reminded himself again that he didn't need to complicate matters any more than they already were. Once her name was removed from his bank records, Ryan knew they wouldn't meet again.

She might well be a con artist, but he could be lenient, even generous, allowing her to walk away from the deed. His gaze moved over her natural, tousled beauty, feeling an unexpected pang. This wasn't going to be as easy as he'd thought.

DRESSED IN A PALE PEACH sundress, Amanda sipped her coffee and stared over the terrace at her hometown. Even its charm and warmth couldn't lift her spirits. She'd ignored the consequences of the time she had spent in Ryan's arms, but now she had to face reality. It was time to say goodbye. They still had to attend the final breakfast, but after returning to San Francisco there was no reason for them to see each other.

You're a big girl, she reminded herself. *You wanted a magical interlude, and you nearly got it. Only one problem with interludes. They end.*

Not one to go back on her word, she intended to keep her end of the bargain. But she couldn't help wondering if Ryan had second thoughts, as well. If so, he hadn't voiced them.

"Got your caffeine fix?" Ryan asked as he entered the terrace.

Glancing up, she allowed her gaze to rove over Ryan's open-necked, banded-collar shirt and close-fitting jeans. His hair was damp, freshly washed in the shower, and its dark length contrasted pleasantly with his golden tan. She felt the effect of his dangerous handsomeness straight down to her toes. He didn't have any business looking that great so early in the day.

She held up her cup. "Almost."

Ryan glanced at his watch. "We should be heading down to the breakfast."

She lifted her eyes and met his gaze, sensing the unspoken goodbyes that echoed in the air, but she made her voice deliberately cheerful. "You're right. We don't want to keep my 'pact' buddies waiting."

Together they entered the dining room, now filled again with numerous tables for the closing reunion breakfast. In unspoken agreement, they chose a table that would easily seat eight.

The waitress poured cups of steaming coffee, and Amanda picked hers up, forcing a smile. "Well, the reunion's almost over and it looks as though we convinced everyone."

"That should make you happy."

"Oh, yes..." Amanda replied brightly, her forced smile straining the corners of her mouth. "I'm...very happy." She clutched the sides of the hot mug, scarcely noticing that it was close to burning her. As the heat penetrated, she released the mug to compulsively fold her napkin into the shape of a duck. "I really appreciate your performance. Everyone believed you. In fact, they liked you."

Their eyes met briefly as Ryan picked up his own coffee mug. "Then, our deal's nearly complete."

Amanda inclined her head to nod, then glanced up in surprise. "Nearly?"

"You still have to sign my loan papers," he reminded her.

"Of course...the papers." She was thinking of their parting, and he was only concerned about his bank loan. Admittedly, she'd agreed, and he'd agreed. And Amanda refused to ask him to reconsider. She had her pride. If he didn't want to continue their relationship beyond the weekend, she wouldn't ask. Still... "Is that all?"

Ryan lowered his mug. "No..."

Her heart lurched.

"Actually, we'll have to remove your name completely from my bank records."

Amanda crumpled the napkin, crushing the duck's head. For good measure, she pulled off its wings, too. Clearly Ryan wasn't wasting time with any messy emotional entanglements. Job's over, deal's done. No need for her to feel any differently, Amanda told herself as she twisted the duck's neck.

The waitress arrived with juice and muffins just as Suzy and John, apparently ahead of the pack, took their chairs. John launched into conversation even before ordering coffee. "Ryan, I'd like to talk to you, before the others get here."

Amanda glanced up from the mangled duck and met Ryan's questioning gaze. Apparently the job wasn't completely over.

"Shoot," Ryan replied.

John was equally blunt, "As I mentioned, I'm interested in your development deal. Liked what you had to say—I know the area, the potential. No piddly stakes—I want to be a major investor."

Ryan's brows rose. "I won't tell you I don't need investors, because I do. But you don't know me, John, or anything about my company. Why are you willing to take this gamble?"

"Because Suzy knows Amanda. And she says if Amanda married you, you must be okay."

Amanda and Ryan drew a collective breath.

"I'd expect you to study the prospectus," Ryan began.

John waved his hands. "Of course. I didn't get this far in business without knowing the basics. You can express me the prospectus. Then I'll sign the papers...but we can do that in the city. That's half of Suzy's plan."

Baffled, Amanda turned to stare at Suzy.

She clapped her hands and nearly bounced out of her chair. "This is the best part. We're going to move to San Francisco! We own a town house there and now we can make it our home."

"San Francisco?" Amanda echoed weakly.

Suzy turned glowing eyes toward John as she picked up his hand. "That's just part of our news. We're going to have a baby."

Amanda reached out impulsively to hug her friend. "That's wonderful, Suzy! I'm so happy for you."

Ryan shook John's hand. "Congratulations."

"Thanks," John replied, pride suffusing his features. "And that's the main reason Suz wants to move to San Francisco. Now that her folks have passed on, there's no need to return to Stanton, and she's not happy in L.A."

Suzy leaned across the table, looking earnestly at Amanda. "I don't have a friend like you in L.A., Amanda. That's why I want to live in San Francisco. This is my first baby. I want to be close to good friends. And now that you're married, you and Ryan can be our child's godparents.''

Amanda felt her throat tighten and knew she didn't dare glance at Ryan.

"My business can be headquartered wherever I choose," John added. "I already have offices set up in L.A. and San Francisco, and I can pick which one I want to work in."

"We'll be able to see each other all the time," Suzy gushed, warming to the subject.

Amanda tried to deflect the flow of the conversation, sensing she would have better luck changing the course of a raging river. "Suzy, you realize I work long hours, that my business demands most of my time—"

"And Ryan takes up the rest of it. I understand all that, Amanda, but there are lunch hours, weekends. Just knowing you're only a phone call away will help."

Amanda couldn't help remembering that it was one of Suzy's phone calls that had gotten her into this mess.

John patted Suzy's hand. "Her mind's all made up. Wouldn't let me sleep all night, talking about it." He glanced at Ryan and Amanda. "Don't imagine newlyweds are used to much sleep, either."

Their gazes flew together, the memory of the aborted evening branding their thoughts.

Suzy chuckled. "Don't mind him. John's just a big tease. I'm so excited about going to San Francisco permanently. I'm contacting a mover first thing tomorrow morning. We should be there by the weekend."

"That seems so sudden," Amanda offered weakly.

Suzy waved a casual hand. "I'll leave the packing to the movers. We have enough furniture in the town house to get by until our other things arrive. John plans to alert his staff first thing tomorrow. Isn't this great?"

Ryan and Amanda avoided looking at each other. "Just great," they chimed simultaneously.

AMANDA PACED THE CONFINES of their hotel room as Ryan folded his clothes into his suitcase.

Her voice crackled with tension. "Well, this certainly puts a fly in the ointment."

Ryan snorted. "Fly, hell. More like a flock of bats in the belfry."

"Are you suggesting that my friends and I are crazy?"

He didn't stop packing. "You consider Suzy's plan rational?"

"Not especially." Amanda's brow furrowed together. "Then, why didn't you just tell John you weren't interested in having him invest?"

Ryan's hands stilled for a moment, then he resumed his packing. "Because I need his investment."

Her eyes widened. "You told me you were getting a bank loan to leverage your deal."

"I am. But I still need a big cash infusion. And it's damn hard to turn down someone like John Meriweather."

Amanda's face grew puzzled. "Why him?"

Ryan met her gaze reluctantly. "Because he can bring in other investors, and right now I'm highly leveraged..."

"And cash poor," she finished for him.

"You could say that," he replied tightly.

Her expression was sober. "Is this deal on the up and up?"

Ryan widened his eyes in disbelief. "Yes. Although after doctoring my bank records, you're hardly in a position to question my honesty."

Ignoring his insult, Amanda spun around, nailing him with an unrelenting stare. "One minor detail. How do we explain our 'non-marriage' to John and Suzy?"

"We don't."

Amanda frowned at him. "I think they'll figure it out pretty soon."

"Not if we're living together."

The words flashed between them, then hung in the air like the ripe scent of an incoming storm.

Amanda's mouth opened, then closed without her uttering a sound.

Ryan abandoned his packing. "It only has to *look* as though we're living together—and it won't be for long. As you already pointed out to Suzy, you work long hours. I work long hours, as well. We won't have to be on display for John and Suzy often, just long enough to get this deal processed. We're talking about a few dinners." He hesitated for a moment, knowing she was prickly where her pride was concerned, also knowing he had to be blunt. "And, with John and Suzy moving to San Francisco, if you don't want your friends to find out the truth, we'll have to look married."

His words must have stung, because her tone was just short of hostile. "Since I created this sham, you mean."

Ryan faced her. "This will work to your advantage as well as mine. Suzy will believe you're happily married. John's investment will put vital capital into my business. And from what I've seen, I suspect Suzy will tire of San Francisco soon enough and she'll move on again. What do you say?"

Amanda raised troubled eyes. "I don't like deceiving my friends."

"I don't mean to point out the obvious, but isn't that what this whole weekend has been about?"

She flinched, then sank into the chair angled next to the bed. "First my friends, then my family, now this. Maybe I should just confess."

He waited, not willing to try to persuade her either way. While John's investment could prove to be just the windfall he needed, Ryan refused to sway Amanda's decision. It was, after all, *her* friends and family they were speaking of. Even though she'd begun this entire entanglement, Ryan doubted she was a master criminal capable of foreseeing all the complications. And, having to follow through on the consequences of her scam might even send her back on the right path.

If Amanda and her friends had been pumping *him* for an investment, rather than offering to invest, Ryan would have clamped the lock on his checkbook, knowing that Amanda intended to play him for really big stakes. As it was, it appeared she'd bungled into something she simply hadn't foreseen.

Amanda pressed a hand to her forehead. "Maybe we could try this pretend marriage thing for a while. I'm probably crazier than Suzy, but I'm not quite ready to tell my friends the truth yet."

Ryan tossed jeans into the suitcase. "It's not as though our lives will really change."

Amanda gaped at him as though he'd sprouted a second head. "Pretending to be married won't change anything for you?"

Feeling a spurt of the resolve he'd clung to for so many years, Ryan met her startled, disbelieving gaze, his voice gruff. "Nothing's ever going to change my life again."

She stared at him. "How can you know that?"

"Because I won't let anything...or anyone change it." Despite all the inherent problems that came with this new bargain, he recognized her agitation and tempered his voice. "And unless you want to put on another performance, *Mrs. West,* you'd better get packed."

AMANDA CLUTCHED HER PURSE in one hand and Mackie's leash in the other, nervously glancing around Ryan's home. Her first impression was pure shock. She'd expected a small bachelor condo, especially considering his financial straits. Instead, he'd escorted her into a luxurious home at one of San Francisco's best addresses. Amanda had agreed to stop at his house first, since they would pass it on the way to her apartment. Ryan had insisted he needed to stop at his house as soon as they reached the city.

As Mackie sniffed each table leg, then stuck his nose into a potted plant, Amanda wondered what she'd gotten herself, not to mention her best friends, involved in. Ryan had been quick to accuse her of being a scam artist, but looking around this magnificent home, she wondered who had conned whom.

An intricately carved, beautifully curved staircase dominated the marble entry hall. Arched doorways led into inviting rooms with ten-foot ceilings, oversized windows and highly polished wooden floors. Tasteful, understated furnishings complemented the Victorian house, allowing the ornate woodwork and medallion-encrusted ceilings to shine. From what she'd seen, it was a remarkable home.

But she hesitated in wandering around the house any farther, since Ryan had disappeared as soon as they'd arrived, casually telling her to make herself at home. Not wanting to intrude, Amanda had kept to the rooms at the front of the house on either side of the entry. She suspected that the kitchen was located in the rear of the house and that the bedrooms were on the second floor, but she didn't want to investigate on her own. Amanda had assumed Ryan would show her around. She wondered what was so important that he'd taken off the moment they had arrived.

Picking up a framed photo of an older gentleman, Amanda guessed he was Ryan's father. The man had Ryan's arrogant, hawklike features, but a trace of sorrow in his eyes softened his expression. Amanda wondered why there wasn't a picture of Ryan's mother, as well.

Hearing Ryan's bootsteps on the marble tiled entryway, she returned the photo to the sofa table and turned expectantly.

But whatever she had expected, it wasn't what she saw.

Ryan stood at the doorway...holding a smiling baby in his arms. The pink-frocked tot waved plump arms in Amanda's direction and cooed charmingly.

Surprised, but enchanted, Amanda moved toward the odd duo. "And who is this?" she asked, letting the baby grab her fingers and smiling at the child's innocent charm. "Is she your niece?"

But Ryan didn't return her smile. Instead, he stiffened

his already ramrod-straight posture. "This is Brianna. My daughter."

"Your..." Amanda stared from Ryan to the baby he held. *He had a daughter?*

She was a beautiful child with expressive, bright blue eyes, beguiling, plump pink cheeks, and her father's dark hair.

"My daughter," Ryan repeated, his voice even, unapologetic, almost challenging.

"You're married?" she asked in disbelief. "You've denied being married at least twice." Amanda tossed her head back, her eyes flashing fire. "Were you planning to start a harem for John and Suzy's benefit? Won't Mrs. West number one have something to say about bringing home another wife? It's not like I'm a lost puppy who followed you home."

Although Ryan's voice remained calm, Amanda could see that he was hanging on to his temper with a rapidly dissolving thread of control. "I'm not married." He glanced down at Brianna. "Not anymore."

Horrified by her quick assumption, Amanda's hand flew to her mouth. Had this tiny child's mother already died? Had she been so eager to believe the worst, she hadn't considered that possibility? No wonder Ryan had been so angry to see her name listed as Mrs. West. It must have been a painful, unnecessary reminder of his loss. Amanda stretched out her hands in sympathy. "I'm so sorry. I didn't know.... I mean I never guessed that you'd lost your wife...and she must have been so young. I don't know what to say, to—"

"I didn't lose her," Ryan responded flatly.

"I'm sure you feel that way, with part of her always alive in Brianna and—"

"I didn't lose her," he repeated. "But luckily she *is* gone."

Amanda stared at him blankly.

"She's not dead," he finally clarified, enunciating the

words as though Amanda had lost both her reason and hearing.

"But you just said—"

"No. You just assumed. I'm not married, nor am I a widower."

Amanda was consumed by questions, but knew she couldn't voice them in front of his child. What had happened to his wife, and why didn't the former Mrs. West have her child?

Since the baby reached her chubby arms in MacDougall's direction, Ryan bent down long enough to let her stroke the dog's back. When he stood, Ryan directed his words to Amanda.

"We'll talk in a few minutes."

Watching him, Amanda glimpsed the kitchen as he walked through the swinging oak door and saw the bottom of another stairwell. The baby's nursery must be located near the rear of the house at the top of the stairs, she thought as the door swung back into place, astonishment making her catalog the house rather than Ryan's surprising revelation.

A baby! The shock of it reverberated again. How could he have made such a glaring omission? And where was the child's mother?

Amanda stared out the bay window in the living room, absently seeing the traffic passing by. The sun was setting, and a twinkle of lights decorated the hillsides. But all Amanda could see was a memory of the night she had almost spent in Ryan's arms, the magical interlude that had nearly swept away her senses. Had Ryan been deceiving her then, as well? If he could conveniently forget that he had a daughter, it would be easy for him to carry out almost any pretense. His convincing deception as her husband had proved that.

Amanda nearly blushed when she remembered her uncharacteristic abandon in his arms. Especially considering how little she'd really known of him. He had a *child,* a beautiful baby girl. How could he fail to mention something so important?

Crossing her arms, absently rubbing them against a chill that had nothing to do with the temperature, she didn't hear Ryan enter the living room until he was nearly behind her. The Oriental rug draped across the floor cushioned his footfalls as he descended from the front staircase.

"Amanda."

She whirled around, startled. "I...I didn't hear you."

"Lost in your thoughts?"

She met his gaze evenly. "Don't you think I have a right to be?"

Ryan pushed one hand through his hair. "I didn't see any reason to involve you. We were going our separate ways—"

"So you just forgot to mention that you have a daughter?"

"I told you I didn't think it was necessary. I'm sure you didn't tell me everything about yourself," he replied tightly, thinking of Amanda's attempted bank scam and the suspicious dealings of her shop.

"No, I concealed the fact that I'm an escaped transvestite, homicidal maniac." She slapped her hands on her hips as she faced him. "But I didn't leave out something as important as a child."

"I'm very protective of Brianna," Ryan replied evenly. His face was impassive, only the tic in his jaw underlining the truth of his statement.

Amanda sighed. With no children of her own, she couldn't completely identify with his feelings, but she suspected his protective streak was wide and deep. "Do you share custody?"

"No." Clearly he did not want to add any details to the aborted answer.

But Amanda needed to know. "So how did you come to be raising Brianna on your own?"

"Her mother wasn't interested in raising babies."

"Did having Brianna break up your marriage?" she questioned softly, knowing it wasn't really her concern, also knowing he had made it her concern.

"Nothing that simplistic. Danielle got what she wanted out of our marriage. And I have what I want."

"She didn't fight you for custody?" Amanda asked, thinking how unusual it was for a mother not to insist on raising her child.

Ryan's brow lifted. "You could say that." His gaze met and locked on hers. "Brianna is *my* child, no one else's."

Amanda wondered where that left Brianna's mother. But she suspected she'd used up her proverbial twenty questions. "That may be so, but you've made her my problem."

The thundercloud on his brow was back. "How so?"

Exasperated, she lifted her hands, then dropped them. "Because you and I are supposed to be *married* for Suzy and John's benefit. Don't you think they'll notice we're a trio instead of a duo?"

Unexpectedly his grin returned. "Don't you *like* babies, Amanda?"

Exasperated, she stared at him. "You're twisting my words. Of course I like babies."

"Then, what's the problem?"

At the moment, her problem was his insistent, obtuse denseness. "You still think we can pull this off? Especially when you didn't trust me enough to tell me you had a daughter?"

"You're running a con, Amanda, and you're asking me about trust? Look, I held up my part of the weekend, which had nothing to do with my daughter. And creating a front for Suzy and John doesn't have anything to do with her, either."

"First—I'm *not* running a con. And second, I can't believe you're so nonchalant. You act as though you've just shown me the family dog, something to be whisked away when he barks too loudly. A child is far more complicated."

"Brianna's a baby, not a mouthy teenager. And Mrs. Buchanan takes care of her."

"It's not her *care* that concerns me," Amanda retorted. "There's more to babies than diapers and formula."

"I'm well aware of that. She's my responsibility, nothing you'll have to worry about. And we only have to make a few appearances with Suzy and John. What's the problem?"

The possibilities assaulted her in waves.

Amanda settled for the most obvious one. "Suzy and John believe we recently eloped—the newlyweds of the reunion. Don't you think they're going to notice that Brianna is what, nine...ten...?"

"Ten," he supplied.

"Ten months old? How do we explain her presence when we just recently eloped?"

"This isn't the Victorian age," Ryan reminded her.

"Okay, maybe not. But why didn't we tell anyone about this beautiful child? What? We were so wrapped up in the reunion that we completely forgot about her? No woman in her right mind will believe that. And Suzy may be pretty wacky about some things, but she won't believe for a minute that I wouldn't have flashed pictures of my baby to everyone at the reunion."

"You're creating problems where there aren't any, chasing runaway chicks before they've hatched."

Amanda clamped her hands at her waist. "Well, your little chick is already hatched. You weren't planning to hide her back in the shell, were you?"

"This is absurd. Brianna isn't your concern. Pretending we're married is. Unless you'd rather walk away right now."

Exasperated, Amanda sunk into a nearby chair. "I don't know *what* I want to do. You may find this hard to believe, but an average weekend for me doesn't include subterfuge, a fake marriage and now learning that in addition to my pretend husband, I have a make-believe daughter."

"It's your call, Amanda. I will not have my daughter used as a bargaining chip." Unexpected anger glittered in his eyes, and Amanda bit back a retort.

Ryan walked to the bar, automatically poured a glass of red wine for Amanda and a Scotch for himself. He handed her the wine goblet, then stared out the window as Amanda had done earlier. He knew it was too much to expect Amanda to blindly accept the fact that he had a daughter and that the baby was entirely his responsibility. Most women considered babies their territory. But not this baby.

For a man who had never wanted to have children, it had been a stunning discovery to learn how much he loved his tiny daughter. Although Brianna's mother hadn't given a passing moment's worry to the possible legacy of hurt and betrayal she was leaving their daughter, Ryan thought of little else.

And now Amanda was demanding answers. Answers he wasn't prepared to share with another woman. Glancing up, he saw the confusion and worry crowding her expression. He passed a suddenly weary hand over his face. It wasn't her fault that his past was so complicated. "This really isn't your problem, Amanda. You can tell your friends that our marriage didn't work out...that we've decided to separate."

Amanda's grip on the wineglass whitened her knuckles. "I know how bizarre this sounds, but I'd be as reluctant to admit I couldn't make a marriage work as I would be to admit I hadn't found a real husband."

"You're talking like you stepped out of a time warp. People have babies without benefit of marriage, and these days divorce is common...nothing to be ashamed of."

She raised fiercely glimmering eyes. "My friends know I swore that when I married, it would be forever. They'll guess in an instant that I'd never walk away from my marriage without giving it everything I could."

Ryan couldn't suppress the skepticism in his voice. "Everyone has childish fantasies about dreams coming true. But this is real life, Amanda. White knights and sleeping princesses belong in fairy tales. So do 'happily ever after' endings.''

"I certainly hope you don't intend to raise your daughter with those tarnished views."

Ryan blinked. "I hadn't planned on laying down the rules of marriage to Brianna until she's at least two."

"Joke if you want. People *need* dreams. Just because yours didn't turn out the way you hoped doesn't mean you should steal your daughter's."

Ryan nearly choked on his Scotch. "Not that it's any of your business, but I'm not stealing anything from my daughter. She'll always have the best."

"In material possessions? That's admirable, I suppose. But she needs more."

Exasperated, Ryan wondered what had turned Amanda from a sexy companion to a wounded mother bear. "She'll have more. Which is the reason I need John Meriweather's investment—for Brianna's future." Ryan deliberately omitted the painful details of just how important the success of this particular venture was. Far more rode on the outcome of his highly leveraged deal than mere money. He glanced upward toward the staircase leading to the nursery. Far more.

"We can give it a try," Amanda finally conceded, sounding reluctant. "I have a few shreds of dignity left to contribute to the cause."

Flooded with relief, Ryan let out a breath he'd been unaware of holding. John Meriweather's participation in this venture increased the odds of success measurably. Ryan saluted the woman who hadn't slammed the door to that opportunity. "It's late, Amanda. Your suitcase is in the car. Why don't you stay?"

Amanda lifted her chin in a defensively challenging posture. "I'm a little old for pajama parties, and there's no other reason for me to sleep here. I'll go along with pretending we're married, but it stops right there. No side benefits from this deal. I have a home and I don't need...or want...another.''

Any remaining expectations that Ryan might have had dissolved under Amanda's steely glare. He couldn't help admiring her pluck. And at the same time, he couldn't help wanting to shred that resolve. He clinked the rim of his glass to hers, already anticipating the next round of their bout.

Chapter Ten

Amanda stood in a corner of her shop examining a new shipment, but she wasn't seeing the well-preserved hurricane lamps. Her thoughts were lost in a dark-haired man and the conflict of emotions he had caused.

Karen Summers, her assistant, continued emptying the crate. "So, when are you going to tell all?"

Startled, Amanda stared at her. "What?"

Karen returned her look patiently. "The reunion. You know, what you've been obsessing about for weeks."

"Oh, that."

Karen rolled her eyes. "Yeah. That little thing. What gives? You were wound tighter than that broken grandfather clock we can't sell and now you can't remember a few details?"

Amanda stalled by digging through the crate with one hand. "I just had the bill of lading a minute ago...."

Karen pulled it out of the notebook in Amanda's other hand. "Diversionary tactics won't work. You're forgetful, but I think you can manage a little info on the reunion."

Amanda sighed as she put the notebook down on the trunk next to her. "I think I got in over my head."

Karen's cinnamon eyes lit up with excitement. "You met someone! I knew it! Reunions are wonderful places to meet. Or is it an old romance you've rekindled? That's even better! Unrequited love that comes full circle and—"

"Whoa! Don't get carried away."

"But you said—"

"I said I got in over my head, which I did." Amanda sighed, then decided she might as well confess the entire thing. After all, Karen would have to know what was going on if Suzy happened to call. One stray word and the jig could be up.

As Amanda related the weekend and what had led up to it, she saw her assistant latch onto the romantic version of the events, which was typical of her personality.

"Oh, this is wonderful," Karen breathed.

"How can you say that? I've lied to my friends and my family. Well, my mother knows the truth, but still... And now I'm pretending to be married to a man so that my friends won't know that I couldn't snag a husband before the reunion. How can this in any way be considered wonderful?"

Karen waved a hand, casually dismissing all these concerns. "But you've met someone you're interested in. And don't tell me he's not interested in you."

A hot flash of the previous Saturday night surfaced, and Amanda could feel the flush of warmth in her cheeks.

Karen pounced. "I *knew* it! And now you've got a great opportunity to see if the relationship works."

"There isn't any relationship."

"Well...that's what this pretend marriage will determine."

"How do you figure that?"

Karen made a distinct sound of exasperation. "Are you just trying to be difficult? Now you can share a home, a relationship, and see if it's meant to be."

"It's only going to be for appearances."

Karen waved her hand in a nonchalant gesture. "Maybe at first. But then..."

"You're impossible!" Amanda plucked at her skirt as her voice quieted. "Ryan was ready to walk away at the end of the weekend. I was thinking of the future—and if that future included an 'us.' He was thinking about taking my name off his loan papers. Not exactly two minds and hearts in sync.''

"Maybe, maybe not. You know men rarely say what they think.''

Amanda pushed a tangle of curls from her forehead. "I hope you're right. The only thing Ryan has said so far is that he believes I'm running a bank scam—so he obviously doesn't trust me.''

"Ah…that only lends an air of mystery.'' Never one to give up on romance, Karen could find a positive angle to almost anything. "Besides, once he spends time with you, he'll get to know the real you.''

Amanda managed a halfhearted grin. "And you think that's a *good* thing?''

Karen swatted her with an ostrich-feather duster. "You spend enough time alone with him, and all you two will be able to think about is each other.''

"You're forgetting his daughter,'' Amanda reminded her.

"Is that a problem?''

"Only in that we could get attached to each other. You know I have a great big mushy spot for children.''

Karen squinted in concentration. "You can deal with that. Sounds like your major concern will be Mr. West.''

"And putting on an act for Suzy and John Meriweather. I know Suzy, she's relentless.''

Karen shrugged. "It sounds like you already have them fooled. And all the little things most married people know about each other comes in time. They won't expect newlyweds to be settled into a familiar routine, even newlyweds with a baby.''

Amanda stared at her friend. "If I didn't know any better, I'd say that Ryan had gotten to you.''

Karen grinned. "Nope, but I'd say he's gotten to you.''

Amanda absently picked up the hurricane lamp, fingering

the crystals that circled the base. "He's not the kind of man I want in my life, Karen. He's too, too…"

"Male?" Karen suggested.

He was that, for sure. "You know the kind of man I want. Someone sensitive, thoughtful…"

Karen sniffed. "A wimp, you mean."

"Karen!"

"Women say they want men like that, but who wants someone you can manipulate like a puppet?"

Amused, Amanda saw the humor in Karen's words. "I think there's a line somewhere between wimp and… formidable."

Karen's expression turned dreamy. "He's formidable? As though he stepped from the pages of the past?"

"Don't get carried away. I didn't say he was a Neanderthal."

"You need a plan," Karen announced.

"A plan?" Amanda echoed blankly.

"Sure, you don't want to let someone like that get away."

"You haven't even met him—how do you even know he doesn't have two heads? Besides, I don't think losing him is going to be a problem." Not when keeping her close meant major investments in his business.

"You wouldn't have taken him to the reunion if you didn't think he'd impress your friends," Karen scoffed.

"True," Amanda agreed.

"When do I get to meet him?"

Amanda tried to think of an excuse. "Well, I'm not sure.…"

"You and I were supposed to go to dinner this week. Why not include Mr. Wonderful?"

Amanda groaned. "I can see you're going to have an open mind about him."

"It's not an open *mind* you need," Karen cautioned. "It's an open heart."

Amanda felt that she'd already opened her heart too

much already. What should have been a simple weekend had already played havoc with her feelings. "*You* are a hopeless romantic."

Karen grinned. "This from a woman who's in a marriage of convenience with Mr. Wonderful?"

MR. WONDERFUL WAS NOWHERE to be found when Amanda visited his house a few evenings later to discuss their arrangement. Mrs. Buchanan's look of anticipation turned to disappointment when she saw that Amanda was alone. Not exactly alone. MacDougall had accompanied her.

"Were you expecting someone else, Mrs. Buchanan?"

"I thought you were Mr. West," the nanny replied, her expression hovering toward disapproval as she glanced at the dog. But disapproval was quickly replaced by the worried look she'd been wearing.

Sensing a problem, Amanda studied the other woman's face. "Is anything wrong?"

"Not exactly wrong. My sister hasn't been feeling well."

"And you're anxious to check on her," Amanda guessed.

"Well…yes, but I'm sure Mr. West will be home soon."

"Would you like to leave now, Mrs. Buchanan?"

"I *am* worried about my sister, but I can wait until Mr. West returns."

Amanda knew the woman didn't live in, yet she worked long hours, caring for little Brianna. Amanda didn't know Ryan's rules, but thought it wouldn't hurt to offer the woman the time she needed. "I'll be here until Ryan comes home, Mrs. Buchanan. I'm sure it would be all right if you want to leave."

"But who will watch Brianna?"

Amanda smiled. "I will."

Mrs. Buchanan looked skeptical, and it occurred to Amanda that the woman probably thought she was Ryan's latest entertainment—not someone to trust a child with. It also made her wonder if Ryan had brought other women home on a regular basis.

Amanda smiled. "Really, we'll be fine."

"I'm not sure what Mr. West would say."

"I imagine he'll understand that you have a life of your own, Mrs. Buchanan."

"If my sister wasn't ill…"

"Please don't worry about us. Brianna and I will be fine."

"I guess if Mr. West didn't trust you, he wouldn't have brought you here to meet his daughter."

Amanda managed to smile, feeling as though her love life was now under the scrutiny of a spinster aunt.

Mrs. Buchanan twisted the handkerchief in her hands. "If you're sure…"

Apparently the woman was going to have to be pried out of the house with a crowbar. "Mr. West should be home soon. I won't be on my own with the baby for long."

That seemed to convince her. "She'll be hungry soon."

"I'm sure I can find what I need in the kitchen."

"Well…"

"I imagine your sister will be glad to see you."

Galvanized by those words, Mrs. Buchanan gathered her things and was soon out the door.

Amanda flipped through a magazine for almost a minute, before she found herself climbing the stairs. With all the intercoms located throughout the house, Amanda knew she could hear the baby's slightest cry, yet she couldn't resist checking on her.

Entering the nursery she'd seen only briefly earlier that week, Amanda was struck by the quiet and sense of cheer. Expecting to find Brianna asleep, she was surprised to see the child sitting calmly in her crib, a fabric-covered book clutched in one hand. When she spotted Amanda, a bright smile infused her plump little face.

"So, you *are* awake. What have you got there?"

Amanda asked as she crossed the room to stand next to the crib.

Brianna promptly held up both arms to be picked up. Unable to resist the little charmer, Amanda obliged. Brianna immediately grasped one of Amanda's unruly curls.

"Like that, huh?" Amanda asked as she strolled across the room. "You're probably supposed to be asleep, but I didn't ask Mrs. Buchanan."

Brianna gurgled obligingly.

Since the child still held her fabric book, Amanda settled in the comfortable rocking chair to "read" the book to her. Brianna trustingly laid her head on Amanda's shoulder. Smelling the child's sweet baby scent, Amanda felt a completely unexpected tugging somewhere in the vicinity of her maternal instincts.

It was just a normal reaction, she told herself as she opened the little book to a picture of a smiling puppy. Brianna chortled as she pointed to the picture.

"Puppy," Amanda responded, enchanted by the baby's delight.

"Puh," Brianna attempted.

"That's right, sweetie. Puppy."

Brianna pointed again at the book, and taking her cue, Amanda turned the page. A bright red fire engine caught Brianna's attention immediately and she waved her hands in excitement.

"You like that, too, don't you?"

Brianna continued pointing, and Amanda took them through the six well-padded pages. And then she started over again as Brianna curled her tiny hand around Amanda's finger. But in short time, she noticed that Brianna's eyelids were drooping, her long lashes feathering against pink cheeks. Amanda considered returning Brianna to her crib, but the child snuggled against her, tiny baby sighs of sleep overtaking her. The baby's total trusting sweetness swamped Amanda, and she continued gently rocking them both.

Amanda found herself stroking the child's dark, silken curls, wondering at the lovely baby and questioning how a mother could have left her. Only the soft lamp lit the room, lulling them both in the cozy quiet.

And that was how Ryan found them. Exhausted after an especially long day, he was alarmed to see that Mrs. Buchanan's car was missing from the garage. Frightened that something had happened to Brianna, he'd rushed up the stairs, then stopped still as he watched Amanda rocking his daughter.

She seemed perfectly at ease, perfectly natural as she stroked Brianna's curls and quietly hummed a lullaby. Amanda's strawberry curls contrasted with his daughter's dark hair, yet the two fair-skinned faces looked as though they belonged together. An image of Amanda with his baby at her breast flashed through Ryan's mind. It was a ridiculous and unexpected thought. Women running bank scams were hardly mother material.

A bitter smile curled his lips. Danielle had forever hardened him against the belief that two people could truly share a marriage and a child. He'd known since his own mother's desertion that there were no happily ever afters. Danielle had been the final confirmation.

Still, Ryan was moved as he watched Amanda gently trace the contours of Brianna's face, then draw her hand through the child's hair. He wanted to dismiss her actions as typically female, but he knew that Danielle had never felt the desire to sit and rock her child.

Amanda glanced up just then, and he saw a spurt of pleasure cross her face when she saw him. Inside, another portion of him thawed. Knowing it was dangerous to let that happen, he made his voice purposely brusque. "What happened to Mrs. Buchanan?"

Amanda put a finger to her lips, gesturing down at the sleeping baby. Her own voice was a whisper. "Her sister was ill, and since it seemed far past time for her to leave, I told her I'd watch Brianna.''

''I pay her well to work whatever hours are needed,'' he replied in a whisper, albeit a gruff one.

''I didn't mean to overstep any household rules, but I was here and willing to watch Brianna. I didn't think it would harm anything to let Mrs. Buchanan go and check on her sister.''

Her words made him feel suddenly small. ''Of course not. But I don't want you to be taken advantage of, either.''

Amanda glanced down at the sleeping child in her arms. ''It's hard to think of being taken advantage of when you're taking care of someone this sweet.''

That thawing attacked him again, and he knew he had to chase it away. ''We can put her to bed now.''

Amanda's gaze drifted up to his face. ''I suppose we have to,'' she admitted, sounding reluctant.

''Don't tell me you'd planned to spend the evening taking care of a baby.''

''No,'' she replied softly. ''Sometimes plans have an unexpected way of changing. A nice way of changing.'' Sighing, she stood up slowly.

Ryan held out his hands, and Amanda carefully placed Brianna in his arms.

''Good night, little one,'' she murmured.

He watched as she moved toward the doorway. As she reached the threshold, she turned back for a moment. ''I imagine you'd like some time with your daughter. I'll be downstairs making some coffee.''

Ryan's big hands gentled as he cradled the baby in his arms, glad that Amanda was perceptive enough to see he wanted this moment with Brianna. The only bad part of working such long hours was that it left little time for his daughter. But, for her sake, he had to work hard. Too much was riding on the outcome.

Instead of putting Brianna in her crib, Ryan settled into the rocking chair Amanda had vacated. Each time he studied his daughter's beautiful face, he wondered again how Danielle could have left her, walked out without a backward glance. But then, that's what she'd planned all along. Knowing that he never planned to marry, Danielle played upon his one weak spot. She knew his distrust had begun because of his mother's desertion, a memory he could never shake. Because of that he could never abandon a child of his own—even if the child's conception had been a carefully orchestrated plan.

And Danielle's defection was Ryan's only regret as far as his daughter was concerned. He planned to provide enough love and support for two parents. But that was proving difficult while working such long hours. So Ryan took advantage of the present. He continued rocking Brianna, talking in a quiet voice to her while she slept peacefully.

Nearly an hour later, Amanda poked her head in the nursery to make sure everything was all right. The coffee had long since brewed, and she couldn't guess what was keeping Ryan, unless the baby had awakened. The sight of him still holding Brianna in the rocking chair surprised her. Seeing such an arrogant, imposing man behaving so tenderly brought a smarting of tears to her eyes.

As she watched, he continued to rock his daughter, who seemed impossibly tiny in his muscled arms. He bent to kiss the sleeping child, and Amanda felt a lump of emotion form in her throat. Oh, my. Everything about Ryan West had been unexpected from the start, but she really didn't know how to reconcile this side of him. Gruff, arrogant and dominating—along with that devilish sense of humor—he still didn't fit her profile of the perfect man, yet there was something about him...

Backing out of the room, she escaped down the stairs. Retreating into the living room, she kicked off her shoes and curled up on the couch, forgetting the coffee she'd brewed. Lost in her thoughts, she wasn't certain how much time had passed when she heard Ryan enter the room.

A trace of weariness colored his voice. "I thought you might have given up on me."

"No, we need to talk about our...arrangement." She sent him a distracted smile. "I made coffee." Glancing at the table, she realized she hadn't brought the carafe in with her.

He didn't comment on her forgetfulness. "How about a glass of wine, instead?"

She nodded in agreement as Ryan selected a vintage from the well-stocked wine rack and pulled out the cork.

He poured two glasses and handed her a goblet. "Nothing like baptism by fire. I didn't expect you to get drafted into taking care of Brianna."

"I told you I volunteered."

Ryan rubbed the back of his neck with his free hand, and Amanda could see the lines of exhaustion on his face. "I appreciate your help."

"Why don't you sit down and relax?"

"Good idea."

A sudden thought occurred to her. "Did you have any dinner?"

"Not that I remember."

She stood as he reached the couch. "I'll just be a minute."

He snagged her hand as she started to leave. "You don't have to make me dinner."

"I never do anything I don't want to." Gently disengaging her hand, she padded out to the kitchen. It didn't take long to assemble a man-sized sandwich for Ryan and a smaller version for herself. She also found some crisp pickles and coleslaw in the refrigerator. From the way the fridge was stocked, it was clear Ryan generally only snacked or ate at work. Other than sandwich ingredients everything else was for the baby. He might have a beautiful house and a lovely child, but there wasn't a sense of warmth, of a home pulled together by caring hands. The house needed a woman's touch.

The notion sidled through her thoughts, then she purposely shook it away. Picking up the plates, she carried them into the living room.

His eyes brightened when he saw the sandwiches. "I won't remind you that this wasn't necessary, but I will tell you it's appreciated."

She offered him a plate and then resumed her seat on the couch. They both ate in silence for a few minutes. Then, satisfied with half of her sandwich, Amanda put her plate on the coffee table.

Ryan paused between bites. "This is great, Amanda. I guess I didn't realize how hungry I was."

"Burning the candle at both ends eventually catches up with you."

"Sometimes it's necessary."

She lifted her brow, hoping for more of an explanation, but Ryan didn't seem pressed to offer one. So she opted to study him, instead. Exhaustion carved lines near his mouth and his eyes looked weary, as well. Amanda couldn't help wondering again what drove him.

"My assistant, Karen, would like to meet you."

Surprise showed on his face as he put his plate next to hers. "Why?"

Amanda made a distinct sound of exasperation.

He passed one hand over his face. "You had to explain about your sudden 'marriage.' Of course. So what did you tell her?"

"That we'll have her over for dinner one evening."

"John Meriweather called today."

Amanda straightened up and stared at him. "And?"

"And he's still interested. Very interested. I faxed him all the details. He said that he and Suzy will definitely be here by the weekend."

"That's why I'm here—to discuss Suzy and John."

Ryan reached out one hand to grasp her hair. "And I thought it was my killer charm."

She slanted him a guarded smile. "Possibly, but don't flatter yourself. I need to know when we'll be on stage."

"At least I'm part of the reason," he mused, twirling her hair in his fingers, then reaching over with the other hand to cup her face.

Her breath seemed to be coming more quickly. And she was unprepared for the sudden flare of desire that struck her. She had thought about her talk with Ryan all day. She would find out about Suzy and John, then return to her own apartment. Amanda planned to keep doing so until the Meriweathers had actually moved to the city and she would have to live in Ryan's house. She'd decided that she could handle this entire situation in a businesslike manner. There was no need to confuse feelings with their charade. But despite those intentions, her feelings were acting on their own—rocketing out of control.

When his thumb edged over her lips, she sucked in a shaky breath. His actions hadn't been a part of her well-thought-out plans. Then his lips settled on hers, his tongue tasting, devouring. He made slow, devastating love to her mouth and her mind moved sluggishly, losing sight of her resolutions.

His hands skimmed over her sides, teasingly grazing her breasts, then moving to stroke the length of her thighs. And the sand beneath her resolution shifted.

His voice was a husky whisper against her throat. "Stay with me tonight, Amanda."

Letting her eyelids fall closed, she nearly allowed that resolution to fade, slip away and finally disappear.

Then she heard the baby's faint cry. Pulling away from him, her eyes pained, Amanda shook her head. "I think it's best for both of us if I don't."

He looked torn, glancing up the stairs toward the nursery, then back at Amanda. "I won't force the issue—I'll take the daybed in the nursery. Stay. We need to talk."

She stood up, purposefully moving away. "Brianna

needs you." Meeting his gaze, she offered him an uncertain smile. "And I need to go home."

He moved fast for a man his size. In seconds he trapped her between outstretched arms. "Brianna's probably having a bad dream. I'll just look in on her and then be right back—" The baby's cry was louder now, contradicting his words.

Amanda gently disengaged herself. "Suzy and John won't be here until the weekend. I don't think I'd better be, either."

Obviously torn, Ryan loped up the stairs as the baby's cries turned into ones of true distress. Reaching the curve in the staircase that angled upward, he turned back. "I wish Mrs. Buchanan hadn't left. What if Brianna's sick?"

Amanda saw her well-formed plans crumbling. If the baby *was* sick and she'd sent Mrs. Buchanan away, it would be on her head. She would have to stay.

When she'd told Karen she was in over her head, she had understated the truth. She was actually closer to drowning.

Chapter Eleven

Sunshine pushed past the drapes, sending insistent beams into the bedroom. Warmed by the light, Amanda opened reluctant eyes. Her gaze skipped across the unfamiliar room, and for a moment she wondered where she was. Realization struck, and she laid back limply against the mattress, grateful that Brianna hadn't been sick, but still feeling like a chump for falling in with Ryan's plans.

Unfocused eyes roved over the furnishings in his bedroom. Sturdy, man-sized pieces of oak dominated the room, and she suspected he'd redecorated after his divorce. Nothing feminine remained in the bedroom.

Deciding she couldn't stall forever, Amanda decided to opt for a bracing shower. It was one of the only cures for her morning fog. She retrieved the robe and bathing essentials Ryan had provided, hoping she didn't shampoo her hair with mouthwash before her focus kicked in.

After a long shower, Amanda dried her hair and then dressed in the clothes she'd worn the day before. Feeling self-conscious, she smoothed the skirt of her outfit and took a deep breath as she opened the door and made her way down the stairs, glancing around for Mackie, who had disappeared before she'd awakened.

Hearing noise from the kitchen, she headed that way, hoping for coffee. She pushed the swinging door partially open and stopped.

Brianna sat in a high chair and big, bad Ryan West was feeding her oatmeal. And apparently loving every minute.

Oatmeal coated the tray of the high chair and Brianna's colorful bib. Ryan talked to the child as he spooned the oatmeal into her mouth. And the two of them punctuated each bite with laughter.

Touched, Amanda watched for a few minutes before clearing her throat and noisily pushing the door open the rest of the way.

Seeing Amanda, Brianna gurgled and pointed eager hands in her direction. Ryan looked surprised as he watched the exchange.

Amanda strolled over to the high chair. "Morning, sweetie. Looks like Daddy's covering you in oatmeal."

Brianna chortled, and Ryan sent her an ironic glance. "It's not as easy as it looks."

Amanda reached for the coffeepot, filling the mug she took from a rack on the wall. She swallowed a bracing gulp before answering. "Admit it, you're having a great time."

Ryan wiped Brianna's sticky chin. "I spend the mornings with her. It's the most time in the day I have to give her."

Brianna gurgled in agreement, her little bow of a mouth curved in an entrancing smile.

"Don't worry, West. I won't give away your secret."

His brow lifted. "I'm not worried about a threat to my masculinity." His gaze roved over her slowly, and she felt its warmth from where she stood. "Can you think of any reason I should be?"

A flash of heat assailed her, and she had to clear her throat to speak. "No, I can't say as I can."

The phone rang sharply, intrusively. Ryan muttered a stifled curse and stood, picking up the cordless phone on the counter.

Amanda tried not to listen to his conversation, but it was difficult not to hear his voice rising, then turning brisk and hard. He had gone from tender daddy—passionate lover to intimidating once again. Amanda drank her coffee, glad she wasn't on the other end of the phone.

He clicked the phone off and set it down on the table with more force than necessary. "Damn."

"Problem?"

Absently he leaned over and slipped another spoonful of oatmeal into Brianna's waiting mouth. "I have to get to the bank right away."

"The loan papers," she guessed, remembering how those papers had brought them together.

"That and another hitch in the financing."

"I'll sign the papers," she offered.

A note of relief flared in his eyes. "Good." He glanced regretfully at his daughter. "But that's not what they need me for today. A deal this size goes through dozens of glitches. And this one blows my time with Brianna."

"Mrs. Buchanan will be here soon, won't she?"

Ryan nodded. "Unless something's held her up. I have a cleaning woman who comes three times a week, but this isn't one of her days. Not that it would matter. She let me know in no uncertain terms that she's not a baby-sitter."

Amanda spoke impulsively. "I can stay with Brianna until Mrs. Buchanan gets here."

"She needs her bath and—"

"I think I can handle a bath. Why don't you go deal with the bank and I'll finish feeding Brianna?"

Ryan's expression was tight. "I don't expect you to take on baby-sitting duties."

"I thought we cleared that up last night. I only do what I want to. Karen always gets to the shop early, and she can handle anything that comes up. And luckily I'm not expecting any big shipments today." Seeing that he was torn, she added a bit of incentive as her eyes roved over him. "While I find your ruffled appearance rather charming, I'm not sure the loan officer will."

Barefoot, dressed in tight-fitting jeans and a loose sweatshirt, his long hair wild, and not yet shaven, he looked like a rake. Karen's words ran through Amanda's mind. *As though he stepped from the pages of the past.* If Karen could see him now, she would know she was right. Ryan resembled a dangerous pirate. And damnably, that only made him sexier.

Ryan glanced down at his clothes as he ran a hand through his hair. "I don't usually shower until after I've fed Brianna her breakfast. There doesn't seem to be much point."

"Then you'd better get moving," Amanda suggested, taking a final sip of her coffee before settling in the chair he'd vacated, turning her attention to the baby. "Okay, sweetie, how about some more cereal?"

Brianna obligingly opened her little mouth and Amanda slipped in a spoonful of sticky oatmeal.

Ryan paused, one hand on the swinging door. "She likes fruit next."

Amanda waved him away. "I'm sure we'll manage."

"MacDougall's in the garden," Ryan offered as Brianna dimpled at him.

"Thanks, I was wondering where he'd wandered off to."

Ryan still didn't leave. "If you're sure—"

"I'm sure you need to get going."

Pushing open the door that swung into the dining room, Ryan finally left.

Amanda wiped the child's chin. "What do you think? Applesauce? Or should we go crazy and have bananas and passion fruit?"

The baby waved her hands, and Amanda took that as assent. Finding a jar of bananas, she opened the lid and offered Brianna a spoonful. "Bananas," she encouraged.

"Ba," the child responded.

"Won't be long before you're talking. Do you know how to say 'Daddy'?"

"Ba," Brianna repeated.

"Oh, I see this is one we'll have to work on. Won't that

be a nice surprise for Daddy? You can say it, sweetie. Daddy.''

"Ba," she replied again.

"Okay, we'll work on it. Right now, I think you just want your bananas." Amanda spooned some into the child's waiting mouth.

After a few more spoonfuls, Amanda tried again. "Daddy?"

"Da," Brianna responded, her huge eyes fixed on Amanda.

"Good girl." Feeling another unexpected spurt of maternal tugging, Amanda smoothed the baby's silky curls. "You're something, aren't you, Brianna. No wonder you've got your daddy wrapped around your finger. I can sure see why." As she continued to feed the baby, Amanda couldn't help wondering if there was any room in Ryan's heart for someone else.

AMANDA RUSHED INTO the shop. It was nearly noon. Karen and Trisha, the young girl who also worked in the shop, would need to be relieved for lunch. Mrs. Buchanan had called, explaining that she needed to take her sister to the doctor. Apologizing profusely, the woman was torn between her duty to Brianna and to her sister. Amanda had taken the decision in her own hands and volunteered to stay with Brianna. What Ryan didn't know wouldn't hurt him.

And Brianna hadn't suffered, although Amanda knew she'd enjoyed bathing and playing with the child even more than Brianna had. She was such a happy baby, sweet and nontemperamental. With a father like Ryan, Amanda wondered how that was possible, but Brianna was all joy. And Amanda had to admit that Ryan had only used his inflexible temper on her at the beginning of their relationship.

Relationship? Had she thought of what they shared in those terms? Ryan had been ready and apparently willing to walk away and never see her again, although he still showed plenty of sexual interest in her. If not for the snag

Suzy and John had thrown them, she suspected she would have seen the last of him.

"Hi! Everything okay at home? Or should I say 'homes'?" Karen asked.

"What? Oh, yes. It's fine. I'm sorry to be so late. I know you and Trish need to go to lunch."

Karen shrugged. "It doesn't really matter. We could have worked something out. We're both pretty flexible."

"And I appreciate it. But I don't expect you to give up your lunchtime and breaks." Realizing she sounded much like an echo of Ryan, Amanda stopped.

But Karen had already moved ahead. She held a clipboard in her hand. "I prepared an invitation list for the tea."

"Tea?"

"For the Spode," Karen reminded her gently. "You sure everything's okay at home?"

Considering it wasn't her home they referred to, Amanda stifled her initial response. "I'm sure. I guess I'm just not used to dealing with babies."

"Or overwhelming men?" Karen guessed.

Amanda met her knowing gaze. "Okay, Sherlock Holmes, knock it off."

But Karen was all innocence. "Just stating the obvious."

Amanda bit her lower lip. "Is it really?"

"Only to me," Karen relented. "You're actually handling everything pretty well. Most women thrown into a mock marriage would be reeling, and now you've got his little cherub to think about, too. You're not the kind of person who can open her heart and shut it as though nothing happened."

Amanda was discovering that was true. "I guess I really am a sap."

"That depends."

"On what?"

Karen smiled wickedly. "On how soon I get that dinner invitation."

AMANDA HADN'T PLANNED on granting Karen's wish so soon, but felt she would rather tackle the dinner before Suzy and John rolled into town, and it wouldn't be long until they arrived. So she suggested an evening later that week. Ryan had been agreeable, saying only that he would invite a friend, as well. Amanda had agreed to his request, mentioning that she hoped their two friends would get along. Too many strangers at a dinner party could be awfully awkward. Especially when her husband was one of them.

Amanda fussed over the table, rechecking the place settings. A pan of lasagna was baking in the kitchen, and she'd made a salad and some elegant appetizers. She wasn't sure why she was so worried about the evening, but this was the first time she'd thrown Ryan together with a friend who knew their true circumstances. And Amanda couldn't help wondering what Ryan's friend, Barry, would think of her, as well.

Ryan was upstairs showering, and Brianna was asleep in the nursery. Amanda lit the tapers and gave the table one final perusal. Just then the doorbell rang. It was like Karen to be early and catch her before she was completely ready.

Amanda spoke as she flung open the door. "You're early." Embarrassed, she stared at the slightly rumpled-looking stranger standing on the doorstep.

"Sorry." He grinned as he held out a bottle of wine. "Will this make up for my gaffe?"

She accepted the wine. "I'm the one who's sorry. I thought you were someone else."

"You *were* expecting me?"

"Of course, please come in. Ryan should be down in a moment."

The man offered his hand. "I'm Barry Daniels."

"Amanda Thorne," she replied, accepting his handshake and then leading him into the living room. "Why don't we open this?"

He gestured to the corkscrew on the mahogany bar. "May I?"

"Certainly."

Efficiently, he popped the cork and then filled two of the glasses she'd arranged. Offering her one goblet, he lifted the other and they took tentative sips.

Barry lowered his glass first. "So, you're the fake Mrs. West."

Spluttering, she choked on the wine. Glancing up, she met Barry's frank appraisal. "I guess you could say that."

"Looks like Ryan struck it lucky, then." Barry lifted his own glass. "To strange beginnings and better endings."

Amanda lifted her own glass uncertainly. "I didn't know Ryan had confided in you."

"We're friends," he said simply.

She took a deep breath. "Then, you know we have to keep up this pretense for a while."

His warm blue eyes, set in a hound-dog friendly face, continued to watch her. "I think it'll be good for Ryan."

"You do?"

"All work and no play…"

Amanda felt a flush of embarrassment.

Barry spoke again, his voice gentle. "I'm referring to his focus on life. He's a little too intense."

That was an understatement. "I'm not sure our arrangement will change that."

"We'll see." He raised his eyes, looking beyond her. "Good to see you've decided to join us, Ryan."

Amanda turned, silently admiring Ryan's freshly showered look. He had chosen to wear jeans, but he'd topped them with a black silk shirt. It was a knockout combination with his dark, potent coloring.

"I see you've met Amanda," Ryan greeted them, his gaze skipping over their wineglasses.

Barry casually turned to pour a third glass. "She's definitely Thorne's best treasure."

Amanda felt a start of surprise as she stared between the

two men. How had Barry known about her business? It didn't seem like something that would have come under the topic of their mock marriage.

Ryan walked smoothly toward Amanda, stopping to stand beside her. "I'm well aware of that."

For a moment their gazes met, and Barry, along with his comment, was forgotten. It astounded her that Ryan could make her weak with simply a glance.

Barry tactfully cleared his throat. "Is it okay for me to dig into this?" He pointed to the tray of appetizers.

Amanda dragged herself back to the present. "Of course, I meant to offer you one."

"Barry usually just makes himself at home, helping himself to things whether I like it or not. You have a good effect on his manners."

Amanda saw a flash of genuine affection cross Ryan's face, and she wondered about it. Apparently this mild-mannered, charmingly rumpled man was a special friend. She wondered how such opposite men could have formed a strong friendship. It seemed that Ryan's intense power and need for control would have blown Barry out of the water.

But Barry seemed unperturbed as he munched on one of the appetizers. "These are great, Amanda. Don't tell me you can cook, too?"

"Maybe you'd better taste the rest of the meal before you decide."

The doorbell rang.

"That'll be Karen." She started toward the door, but surprisingly Ryan joined her.

Karen looked properly impressed as Amanda introduced them. In fact, Amanda could read the wheels spinning, especially when her friend winked and shot her a thumbs-up sign as soon as Ryan turned around.

"He's great," Karen whispered as they followed Ryan into the living room.

Ryan gestured to Barry. "Karen, I'd like you to meet my friend, Barry Daniels."

Barry glanced up, the appetizer in his hand forgotten midway to his mouth as he stared at Karen.

Amanda and Ryan looked from Barry to Karen. She, too, seemed frozen in place.

"And, Barry, this is Karen," Ryan added unnecessarily.

Amanda tried to ease the awkward situation. "Won't you come in and sit down, Karen?"

Karen simply stood without answering, staring at Barry.

"Amanda's appetizers are delicious." Ryan gestured to the tray.

When her friend still didn't reply, Amanda tried again. "Karen, would you like some wine?"

Finally Karen came to, her face flushed, her eyes dreamy. "Wine? Yes, that would be nice."

Ignoring their hosts, Barry hastily poured another glass, then practically jumped from the bar stool to offer the glass to Karen. Their fingertips touched, and Amanda began to feel like a voyeur. Catching Ryan's amused gaze, she placed a gentle hand on his arm. "Perhaps we should go check on the dinner. I imagine Barry and Karen can entertain themselves."

"Sure looks like it," he muttered.

Barry and Karen didn't glance their way as they moved toward the kitchen.

Slightly uncomfortable with what she'd witnessed, since it reminded her too much of her own unresolved situation with Ryan, Amanda rattled a few unnecessary bowls, then checked and rechecked the lasagna.

Ryan draped his hands around her waist and pulled her away from the stove before she could open the oven again. "The lasagna is fine."

She pushed at an unruly curl. "I don't want it to—"

"It won't."

"Burn," she finished, letting the word trail away.

He traced the outline of her lips, then the contour of her cheek. "I can't promise I won't burn, though."

She repressed a groan. "We have company, you know."

One corner of his mouth lifted in a sardonic grin. "Somehow, I don't think they'll miss us."

"They do seem rather taken with each other," she responded, trying to steady her voice and her shaky breath.

Amusement continued to curl his lips. "I think that's a relatively safe statement."

Safe and Ryan didn't go together. And the weakness flooding her was proof of that.

He tweaked a lock of her hair. "Don't you think we should give them some time alone?"

Amanda tried to back up, but found herself pressed into an uncompromising wall of steel. The refrigerator, she remembered vaguely. "Alone? I... I don't want to seem rude."

He began nibbling on her lips, easing them open. "Oh, I don't think they'll feel you're being rude."

His arms trapped her in place, and using only his mouth, he melted her reserve. When he planted a trail of kisses beneath her chin and down the sensitive skin of her neck, she shivered, then wound her arms around him, pulling him closer.

It was madness, her logical side argued. This man will walk away when he doesn't need you any longer. He's already told you that, loud and clear. He is not the kind of man to share your life. But logic was overpowered by desire. In fact, it ran a poor second.

Pouring herself into the kiss, Amanda forgot her guests, the lasagna and certainly all the resolutions she'd been clinging to. Ryan teased her breasts with a sure touch, then skimmed over her back, resting finally on her derriere, pulling her close enough to feel the rough indention of his belt buckle, the fullness of his sex.

Heat rushed through her blood like molten steel. There was nothing gentle in his kiss. Like Ryan himself, his touch was powerful, controlling. And every nerve in her body responded.

The kiss seemed endless, and when Ryan finally drew back, she saw desire laced with regret. And part of her heart stood still.

"I nearly forgot we have company," Ryan explained, his forehead tilting forward to touch hers.

Relief flooded her. Having completely blocked out the other couple, Amanda was glad Ryan hadn't. She was even gladder that Ryan hadn't been regretting the kiss.

Somehow, this simple charade had spun far out of control.

Her own voice was shaky. "I'd better check on dinner."

Reluctantly, he released her and she turned around to face the refrigerator. Amanda felt his eyes watching her as she pulled the bowl of salad from the refrigerator. "I'll toss this and we can serve dinner in a few minutes."

He peered over her shoulder into the refrigerator. "I don't suppose you have a cold shower in there."

Unsettled, Amanda managed to laugh. "No, and I hope nobody else here needs one, either."

Ryan followed her gaze toward the kitchen door, pasting on a mock scowl. "I could always turn the hose on them, if they're not ready for dinner."

Amanda kept her gaze on the salad as she mechanically tossed it. "I don't think that will be necessary."

Surprising her, Ryan stilled her hands, picked one up and lightly kissed her knuckles. "Then, they don't know what they're missing."

Picking up the salad bowl, he backed out of the kitchen, raising his voice. "Okay, you two, we're ready to eat."

Stunned, Amanda stood for a moment holding the salad tongs blankly in her hands. The tender kiss on her fingers still tingled, and she reached with her other hand to touch that same place. She expected the desire, the passion, but his tenderness unnerved her.

"You coming, Amanda?" Ryan said, poking his head in the kitchen.

Dropping the tongs, she made a stab at smoothing back her hair. Trying for composure, she offered Ryan a tentative smile. "I'll be right in."

He disappeared, and she sagged briefly against the counter. Oh, this man was making mush of what used to be her controlled feelings. Knowing everyone was waiting, Amanda plastered on a smile and entered the dining room. Karen and Barry sat side by side, not even noticing as she came in.

Glancing at her friend, Amanda felt a little of her tension dissolve. Karen was completely wrapped up in Ryan's low-key friend. She suspected they could have left them alone for the rest of the evening and neither would have noticed.

Barely touching their dinners, Karen and Barry were too distracted to do much more than answer the questions Amanda and Ryan offered by way of conversation. Turning down offers of dessert, they both rose quickly at the end of the meal.

"Wouldn't you like coffee?" Amanda asked, looking at the untouched cheesecake she had lovingly prepared.

Karen's flushed cheeks deepened to an even rosier shade. "I really should be going. I want to catch an early bus home."

"Why don't I drive you?" Barry offered. "I'm going that way."

Amanda and Ryan exchanged glances. No one had mentioned where Karen lived, and Amanda knew for a fact that Karen never worried about catching an early bus. Amanda suspected they had hatched this plan while she and Ryan had lingered in the kitchen.

"That would be lovely," Karen offered. Belatedly, she glanced back at Amanda and Ryan. "If they don't mind you leaving early, too."

Before either could answer, Barry jumped in. "Ryan won't mind. He and Amanda will be glad to be rid of me."

"Don't you want to see Brianna before you go?" Ryan asked him dryly. "You're always such a devoted godparent."

Distracted, Barry barely glanced in his direction. "Give her a kiss for me. I don't want to wake her up."

"It was great meeting you, Ryan," Karen offered, already slipping toward the door.

Amusement shaded Ryan's features, and he looped an arm around Amanda's shoulders, glancing between his friend and Karen. "I imagine I'll be seeing quite a bit of you."

They exited hastily, and Ryan turned Amanda around to face him. "No doubt about it. They didn't get along at all."

Catching his amusement, she grinned as well. "Gives a new meaning to the word 'awkward,' doesn't it."

His arms snaked around her, pulling her close. "I thought they'd never leave."

Even though it had been the shortest dinner party Amanda had ever hosted, she found herself agreeing, persuaded once again by Ryan's touch. And even that thought fell away as he reached out to flip the light switch off, plunging them into darkness, taking her fragile feelings with him into the night.

A sudden cry pierced the darkness. As they increased in volume, Brianna's cries nearly drowned out Ryan's muffled curse as he reluctantly released Amanda.

Her hand was shaky as she turned the light back on. In the sudden glare she saw the passion in Ryan's eyes and wondered how the evening might have ended had Brianna not awakened. As he climbed the stairs to check on the baby, Amanda grabbed her purse and fled, afraid to examine the possibilities.

Chapter Twelve

Karen's voice and expression were dreamy, unfocused. "Barry's magnificent," she murmured.

Amanda hid her amusement. "What did you think of Ryan?"

"Oh, he was nice, too."

A far cry from Mr. Wonderful. "I thought you believed he was the best thing that happened to the male species since Lancelot."

"For you, he is." Karen hugged her arms to her sides. "I just prefer a different sort of man."

Amanda considered strangling her friend. Karen had been the one to expound on the virtues of the darkly compelling male, and now she was attracted to the exact reverse of her own ideal. In fact, she and Karen seemed to have flip-flopped their preferences for men, winding up with their opposites.

"I see." She cleared her throat. "Does this mean you'll be seeing Barry again?"

"Oh, I hope so." Karen sighed, then seemed to gaze off at unseen stars. "After he took me home, we talked for hours. I've never met anyone like him."

Amanda was pleased for her friend. Karen had been chasing her romantic dream for years. "I'm glad for you."

"And I'm glad for you. Ryan is perfect for you. Maybe it was kismet the way you met."

"It was a computer error," Amanda reminded her.

"Oh, yeah. Like either of us believes that."

Speechless, Amanda could only clamp her mouth shut on a denial. She, too, believed it had been more.

Then Karen switched gears. "I hope Barry calls."

Amanda thought that only a breakdown of every phone line in the city would prevent it.

The door jangled, indicating a customer. Amanda turned with a smile and saw Barry walking toward her, carrying a bouquet of flowers. She greeted him warmly. "Hi."

His gaze lit on her for a moment. "Hi, Amanda."

At the sound of his voice, Karen turned around, her entire countenance changing, lighting up into a soft glow. "Barry."

He smiled shyly, holding out the flowers. "These are for you."

Karen accepted them, taking a moment to inhale their delicate fragrance.

Barry's eyes never left Karen's face. "I thought you might be free for lunch."

It was early, and Karen turned to Amanda, obviously prepared to plead for an early lunch hour.

Amanda smiled because it was difficult to do anything else while watching them. "Go ahead. Trish and I have everything covered here."

Karen didn't ask a second time. She reached under the counter for her purse, then scooted past the cash register to stand next to Barry.

"Have fun," Amanda called out as they left.

Neither heard her words, completely absorbed in each other. The door shut behind them, and Amanda couldn't repress a sigh. She suspected Karen had met her white knight, a slightly rumpled one, but apparently the man to fulfill her dreams. In their long association, she'd never seen Karen respond this way to a man. And the fact that he was equally bowled over by her looked as though it spelled a sweet future.

An hour later, when Amanda heard the bell again, she wondered if Karen was returning. Trish was at the front of the store tending the register while she was handling a curious customer.

The woman was picking up a valuable glass, one of a rare set of six. Crystal martini glasses with silver overlay, inscribed with the Tokyo Golf Club initials and insignia, dating from 1940, they were an unusual collectible.

"Is it $300 for the set?" the woman asked.

Amanda withheld her sigh. Apparently the woman wasn't a serious collector. "No, ma'am. They're $300 each and I won't break up the set."

The customer huffed up and widened her eyes. "Well, that's a little more than I want to spend."

Amanda could tell from the woman's expression that she thought the price was outrageous, but she also knew that one of her regulars, serious collectors, would be delighted with this find.

"We have less expensive glasses all through the shop. I'd be happy to show you some."

The woman pursed thin lips, her bony face drawn into a frown. "That won't be necessary. I'll look on my own."

Amanda hid an amused smile. She suspected the woman was going to try to find the most expensive items in the shop so that she could report to her friends that Thorne's Treasures dealt in highway robbery.

Still smiling, she turned, then stopped in surprise to find Ryan directly behind her.

"Eighteen hundred for half a dozen glasses." He clucked his tongue in mock disapproval. "No wonder that woman looked like you were offering her arsenic."

"We have a lot less expensive items...and some that are quite a bit more. She's obviously not a serious collector."

Ryan picked up one of the glasses in question. "Only the serious ones buy the real expensive stuff?"

Amanda cocked her head, considering. "Usually. But then sometimes someone will wander in, be taken with a valuable piece and buy it just because they like it. This business isn't an exact science. Not that the stock market is, either, but even though collectibles are great investments, it's not always a logical process."

"But you probably don't have that many valuable pieces, do you?" Ryan asked, testing the waters, thinking of the latest transactions of hers that had been uncovered, papers that were even more incriminating.

"Well, actually, yes." She pointed out a beautifully carved curio cabinet as she walked toward it.

"This piece?" he asked, examining the fine craftsmanship of the mahogany, a wood rarely seen anymore.

"Actually, it's valuable, too, but I was referring to the collection inside." Withdrawing a small, old-fashioned key from the group on her chain, she unlocked the glass door. "It's Steuben Glass—extremely rare and valuable. You're more likely to find it in a museum than a store. Which is why it's under lock and key." Then she unlocked and pulled out the wide drawer located beneath the glass. "And in here I have a good selection of fountain pens."

She wasn't kidding—there must have been more than a hundred pens in the drawer. He picked up one that looked fairly old. The marbled burgundy of the big barrel appealed to him. "How much is this one?"

"More than you'd expect. It's an early Parker—$3500."

Ryan sucked in his breath in surprise. More than a hundred pens in the drawer, the collection was valuable and took up only a tiny space in her crammed shop. "Are they all this price?"

She shrugged. "Some are. But for the most part, they're all valued differently."

"Oh, so this one's on the high end?"

"Actually, no. It's on the low end." She pointed to a few pens near the edge of the drawer. "See, these have silver and gold overlay." Then she pointed to one in particular. "And this one is both older and extremely rare. Waterman came out with a similar pen in the 1920s, but this one predates it considerably, and it's one of only a few ever made by this lesser-known manufacturer.'' She smiled again. ''But there are three or four pens in here that aren't quite as costly.''

Barry's assessment of her stock had been correct. And as his report stated, it didn't align with her profit margin, especially when you considered the pricey European antiques he'd spotted throughout the store. Even though they hadn't been tagged, he knew from decorating his own home that the pieces were extremely valuable. ''And you have customers who buy things this expensive?''

''Oh, yes. For serious collectors, the Steuben in particular is a real find. Especially when there are plenty of dealers who don't look too closely for authentication.''

Ryan hated to think how much the Steuben must be worth. Yet she'd tossed off the authentication issue without much apparent thought. Were they on tricky ground? ''But you verify your merchandise?''

Amanda relocked the cabinet. ''I wouldn't be in business long, otherwise. Word gets around.''

''So you know of other dealers who don't mind passing a few fakes?''

She shrugged. ''Not well.''

He wondered at the casualness with which she dismissed the shady dealings. Was this another avenue for making illegal funds—dealing in forged collectibles? It could explain why her figures didn't tally.

She turned a brightly innocent face toward him, and he was instantly reminded of how convincing Danielle had been. Amanda's smile was tentative but curious. ''Now that we've taken the tour, just what are you doing here?''

One black brow cocked impudently. ''Not delighted to see me?''

''Just surprised,'' she replied diplomatically, wondering if he had come to ask her to lunch. A seed of excitement took root as she waited for his reply. Perhaps he hadn't brought flowers, but...

"Actually, I came by to see if you'd go to the bank with me. We have some more papers to execute."

Disappointment flared, then she resigned herself. After all, this was what she'd signed on for.

PAPERS ENDORSED, Ryan and Amanda left the bank, blending into the crowds that spilled across the sidewalk.

"Where would you like to eat?" Ryan asked, scanning the street for possibilities.

"Eat?"

Hearing the surprise in her voice, Ryan glanced at her face and saw that it wore a matching expression of astonishment. "You know. Open your mouth, insert food, chew." When she continued to look amazed, he narrowed his eyes, studying her for the reason. "You *do* eat lunch, don't you? That meal in the middle of the day?"

She cleared her throat. "Of course."

"I thought so. I did drag you away right at noon."

"But you don't *have* to take me to lunch."

"No. But we *have* to eat, don't we? How about Japanese? I know a great place with a revolving—"

"Sushi bar," she chimed in at the same time. "I know the place. I love it."

"We can catch a trolley a block over." Ryan picked up her hand, relishing the feel of her cool fingers in his.

Like most people who lived in San Francisco, Ryan regarded trolley cars as transportation rather than as the romantic images most tourists considered them to be. Yet, with Amanda beside him, it did seem romantic. Feeling like a Rice-a-Roni commercial, Ryan hung onto the side of the crowded trolley car with Amanda. The wind ruffled her unruly mass of curls, but Ryan thought she looked sexy. In a blink of an eye, he could picture that same hair fanned across his pillow.

The trolley headed down a steep hill, pushing Amanda's body into his. When she didn't jerk away, he allowed himself to enjoy the sensation. Those incredible eyes of hers that resembled lush, verdant wild grass now sparkled. Her cheeks were flushed to an entrancing pink, and the freckles that danced across the bridge of her nose glowed in the sunlight. God, she was something.

They were passing Chinatown, alive with its own scents, sounds and crowds of scurrying people. The trolley stopped to let a load of people off at the popular destination. An equally large group boarded, taking their places.

"I know it's a touristy thing to say, but I just love Chinatown," Amanda confessed. "I've probably seen every piece of jade in every store."

"There *are* worse things. I prefer Golden Gate Park, myself."

"Rollerskating?" she guessed.

"On Sundays, when they close it off from cars." He studied her face. "Don't tell me you like that, too."

"Actually, I prefer Rollerblades, but yes, I like it. There's an art exhibit at the park now, and for me, going to one after skating is like dessert after a good meal."

Ryan searched his memory. "The Monet exhibit?"

She shook her head. "No, that moved on quite a while back."

He grinned ruefully. "Since Brianna's arrival on the scene, I don't get around as much as I'd like."

Amanda tilted her head in his direction. "You have Mrs. Buchanan."

"But she's not Brianna's parent. And the kid's already been shortchanged with having only a father. I don't want to reduce the number of parents to zero."

A thoughtful expression crossed her face. "Brianna knows you love her, and I think that's what counts. In fact, I'm not sure when I've ever seen a more contented child."

Inordinately pleased, Ryan couldn't prevent a satisfied smile. Brianna was the most important thing in his life. "You're pretty good with her yourself."

Amanda's voice was quiet. "She has a way of getting to you."

Ryan wondered briefly if she was becoming too attached, but they had reached their stop, and he held out his hand to Amanda as they stepped down.

"I'm starving," Amanda announced as they walked uphill toward the restaurant. "And sushi sounds better than the yogurt and banana I brought for lunch."

"You eat in often?"

Amanda shrugged. "We have three people to rotate lunch, and I always make sure Karen and Trish have a full hour. Usually it's easier if I stay in."

"All work, and no play…"

Her eyes flicked upward, meeting his, and he saw the quick flare in them as he spoke.

Then they were inside, headed down the stairs to the restaurant. Quiet, softly lit, the restaurant was decorated in pleasing reds and blacks. The novel rotating sushi bar was in operation, the expert chefs preparing traditional Japanese dishes as interested patrons watched. Chairs circled the round bar that provided an ample eating area. Sushi, sashimi and nori-maki, along with garnishes of wasabi and gari—spicy horseradish and vinegared slices of ginger—passed in front of the diners, traveling in continuous circles as the chefs replaced emptied selections.

Ryan guided Amanda to two chairs slightly away from the rest of the crowd. The vast, intriguing array of food revolved by as they watched. Delectable dishes of sauces were placed in front of them, and they tried to decide what to choose.

For some inexplicable reason, the octopus and eel had them trying to stifle a fit of giggles. A connoisseur of sushi, Ryan had never found any amusement in the exotic choices, but with Amanda at his side, there was a subtle shift in his perspective. A playfulness that she alone brought out in him.

Ryan tried to straighten out his own expression. "If we don't knock it off, they're going to kick us out."

"You're right." Straightening her shoulders, Amanda

glanced at the eel on her plate, obviously trying to look serious, but failing miserably. "I hope this isn't the electric variety."

Ryan rolled his eyes as he tried not to laugh. "I don't think they'd intentionally provide us with any more energy."

Her eyes danced. "They'll probably limit us to seaweed and rice."

"Or a nice, calming tofu soup."

Amanda sighed as she watched the delicious-looking dishes spin by. "I hope not. I'd like to taste everything."

"Unless your stomach's a bottomless pit, I don't think you'll manage dozens of varieties."

She reached for a dish that looked particularly exotic. "Maybe not, but I'm going to have fun trying."

He glanced at the dish she'd chosen and impulsively picked up a portion. Her mouth opened in a surprised "oh." He took the opportunity to place the bit of seaweed-wrapped rice and cucumber in Amanda's mouth, his fingers lingering near her lips, enjoying the sensuality of the intimate gesture.

She seemed frozen in place.

Unable to resist, he traced a line up the curve of her cheek. "Is it good?"

Her voice wasn't quite steady. "I think I forgot to chew."

His thumb eased over the tip of her chin. "Any reason why?"

Ryan could see the confusion crowding her expression.

"I guess I wasn't as hungry as I thought," Amanda managed to say, the forgotten sushi still resting in the dish.

"And I don't think I realized just how hungry *I* was."

He watched as Amanda swallowed with difficulty.

"Ryan—"

"Do you *have* to get back to the shop right away?"

"Not exactly—"

"Then, how about Chinatown?"

In her confusion, she dropped her chopsticks and they both bent over to retrieve them, their eyes meeting as he handed her the utensils.

"Chinatown?"

It was easy to smile at her confusion. "You *did* say you loved it."

"Do you have time?"

"I can steal away for a few hours." It had been a purely impulsive offer. Normally he would have rescheduled his canceled meetings, crammed more work into the day, but something else was tugging at him, pulling him toward playing hooky with Amanda.

"Today's a special day," he continued as they rose from retrieving the chopsticks.

Once again sitting upright, she looked at him carefully. "It is?"

"You're taking up residence at the West home, remember? And after Chinatown, we can pick up MacDougall and your things."

She swallowed carefully. "That is today, isn't it?"

"Suzy and John will be in town tonight," he reminded her.

Abandoning the remainder of her untasted lunch, Amanda propped her chopsticks on the porcelain holder.

"Don't you have at least a dozen varieties left to taste?"

She shrugged. "Maybe some other time."

Seeing that his reminder about the Meriweathers had upset her, Ryan talked her into tasting a few more choices, smoothing over the awkward moment as they lingered over cups of hot tea.

Knowing they were stealing time from crowded schedules, Ryan hailed a cab to take them to the gates of Chinatown as they left the restaurant.

"Where would you like to stop?" he asked as they approached Dragon Gate.

"It doesn't really matter," she replied, still uncharacteristically quiet.

"Hey, Chinatown's your place."

A ghost of a smile flickered. "I *do* love it," she admitted. "I always get so caught up, I forget everything else."

The sounds and smells of the crowded area rushed through the open windows of the cab. "Then, it's your call. Where do we stop?"

She shrugged, a reluctant grin tugging at her lips. "Anywhere."

"You don't have a preference?"

The grin was in full bloom. "I love it all. It really doesn't matter. Just pick a place to stop."

Doing just that, he watched her light up as she stepped into the scurrying mass of humanity crowding the streets. Although not a shopper, Ryan always caught the contagious feel of energy that filled the bustling streets. As he glanced around, Amanda captured his hand, tugging him toward a nearby shop that specialized in jade. Figurines filled the window, and as he soon saw, lined the shelves, as well. A courteous clerk offered her assistance, but Amanda smilingly refused. Instead, she studied the beautiful sculptures and Oriental artifacts.

Without warning, she darted from the jade store into a nearby shop that sold a variety of goods. She was drawn to the happy coats—knee-length silk robes that were fancifully embroidered, along with intricately carved teakwood boxes and cloisonné jewelry.

But she didn't linger long, instead pulling him into a variety of shops. He couldn't predict what would interest her. Randomly, she chose an Oriental antique shop, produce and fish markets, a store that sold only silk goods, and a shop where she talked him into a gooey dessert.

He found himself fascinated by the swing of her glinting strawberry hair, the light of excitement in her unusual eyes, that outrageously sexy dimple, the flirty skirt that allowed a generous view of her incredible legs. And even more so, the excitement that she carried with her like a ticket into a fun, new world.

How long had it been since he had allowed himself a few hours of simple pleasure? He couldn't even begin to remember. Since Danielle's departure, he had been caught in the dark web of heavy responsibilities. And, much as he hated to admit it, Amanda was yet another means to an end in that set of responsibilities.

Laughing as they finished the sugary treat, Amanda spied a herb pharmacy. "We *have* to go in there," she insisted, dragging him along.

Pungent, sweet, acrid, spicy, the sharply distinctive odors assailed them as they entered. At the far end of the shop an ancient herbalist filled prescriptions for his patients, while the walls held cures for everything from arthritis to warts. They poked around in bins of strange-looking roots, and shook clear bags containing mysteriously fascinating yet indiscernible products.

Amanda picked up a box of ginger tea for upset stomachs—always a good staple to have at the shop, along with some ginseng for improved brain power.

Ryan's mocking glance landed on her last choice. "Think you might need that?"

"I was a Girl Scout—it pays to always be prepared."

As she spoke, their gazes collided on the next display. A potion guaranteeing love, fertility and sexual prowess. Her words seemed to still ring between them. *Be prepared.*

The frivolity they had felt changed as quickly as the tension that now pulsed between them.

"You be wanting this?" An elderly Chinese woman, smiling broadly to reveal a gap-toothed smile, patted her own flat stomach as she gestured to the display.

"N-no…" Amanda stuttered.

The woman's lined face smiled with age-old wisdom. "You two have look of love, not long till your babies come along."

Amanda stared at Ryan, seeing his matching expression of turmoil.

"Thank you," Ryan answered the clerk. "Your kind thoughts are appreciated."

Amanda saw that he managed to remember the courtesy those of Chinese ancestry cherished, despite the awkward circumstances. Paying for their purchases, then moving out of the shop, Amanda made all the correct responses, yet her mind was apparently stuck in the same groove, the replay mode. Because the woman's words kept sounding in her mind. *"You two have look of love...."*

Could the wise old woman have seen something neither she nor Ryan realized? Or was she simply latching onto what she wanted to hear?

Chapter Thirteen

Suzy and John had been delighted with Brianna the first time they had met her, waving away Amanda's awkward attempts to explain why they hadn't told anyone at the reunion about her.

In town now for several weeks, Suzy and John had practically adopted the baby along with Amanda and Ryan, dropping over often. Suzy constantly regaled them with tales of the move and her plans to redecorate the town house, while John sat contentedly at her side not seeming to mind that she dominated the conversation.

This evening, as they all sat drinking wine in Ryan's spacious living room, Suzy turned her full attention on Amanda, her voice oozing drama. "Now, I want to hear all the details about how you and Ryan found this wonderful house, and whether this beautiful furniture came from Thorne's Treasures. I'd like to look at some things in your shop—see if I can decorate my town house to look this great."

Before Amanda could concoct a reply, Brianna, bless her, began to fuss. "She's such a good baby, she never cries," Amanda improvised. "She must be hungry or wet. Let me check and I'll be right back."

Suzy turned her hundred watt attention on Ryan. "I bet you're so proud you could pop. Two such beautiful ladies in your life."

Amanda had the satisfaction of listening to Ryan trying to scramble for something to say. Then she was out of earshot as the kitchen door swung behind her. With Brianna snuggled comfortably on her hip, Amanda filled a bottle and slid it into eagerly waiting lips. Then, checking the baby's diaper, she found it to be very soggy indeed. No wonder the baby had put up an unexpected fuss.

Using the backstairs, Amanda escaped to the nursery, letting Ryan fend for himself as she leisurely changed Brianna, then settled in the rocking chair while the baby finished her bottle.

"You're lots more fun than the grown-ups," Amanda told the child, who gurgled contentedly.

Amanda rested her cheek against the baby's soft hair, struck as always by the child's utter sweetness and trust. Running her hand over Brianna's arm, she felt tiny fingers clutch her own, then nestle in her grip. She wanted to believe that Brianna cherished this connection as much as she did. Amanda had formulated excuses to spend more time with the child, visiting on her lunch hour when Ryan wasn't home, then returning to the house early each night. How was it possible to grow to care so much about a small stranger?

But the tightening in her chest confirmed that Brianna was no longer a stranger, someone else's baby to play with and then return. It was as though her own biological clock had kicked into overdrive, sending every maternal instinct to the surface. Brianna turned her head to snuggle closer in the curve of her shoulder, and Amanda felt her throat tighten.

It was going to be so difficult to walk away from this precious child. Not to mention Brianna's father, a man who still refused to give their relationship a chance.

"What am I going to do, punkin?"

Brianna kicked her feet in reply as her lids started to droop.

Knowing the child needed to be put to bed soon, Amanda

sighed. Repositioning the baby in her arms, she reluctantly returned to the living room to rejoin the adults. "Brianna has to go to bed soon, so she came to say good-night."

"I can put her to bed," Ryan offered, rising, obviously ill at ease with hosting a constantly chatting Suzy.

Amanda smiled sweetly at him. "That's all right, dear. I'm sure you and John have more business to discuss."

John cut off any reply Ryan planned to make. "That'd be great, if you don't mind, Amanda. I still have a few more items to go over with Ryan."

Amanda kept her smile so sweet she half expected molasses to drip down her chin. "Of course not, John. I'll be glad to give you some time."

Suzy jumped up at her last words. "Do you mind if I tag along? It'll sort of be like mothering classes. I never thought being the youngest in the family was a handicap." She giggled. "After all, I got spoiled rotten, but I don't know a thing about babies. And who had time during high school to baby-sit? Between cheerleader practice and dates, I barely had time to study."

"It's pretty dull, Suzy. Just changing diapers, putting on pajamas and—"

"That's okay," Suzy interrupted. "It's the everyday stuff I need to learn."

Glancing at Ryan, Amanda saw the amused smirk on his face.

Resigned, she smiled at Suzy. "We'd love your company."

Trailing beside them, Suzy chatted nonstop. Still, she wasn't as much of an intrusion as Amanda expected. There was an awkward moment after putting Brianna in her crib when Amanda had to search for pajamas under Suzy's watchful gaze. Ryan always insisted on performing the bedtime ritual, and Amanda had no idea where the nightwear was stored. But it was Suzy who offered a saving explanation after Amanda tried to find a rational reason for the search.

Shrugging, Suzy seemed unconcerned. "I imagine her nanny puts away her things. Didn't she leave early tonight?"

Amanda grasped that excuse. "Yes, her sister's been ill."

"She usually puts Brianna to bed, doesn't she?"

Caught in a moral dilemma, Amanda hesitated. Brianna intervened once again, uttering a tiny, dissatisfied cry.

"What's the matter, sweetie? Tired, huh? Let's get these jammies on, then we'll have a bottle, okay?"

Brianna held up her little arms, touchingly eager to comply.

Suzy watched intently as Amanda undressed Brianna, put on a fresh diaper, then redressed the baby, securing her in footed flannel jammies.

"Why don't you sit in the window seat?" Amanda suggested, as she settled in the rocker, preparing to give Brianna her bottle.

"Sure." Then Suzy was uncharacteristically quiet as she watched Amanda and Brianna. Her voice was soft when she spoke again. "I still can't get over it. I don't know how you kept such a delicious secret at the reunion. It's obvious how much you love her."

Amanda glanced at her friend in surprise, then down at the sweet face of the baby, who once again had nestled her head trustingly in Amanda's shoulder. How had she taken a slice of her heart so quickly?

Brianna's lips reposed in a satisfied bow, her cheeks flushed a delicate pink. Unable to resist, Amanda smoothed her silken baby curls. "She's something," Amanda admitted finally.

"I know you probably think I'm so spoiled I won't appreciate a child, but I want what you have with Brianna." Suzy leaned forward earnestly. "I want to know that unconditional love everyone talks about. I can see it in your face when you look at her." Suzy glanced at her own stomach, a tiny bulge barely noticeable. "I'm going to have a real little person like that. Someone to love and depend on me.''

Amanda tried to digest Suzy's words, wondering if her friend was right, then feeling more of her heart fall under attack. Brianna sighed contently in her arms, and Amanda couldn't resist holding her a little closer as she spoke. ''John loves you, Suzy.''

''I know. But he doesn't depend on me. And a baby will.''

''They're so trusting,'' Amanda admitted in a soft voice, still full of wonder at the baby's purity and innocence. No wonder mothers were so fiercely protective of their children.

Suzy's face filled with admiration. ''I want to learn to be a really good mother like you. I want that sense of love you three share.''

Amanda buried her face in the baby's hair. Suzy was not only treading on every fragile, unexamined emotion, she was putting them under a microscope.

A seed of hope was growing despite her innate caution. Was there something more between the three of them? Between herself and Ryan? Something Suzy had seen? Something the old woman in Chinatown had sensed, too? Or was she just deluding herself, wanting to believe Ryan looked at her with more than lust in his eyes? That she, too, could become part of this tiny family?

''I'm not going to stay jealous,'' Suzy admitted frankly. ''Because I think I can achieve this kind of family, too. And Lord knows I'm no career woman. Thank God John's got money. It would have been hard for me to marry a poor man.''

Amanda's lips twitched. Suzy was, if anything, brutally honest about everything—including herself. ''John's pretty lucky, too.''

Suzy smiled, her bubbles effervescing again. ''Thanks, Amanda. You're one of the few people who really know me, and still like me.''

"There's a lot more to you than surface fluff, Suzy, and I know it."

"Well, don't tell anybody." Suzy threw her head back in a mock regal gesture. "I don't want to give up my pampered status."

"Not much chance of that with a devoted husband like John."

Suzy's smile reeked of satisfaction. "True. But then you know how that feels. You have your own white knight."

Perhaps dusty gray, Amanda acknowledged in silence. But she dredged up a smile. "Suzy, I'm sure you'll be a wonderful mother."

Suzy looked uncertain, an uncommon state for her. "There's so much I don't know."

"But you know the most important thing—that your child and family have to come first. Everything else will fall into place."

The furrow in Suzy's brow relaxed and her lips curved upward. "I guess you're right. You probably didn't know everything about Brianna the first time you took care of her."

"You can say that again." Amanda kept her tongue tucked firmly in cheek. Then she stared down at Brianna's drooping eyelids, the tiny fingers clutched protectively around her hand. "But they surprise you. It's amazing how fast they get under your skin."

"I can see that." Suzy smiled as she rose from her perch on the window seat. "I'll leave you alone now. I suspect this is a special time for you and Brianna. I'll go raid the fridge. It may be a cliché but I'm starving *all* the time." Tiptoeing to the door, Suzy blew the baby a kiss and then disappeared.

Amanda knew she could place Brianna in her crib and in all likelihood the baby would drift quickly off to sleep. Yet she continued rocking, carefully easing the nearly empty bottle from almost lax lips. Brianna's eyes struggled to open, then lowered to shadow pinkish ivory cheeks. Oh, she would be a heartbreaker some day. A start of unexpected tears reminded Amanda that the baby already was. Again she thought how terribly difficult it was going to be to bid this innocent goodbye.

Amanda continued the gentle rocking, far beyond the time Brianna slipped into a deep sleep. Her baby scent of lotion and powder filled Amanda's senses. Knowing she couldn't rock the child all night, Amanda reluctantly rose and placed Brianna in the crib, reaching for a cuddly stuffed lamb—the first thing she'd bought for Brianna. After winding the crib toy, she placed it gently on the mattress, smiling as the woolly lamb played a soft lullaby.

Amanda started to pull up the soft pink quilt, but Brianna whimpered in her sleep. Amanda patted her diaper-padded rear, then rubbed her back in soothing circles. Brianna sighed contentedly, then slipped back into baby dreamland.

"Oh, little one, you're stealing my heart." Covering her securely, Amanda flicked on the night-light as she dimmed the lamp. With one backward glance, she left the darkened nursery, realizing she really needed to rejoin the others.

Not certain how Ryan was faring with Suzy, she was surprised to hear easy laughter spilling out from the living room.

Suzy glanced up just as Amanda entered, and the vivacious blond clapped her hands. "I've been filling in Ryan on just what a character you were in high school. I can't believe you didn't tell him about your checkered background."

Amanda took the wineglass Ryan offered. "Being president of the Scots club hardly qualifies as a checkered past. Technically, that would be a plaid past."

Suzy waved nonchalant hands. "And you didn't tell him you were captain of the drill team."

"I should have guessed, with those legs of hers," Ryan added, his gaze lingering appreciatively over her legs while he draped a casual arm around her waist.

Amanda felt the warm beginnings of a blush.

"Bet you didn't guess she spearheaded the sophomore class's wildest accomplishment..." Suzy paused for dramatic effect. "Painting the town water tower pink and purple."

Ryan glanced at Amanda, his face subtly ironic. "I didn't peg you for the criminal type."

She purposely arched her brows, wanting to tell him that she knew he still suspected she was. He hadn't let the issue of his bank records rest. Instead, she smiled at her friend. "Suzy had better be careful or I'll start spilling her secrets."

"I've already bragged about mine. But nobody's pulled off your feats." Suzy turned enthusiastically from Amanda back to Ryan. "The school planned a field trip to the Museum of Natural Science in San Francisco. Amanda called the supervisor of buses, pretended to be the teacher in charge and told him the destination had been changed to Chinatown. Of course, by the time the buses stopped and the doors had been opened, the chaperons had no way of corralling a hundred and forty teenagers high on a taste of freedom. The Stanton High senior class didn't leave a stone unturned in the city. It was great!"

Ryan's eyes were amused, yet challenging. "Quite an accomplishment, Amanda. I'm surprised you didn't find a line of work that could make use of your...unique... talents."

"I considered bank larceny, but it involves such a tiresome group of cohorts."

Ryan's grin faded. "I know that's been my experience."

Suzy and John looked on, puzzled by their exchange. John rose, holding out a hand to Suzy. "It's late. I'll see you at the property tomorrow morning at ten, Ryan."

Amanda felt a sense of relief. If the business deal could be finalized soon, perhaps they wouldn't have to continue on as Lucy, Ricky, Fred and Ethel.

"This has been a wonderful evening," Suzy said with a

satisfied sigh as they walked toward the entry. "I can't tell you how valuable it is to see you both with Brianna."

Amanda realized she'd forgotten Little Ricky. Or in their case, Brianna. This masquerade was getting to be tiresome. But as the door closed behind them, Amanda was hit with another unsettling truth. Once the masquerade ended, her time with Ryan would also end.

Chapter Fourteen

"A few dinners for appearance's sake," Amanda said glumly into the post-breakfast silence, as she downed her fifth cup of coffee, obviously trying to wake up with a megadose of caffeine. "It was going to be so easy."

"You're leaving out the 'you said,' aren't you?"

"If I wanted to pick a fight, I'd say yes. But the truth is, I wanted to pretend to be something I'm not, so I don't have any room to talk. I just didn't realize that Suzy and John would want to be our Siamese twins."

"I think that would be quadruplets."

"Don't quibble. You know I'm still functioning in morning mode. The truth is if we don't cooperate, you'll lose your investor and my cover will be blown."

"Is that still so important?"

Amanda peered over the rim of her mug. "You said it could make the difference in the success of your business deal."

"And your cover?"

"I'm beginning to think I should have stuck to painting water towers and rerouting buses."

Ryan studied her face. "The problem with deception is that it builds on itself."

Amanda slowly lowered her mug of coffee. "Does that mean you're ready to give up the game?"

Ryan lifted his brows. Over the last several weeks she'd

had to drag nearly all of her clothes from her now ne-
glected-looking apartment, along with everything else she
needed for daily living. He knew how difficult the situation
had become. "You're the one making most of the sacri-
fices. What do you want?"

"More coffee," she muttered.

Ryan didn't intend to give her another easy out like this
one. He'd struggled again the previous night with his con-
science while cramping his too-tall body into the nursery
daybed. He glanced at her, knowing she was scarcely
awake. It was hardly fair to issue an offer she was unlikely
to remember.

Still, since she hadn't bolted and run, Ryan intended to
see if they might not find more comfortable sleeping arrangements. Even though their agreement would soon end,
there wasn't any reason they couldn't *enjoy* their time together.

Thinking just how much he would enjoy that time, he
let his gaze linger on Amanda's still sleep-flushed cheeks.
A light dusting of makeup couldn't disguise their freshness.

His lip curved in amusement as he saw that she had once
again forgotten to remove her fuzzy slippers. Although
dressed in a tailored, sleek jacket and slim skirt, her nylon-
clad feet were still encased in hot pink bunny slippers. He
wondered how she'd managed to arrive at her shop each
day in proper shoes when she'd lived alone.

He had come to be unofficially in charge of making sure
she remembered her shoes, purse and other essentials. One
morning she had tucked her shortie nightgown in her skirt,
thinking she'd donned a blouse. When he'd pointed out the
mismatched outfit, she had admitted with a yawn that she
really wasn't a morning person.

Although he considered her response the understatement
of all understatements, instead of being annoyed, he
thought her forgetfulness and early morning daze were surprisingly charming. Especially since she so openly ac-

knowledged both traits. He'd even begun checking to be sure she had her keys and trolley fare.

And he'd come to look forward to her bemusing, casual kisses as she left each day in her befuddled state. At first, he'd been concerned about her morning fog, but then realized she successfully operated on automatic pilot. Her assistant Karen assured him that Amanda had done so for years.

He remembered how his ex-wife had slept with night-blinders on her eyes, sleeping like the dead until nearly noon, and becoming furious if he dared awaken her before then. Of course, their time together had been mercifully brief—only the duration of her pregnancy. Danielle hadn't bumped comically into the furniture, tried to wash her hair with bubble bath, or brush her teeth with a tube of baby ointment.

And he didn't understand why he found all these oddball qualities so endearing. Or why he liked the way Amanda would smile sleepily or kiss him when he gently steered her out of harm's way.

It seemed he understood less and less, especially as the evidence against her piled up. With a frown, he remembered the stack of papers detailing imports and exports that Barry's men had provided. Papers that didn't paint a pretty picture of Thorne's Treasures.

Amanda interrupted his thoughts. "I'd better get to the shop. I've had enough coffee to be launched to Jupiter and I'm still in a fog." A tiny yawn punctuated her statement.

"Shoes, Amanda."

She glanced down at her slippers. "I thought I'd put them on."

He didn't hide his smile, knowing she was still too fuzzy to mind. "Upstairs. Might as well get your purse while you're up there."

"Good idea." She wagged her fingers at him as she navigated toward the stairs, nearly tripping over MacDougall as he wisely darted out of her path. "Did we stay up extra late last night?"

"Yup." Not that it mattered. She wasn't a morning person even after twelve hours of sleep; however, she wasn't usually this out of it after a decent amount of sleep. But last night, the Meriweathers had stayed particularly late. And then Amanda had gotten up with Brianna in the night, even though he slept only a few feet away.

Ryan heard a few bumps coming from the master bedroom and hoped Amanda's shins hadn't taken too much of a beating. Mrs. Buchanan was upstairs with a freshly bathed Brianna. Normally, Amanda rose in time to share breakfast and bath time with them, but knowing she'd had only a few hours' rest, he'd purposely let her sleep.

The bumping stopped, and he heard his daughter squeal with delight. He could imagine Amanda tickling the baby's tummy and blowing kisses.

Glancing up a few moments later, he saw her walking down the stairs, holding Brianna's stuffed bear instead of her own purse.

"You have everything you need in your purse?"

She nodded as she tried to stifle a yawn.

Ryan grinned. "Maybe so, but I'd take the leather one, anyway. Bears went out last year."

She stared dumbly at the stuffed animal. "Brianna probably can't figure out what to do with my purse, either."

As she retrieved her purse, Ryan found her raincoat and umbrella, knowing rain was expected. Also, knowing she would forget both.

Descending the front staircase this time, Amanda clutched her purse and headed toward him. "Thanks for the accessory tips."

"This year, real estate. Next year, I tackle the fashion world."

Her soft lips landed on his, feathering a breathy kiss.

He took time to enjoy, then held out her coat. She automatically stuck her arms in the sleeves. He belted the coat, then handed her the purse she had forgotten on the entry table along with the umbrella.

"Keys?"

She dug around inside the purse, held them up, then dropped them back inside.

"Trolley fare?"

She tried to locate her wallet, failed and meantime he dug some bills from his pocket and stuck them inside the purse.

"Don't take any candy from strangers," he cautioned, enjoying the soft, unguarded look she wore.

"I know. And play nice with the other kids," she murmured agreeably.

His smile broadened. "And if you manage to follow the crumbs home tonight, we'll take a cruise of the bay one night next week."

She nodded, clutching her purse and umbrella, leaning over to offer one more unguarded kiss. "Nice. You're nice, too, Ryan."

"We're both nice," he agreed, opening the door and making sure she turned the right direction once she reached the sidewalk.

She seldom remembered what happened in the mornings. It all seemed like a vague daze. Which allowed him to enjoy the time, knowing he didn't have to regret the silliness, the openness. To explain that despite either, he still couldn't allow this woman into his life.

A smile lingered on his lips as he thought of the cruise he was planning, knowing it would still be a surprise to Amanda. There were definite advantages to a woman who wasn't a morning person. His smile broadened. Definite advantages.

MacDougall, greeted, petted and appeased, happily chomped a chew toy in the corner of the room as Suzy gushed over Brianna, once again captivated by the beautiful child.

Sighing with regret, she reluctantly handed Brianna back to Amanda. "She is absolutely precious." Suzy glanced happily down at her own stomach. "I knew it was the right decision to move here."

Amanda stroked Brianna's plump leg, comforted by her tiny presence. It had now been close to a month that Suzy and John had been in town, and they'd spent nearly every evening together. This cat-and-mouse game of tension was about to send Amanda over the edge.

But Suzy was practically bouncing in her chair, not noticing that Amanda didn't reply. "I can't wait to tell you both my news."

Ryan and Amanda exchanged an uneasy glance.

Suzy was all secrecy and smiles, like a child who had peeked into every Christmas package. "John and I have a surprise for you." She paused for effect. "We know how hard you've both been working...and since we didn't give you a proper wedding present, we're giving you a trip to Carmel!"

"This isn't a good time," Amanda began. "I can't leave the baby and..."

"Amanda's right. It really isn't a good time," Ryan chimed in.

Suzy waved aside both protests. "It's only a weekend—*this* weekend, in fact. I took the liberty of calling Mrs. Buchanan and she's available to watch Brianna."

Ryan met Amanda's gaze. It was her call. A weekend in romantic Carmel. Watching her, he remembered it was one of her favorite places.

Amanda shifted her gaze away, directing her attention to Suzy. "We appreciate the generous gift, but it's really not necessary. Ryan and I weren't planning a trip just now."

Just the slightest bit of a pout showed on Suzy's face. "But you don't understand. We're going, too. Just the four of us. Now that we're settled, we want to take a trip with our best friends."

Ryan met Amanda's gaze. Apparently it was showtime.

THE DAYS BEFORE the weekend flew by. Amanda turned into a classic mother hen, fussing over Brianna constantly as though they were leaving for a month rather than a few days.

Even though Ryan assured her that the weekend would pass quickly, Amanda insisted on cramming in as much time as possible with the baby. One afternoon he came home to find that Amanda had packed a hamper, insisting that they have a picnic in the park. Ryan had never taken Brianna on a family outing before, and a picture of what he'd missed out on struck him as Amanda turned the time into a family moment.

It was a week of discovery. The day before they were to leave, Amanda dressed Brianna in a miniature sailor suit and the three of them dined in a family restaurant on the wharf where Brianna could watch the seals climbing on the pier in the fading sunlight. Brianna squealed with delight, both at the seals and the spaghetti sauce she smeared all over the high chair. Although Ryan would normally have closeted himself in his study, poring over reports, he had to admit he was glad that Amanda had insisted on the outing.

Her genuine concern about leaving the baby behind as they left for the weekend also touched him. Finally even Mrs. Buchanan told Amanda that the baby would be content under her care.

When Friday arrived, Amanda fretted endlessly until Ryan had to drag her away. "If you'll leave, we can call the baby every hour on the cellular."

"What if Mrs. Buchanan's sister gets worse? What if—"

"What if you get in the car. I doubt NASA had this much trouble launching the last satellite." Taking her weekend bag in hand, Ryan stashed it in the trunk, then propelled her to the passenger's side of the car.

"But—" Amanda began.

"I appreciate your concern. Brianna would, too, if she understood it, but she'll be fine." He gently but firmly closed her door, then leaned forward to speak through the window. "Let's just enjoy the weekend."

Amanda opened her mouth to protest.

But Ryan closed it with his words. "Think of it as a romantic getaway."

She didn't look convinced, but at least she wasn't jumping out of the car to check on the baby. "A romantic getaway? With Suzy and John as our chaperons?"

Ryan took a chance, knowing he was treading on prickly ground. "They won't be in our hotel room at night."

"Are you sure?"

"Relatively."

Ryan crossed to the other side of the car and got in as Amanda settled back, muttering as she fastened her seat belt, "I wonder how Lucy ever got pregnant with Fred and Ethel around all the time."

Bursting into laughter, Ryan nearly jerked the car into the wrong gear. Reluctantly, Amanda joined in with a smile. And Ryan hoped it meant this time they really would share the hotel room. In all aspects.

Nothing else had changed. She was still a woman he could never trust, and because of that he knew they could have no future together. But there was today...and the rest of their romantic getaway.

Chapter Fifteen

Amanda had to admit she liked the hotel Suzy had chosen, even if she could have choked her friend for forcing this weekend. Designed, decorated and furnished in a European style, it reeked of old-world charm, elegance and romance.

It seemed like a bizarre déjà vu experience to walk into the hotel with Ryan, an experience that became even more intense when they entered their room. The last time they had been together in a hotel, they had begun as strangers. Strangers who still planned to walk away from each other.

"Thinking how different this weekend is from the first?" Ryan accurately guessed, placing his hands on her stiff shoulders.

So very different. But Amanda couldn't tell him that. Not when he didn't reciprocate her feelings. "Only in that Suzy and John shouldn't be any more difficult to convince now than at the reunion. You might not have noticed, but Suzy tends to be rather self-involved, so if we don't make any major flubs she won't catch on."

Ryan's brows lifted in mock surprise. "Did you major in understatement during your college days?"

But Amanda found she couldn't smile. "No. Fraud was more to my liking."

A knowing, guarded expression she'd grown to recognize flashed across his face. "I don't suppose you're going to let me forget about that."

"I think we only forget what we choose to."

He didn't question her odd response. Instead, his hands moved to her vulnerable collarbones and to the spot between them where her pulse beat, its rhythm becoming uneven. "Nothing I can say...or do...to make it up to you?"

"I might consider opening negotiations," she replied, her voice becoming thready.

His fingers moved to the buttons on her blouse, and he slid the first one from its fastening. "Consider them opened."

Breathing was suddenly a painful thing as Ryan's lips swooped down against hers.

It was all Amanda could do not to melt into his arms, forget any consequences and let him sway her with his persuasive touch. Instead, she broke away. "I think we'd better check out Carmel."

"I'd rather check you out."

Amanda grabbed her straw hat and held it between them as a feeble defense. "Which is why I told John and Suzy we'd meet them for lunch."

LUNCH WITH SUZY AND JOHN was more than tolerable. With the tension that had begun in their room, it wasn't difficult to pretend for the Meriweathers. Instead, it was easy to sit closely side by side, for their hands to stray together often.

"Amanda, was Brianna all right?" Suzy asked as she lowered her glass of milk.

Amanda flushed, knowing Suzy was referring to her call home the minute they had entered the hotel.

Ryan answered for her. "Brianna was fine then. She was also fine when Amanda called from the car, and I imagine she'll be fine when Amanda calls her later when we get back to the room."

"I didn't say I was going to call again," Amanda protested.

"You plan to, don't you?" Ryan asked, mild amusement

flirting in his expression. There was always an edge of danger in his demeanor, with which the humor somehow blended well...even irresistibly.

Knowing she planned just that, Amanda refused to answer.

Suzy stepped in. "Ryan, you know all mothers are worrywarts. Amanda's just a normal mother who loves her child. You men are so callous about things."

Amanda's gaze collided with Ryan's.

John snorted. "Suzy's already planning my daddy-baby days. Ryan, you're lucky Amanda's not making *you* phone the baby."

Suzy huffed at her husband. "Ryan's lucky he found someone like Amanda who's a wonderful mother."

Ryan's expression didn't change, only a slight tic in his jaw revealed his strain. "You're right, Suzy."

She beamed at him, as always loving a man's approval. "And we have another surprise for you."

Amanda felt her stomach sink. She hoped the Meriweathers hadn't chartered the Concorde for a quick trip to Paris.

"This trip's for you two. But we knew you two workaholics wouldn't come unless we dragged you here. So tomorrow John and I are spending the day in Monterey—alone." One of her eyes dropped in a leisurely wink. "Leaving you two on your own tomorrow."

John picked up his wineglass and raised it in Ryan's direction. "You'll find that if you sift deep enough, Suz has *some* good ideas."

Ryan grinned at them both. "We don't want to cut the lunch short, but Amanda has another call to make."

John glanced over at Suzy. "We were planning an early afternoon ourselves."

Suzy met John's gaze, her own look both pouty and provocative. "Yeah. We love you guys, but we thought you'd never leave." As they blinked in surprise, Suzy turned back toward them for a moment. "And remember, we won't be seeing you tomorrow."

As they walked away, Ryan leaned over, his lips near Amanda's ear so only she could hear him. "Promises, promises."

A GENTLE BREEZE SWEPT the white sands of Carmel beach. Driftwood and moss-shrouded trees decorated the uncrowded, pristine shore. There was something calming about Carmel, radiating a very different mood than San Francisco. Carmel evoked images of long walks, drawn-out discussions over endless cups of rich coffee, a return to a time when appreciation was neither money- nor power-related.

Carmel made Ryan want to kick back, forget the pressures he'd left behind in the city and pretend he was part of the culture that lived to appreciate each moment. Moments such as watching a beautiful woman like Amanda. The breeze ruffled her hair, teased the folds of her cotton skirt and caused her provocative scent to drift upward.

They walked side by side, arms and shoulders grazing with every other step. Then Amanda stopped abruptly, pouncing on something she found in the sand.

Holding up a sand-covered bit of shell, she grinned. "Can you believe it?"

Ryan stroked his chin as he pretended to study her find. "A shell on a beach? That *is* something to write home about."

"Not just any shell. It's a sand dollar."

"Which if I remember correctly, you can buy at most shell shops."

She rolled her eyes. "Everybody knows those shells don't count. Only found shells count."

"This *will* be a blow to the retail shell market," he replied gravely as he enjoyed her mock indignation.

She wrinkled her nose, making her freckles dance. "You have no imagination."

His gaze drifted over her slowly. "Oh, you'd be surprised at the things I imagine."

A charming blush stained her cheeks. "There *are* other things that are important."

His fingers reached to touch one curl ruffled by the breeze. "Such as hair that feels like silk."

Releasing her hair, he skimmed his fingers over her lips. "Or a mouth that tastes like wild honey."

Seeing the flutter of her pulse at the hollow of her throat, Ryan felt pleasure drift slowly through his veins like warmed molasses. His fingers traced the outline of her lips again. "And to know that same mouth smiles more easily than it frowns."

Meeting the incredible green of those emerald eyes, he saw the confusion there, knowing he had caused it. He wished they had met at a different time, when his life wasn't so complicated, when he wasn't already trying to erase the results of a woman's deceit. But then there would be no Brianna. And Danielle, along with the legacy of mistrust she'd left him, had also given him his daughter. It wasn't a trade he regretted.

But as he stared at Amanda, he felt another kind of regret, knowing he could never offer her more than the moment.

Unable to resist, he stroked the velvety skin of her cheek. Then he picked up her hand, leading them once again down the length of the beach.

Amanda stopped to slip off her sandals. "Why don't we walk closer to the water?"

Since he'd shed his shoes on the dock, Ryan readily agreed. Together they watched the waves tumble toward them, burying their toes in the fine-grained sand.

Amanda wiggled her feet in the water. "Oh, I wish we'd planned to swim. I want to get wet all over, not just my toes." Because of the clouds scuttling in the sky, they had expected a storm and hadn't brought suits.

Ryan smiled at her indulgently. "It'll probably be clear tomorrow."

Amanda slanted an arch glance at him. "I didn't know meteorology was one of your talents."

"It doesn't take an expert to find the weather channel on TV."

"And I was beginning to think you were the man of a million careers."

Ryan pulled a comical face. "At least it would keep you from being bored."

"You might be a lot of things, Ryan West, but boring isn't one of them."

Her fresh, saucy grin flashed, and he wanted to reach out and capture that sense of fun. To keep some of it for his own once she was gone. "That wouldn't be a compliment, would it, Miss Thorne?"

"That's Mrs. West to you, boyo," she replied impudently, splashing a small bit of water on his jeans.

"Be warned, I splash back. My sainted nanny tried to break me of the habit, told me little gentlemen didn't splash ladies, even if they splashed first, but it was a hopeless cause. I still splash back."

She tucked the corner of her lip into a daring smile, then splashed him again. "*My* mother always said I was a slow learner."

Instead of splashing more water, he pulled her close, dampening her clothes with the water she'd splashed on him. "We reserve special punishment for those who flaunt the rules."

Her giggle bounced around them. "Mother never told me about that."

"Didn't she warn you about big bad men like me?" he asked in an overly intimidating voice, shading the inflection with laughter.

"She said most of you were mush underneath," Amanda replied, batting her eyes in an exaggerated motion.

"Is that all she said?"

Amanda curled her fingers over the longish hair that grew over his neck. "No, she said to run away as fast as I could."

He bent to nip her ear. "You're not moving."

"I seem to be paralyzed." A deep, throaty laugh punctuated the words. "Think I can find a big, strong man to rescue me?"

Placing a hand beneath her legs, he scooped her up and into his arms. "Sure there aren't any railroad tracks close by? After the villain straps you to the tracks, I could untie you just before the express train is due."

Amanda's eyes softened. "You don't have to try that hard to be my hero."

Silence pulsed between them as the words faded and only their gazes spoke. Ryan lowered his lips to hers, tasting the wild honey he hungered for, then a deeper, darker flavor, one that pulled at him, drew him like no other.

Caught in the embrace, Ryan didn't recognize the rain falling around them until the water sluiced over their faces, drenching their skin and clothes. Still Ryan didn't release Amanda, wanting to hang on to this moment, to stamp it in his memory.

When he finally pulled away, his throat thickened at the expression on Amanda's face. Sober, unblinking, despite the rivulets of rain that slid from her forehead down her cheeks, it was clear she was affected as well.

"It's raining," she commented numbly.

Ryan carried her up the beach, drawing her beneath the shelter of one arm as they moved toward the dock. "You said you wanted to get wet all over," he finally replied.

"So I did."

Reaching the dock, he lowered her feet to the planked floor, seeing that her thin cotton top was now plastered to her skin. "I like the wet look."

Suddenly she reached up to touch her hair, obviously embarrassed. "I must look like I'm wearing a fright wig. This wild hair is bad enough when it's dry—"

Enchanted, Ryan reached out to touch the tousled curls. "You look...fine."

He had lied. She didn't look fine. She looked like an untamed savage beauty, radiant in her element.

The cool rain made her ivory cheeks resemble finely chiseled marble, and her eyes shone like rare jewels. Unable to resist, he drew one hand over her face, then dropped it to his side at the rush of emotions crowding him.

Her eyes fastened on him, questioning, beckoning.

Ryan remembered how convincingly Danielle had portrayed an honest, loving woman, too. How she'd made him abandon a lifetime of caution, much to his eternal regret. Was Amanda an actress of equal talent? Torn by the possibility, he retreated to the practical. "You're probably freezing. We'd better get back to the hotel."

Nodding her agreement, Amanda walked with him down the dock and onto the road, keeping beneath the canopies of the giant trees lining the street.

Rain dripped mournfully from the moss clinging to the tree bark, and Ryan sighed, knowing the sad sight matched his mood perfectly.

These times with Amanda were only making things worse, reminding him that he'd known the bitter truth about women since his own mother's desertion. Though he still didn't know the whole truth about Amanda, he couldn't let down his guard. Yet he drew her a bit closer, lifting the hair from her forehead, then dropping a gentle kiss on her lips before walking hand in hand down the road.

ARRIVING BACK at the hotel, they were met by the anxious bell captain. "Mr. and Mrs. West, I'm so glad you're back! We've been searching all over for you. There's an urgent message for you at the front desk."

Ryan broke into a run. Amanda wasn't far behind.

The clerk handed him the message and turned the telephone toward him so that Ryan could dial the number.

Amanda clenched her hands together, releasing them

only to absently accept a towel from the bell captain. Watching Ryan's grim face, she felt her heart lodge in her throat. Covering her mouth with one hand and biting on upraised knuckles, she tried to stifle the thought that crept through her mind. What if something had happened to Brianna?

When Ryan hung up the phone, she clutched his arm.

"Brianna's fine."

Amanda felt a rush of relief sweep over her as she tried to concentrate on the rest of Ryan's words.

"It's Mrs. Buchanan."

Startled, Amanda's eyes widened. "Is she…"

"It's her sister. She took a sudden turn for the worse, and she's being prepped for emergency surgery." His eyes met Amanda's. "Apparently, it doesn't look good. Mrs. Buchanan wants us to come home right away."

Amanda was already heading toward the elevator, flinging the words back over her shoulder. "Of course."

Moving rapidly, they were out of the hotel less than half an hour after talking to Mrs. Buchanan, taking time only to leave a message for the Meriweathers. Arriving home in record time, they were greeted by a frantic Mrs. Buchanan and a worried-looking MacDougall who circled them repeatedly.

Amanda distractedly patted his head. "It's okay, Mackie."

Mrs. Buchanan continued to look distressed as Ryan helped her into her coat. "I feel terrible leaving you in the lurch like this, ruining your holiday and all, but she's my only sister and—"

"Don't worry about us, Mrs. Buchanan," Ryan interrupted her gently. "Just take care of your sister. She needs you the most right now."

"I've taken care of babies and little ones all my life. Never once did I desert my job, but now—"

"You're not deserting," Amanda reminded her. "You

called in the reinforcements and we're here now. Would you like one of us to drive you to the hospital?''

Mrs. Buchanan shook her head. "No, I'll be needing my car, I'm sure. You're good people to be so understanding. I won't take off a minute longer than is necessary."

"I'm sure you won't," Ryan replied.

"Be careful driving," Amanda cautioned as the woman scurried toward her car.

Mrs. Buchanan bobbed her head as she scooted inside the car, turning on the key before her door closed, then reversing quickly into the street.

"It's amazing how fast everything changes," Amanda commented. "One minute we're on vacation, and the next everything's upside down."

Ryan watched the car disappear before turning back inside. "Things won't change that much. Mrs. Buchanan's a good sitter, and Brianna likes her, but I'm sure the agency I got her from can find a temporary replacement without any trouble."

BUT THEY COULDN'T. And neither could any of the other agencies Ryan called. Amanda watched him spend a frustrating morning on the phone, only to discover that Mrs. Buchanan had been a national treasure, and the agencies didn't have any spares. Offers were made to place him on waiting lists. Lists that couldn't promise a replacement for months.

Ryan pushed his fingers through tousled hair as they left the kitchen. "I can't believe it. In this entire city there's not one qualified person available to take care of a baby."

Amanda cleared her throat. "Maybe *one*."

Ryan stared at her through fatigue reddened eyes. "And who might that be?"

"Me."

"You?"

She straightened up defensively. "You needn't sound so surprised. It's not as though I'm a total incompetent."

"I'm not implying that you are. But you have a business to run, remember?"

"True," she replied as her tone gathered enthusiasm. "But I thought this out last night…in case you couldn't find someone. Karen already mentioned wanting to work more hours so she can save some extra money. Trish has always been willing to work extra hours when needed. And I can hire one more part-time clerk."

"You love your work, but you're willing to forget about it to take care of a baby?"

"It's not just 'a baby,'" Amanda reminded him gently. "It's Brianna. And I'll still have plenty of input in my business. We have a computer, modem, fax and phone in the study. I won't exactly be out of touch."

Ryan rubbed the morning stubble on his chin, looking torn and frustrated as he stood barefoot, wearing only jeans and a shirt he hadn't found time to button. "We'll take turns watching her. You'll have to get to your shop on a regular basis or we find another way," he warned. "And we'll keep looking for a replacement. I won't ask you to compromise your business." He walked to the bottom of the stairs and paused. "I'll take care of Brianna today. You need to check on your shop—especially if you plan to run it from the house."

Amanda stared at him, wondering what he was leaving unsaid, guessing whatever it was had prompted his stern manner. Also, guessing he felt the situation was slipping out of his hands.

But even as she tried to analyze his reaction, doubt assailed her. So much of him remained a mystery. Amanda knew he shared her growing desire, but he'd shared little else about himself. While he'd met her family, she hadn't heard a word about his. In fact, his past remained a closed book.

Ryan headed up the stairs and Amanda studied his retreating form, her doubts multiplying—what did she *really* know about this man?

Chapter Sixteen

"Come on sweetie, you can say it. Daddy."

Brianna reached for one of Amanda's earrings and tugged.

"You're all girl, aren't you?" Amanda sighed as she removed the curious little fingers. "But you're still too young for jewelry. And makeup is completely out of the question."

Brianna stretched out her hands toward Amanda's necklace, and Amanda deftly avoided the maneuver, directing the child's attention to the tiny chunks of fruit in her bowl.

"Since you seem to have a newfound liking for jewelry, tomorrow I'm not wearing any," she informed her little charge. "And we're going to work on saying daddy. You can do it. Daddy."

"Dud," Brianna replied.

"Don't let him hear you say that. I don't think your father would like being called a dud. But you're getting there. Another few days and you'll have it down pat."

Brianna happily raised up her hands, palms outward.

"You think I meant patty cake, huh? I didn't, but that's okay." Amanda glanced at the nearly full bowl. "I think you're tired of peaches. I know I would be. I think Mrs. Buchanan must have bought fifty jars of the same kind of fruit. Must have been on sale. But we'll outfox her. Tomorrow we'll go shopping in Chinatown. We'll find fruits Mrs. Buchanan doesn't even know exist.''

Holding up her own hands, Amanda took them through a routine of patty cake. Finished, she had to wipe four sticky hands. Glancing at the clock, she realized it was time for Brianna's nap. She'd rearranged the child's schedule so that Brianna could have a little more time with Ryan when he came home each evening.

Brianna had adapted well to the change in caregivers. Amanda wasn't sure if the child missed Mrs. Buchanan, but her contented, sunny disposition hadn't wavered. It had taken Amanda a few days to get everything under control, since it was a far larger task taking care of a baby full time rather than for a few hours. That, along with coordinating the running of the shop from home, had been a challenge. As Amanda looked into Brianna's expressive blue eyes, she knew she'd made the right choice.

The doorbell rang suddenly, and Amanda smiled at Brianna, scooping her up and carrying her into the entry hall where she placed her in her walker. With Mackie close behind her, Amanda opened the door.

A tall, stunningly beautiful woman stood on the doorstep. Perfectly coifed and made up, she looked as though she'd come directly from a photo shoot.

Amanda ran a self-conscious hand over her own less-than-immaculate T-shirt and jeans, feeling suddenly inadequate. ''Can I help you?''

Despite the woman's beauty, her expression was aloof. ''Is Ryan in?''

Amanda gestured toward the hallway, empty except for Brianna and Mackie who stood defensively in front of the baby's walker. ''I'm sorry, no.''

The woman barely spared the baby a glance, before sweeping her cool eyes over Amanda. ''In some respects, I must say that Ryan's taste in nannies is improving.'' Her glacial expression didn't waver as Brianna gurgled at the dog, waving plump little arms.

Amanda started to correct her, but the woman cut off her words.

"Tell Ryan that his time is running out." Her gaze flickered momentarily toward the hallway. "I may be forced to repossess my security."

Amanda's eyes flew toward Brianna as she felt an unwelcome chill. Then she met the woman's gaze. "Can I tell Ryan who the message is from?"

"Oh, he'll know." The woman turned to leave.

"But—"

She angled her face back for a moment. "Just tell him."

Amanda considered calling Ryan, then decided she didn't want to disturb him with the enigmatic message. With a stab she realized that the woman could be someone he was interested in. Certainly she and Ryan had not questioned each other's entanglements. Still...for a moment Amanda had been sure the woman had been referring to Brianna.

Settling into the rocking chair, Amanda absently stroked the baby's satiny cheek, thinking once again of the woman who had abandoned her. She wondered if Ryan still loved Danielle. Had she been as beautiful as the woman who had appeared at the house? Although he'd spoken only briefly about his ex-wife in a brusque tone when he explained why she wasn't part of Brianna's life, Ryan could be covering up how he felt about Danielle. After all, she was the mother of his child.

Glancing down at Brianna, Amanda saw that she'd drifted off to sleep, lulled by the rocking motion. Her long lashes feathered over porcelain cheeks, her lips relaxed, and a tiny, gentle sigh emerged. Knowing she should put Brianna in the crib, Amanda continued rocking her instead, reveling in the freedom to care for the baby as she pleased. No Mrs. Buchanan or Ryan to take over, she could hold the soft, warm body as long as she wanted, inhaling her fresh baby smell, storing up the memories.

RYAN ENTERED THE HOUSE, loosening his tie. Aware suddenly that soft music drifted from the stereo in the living room, he listened for a moment. The house was so different these days. Once a quiet shell, it now radiated with warmth.

Putting his briefcase on the hall table, he reached for the mail and then paused. He lifted his head, sniffing the air. If he didn't know better, he would think he was smelling fresh bread. He decided it must be his imagination. Accustomed to grabbing something while he was out, or making a sandwich when he came home, he didn't expect to walk in to mouth-watering aromas.

Shaking his head, Ryan glanced again at the mail. But in a moment, he lifted his head again. It was more than bread. The pungent aroma of sautéed garlic and onions wafted toward him. Curious, he dropped the mail and headed for the kitchen. Pushing open the door, he was surprised to see Amanda, a huge apron engulfing her slim frame, as she stirred and then tasted the contents of the sauté pan.

His glance roved around the kitchen. No longer immaculately sterile, fresh flowers filled a vase on the table, loaves of bread rested on a cooling rack and the cutting board was littered with chopped vegetables. The all-white kitchen was splashed with color, including the fire-haired woman who busily checked the contents of the other pots on the stove.

Letting the door swing closed behind him, Ryan walked inside. Amanda turned at the noise and her smile flashed. "Glad you're home early. I wasn't sure when you'd be here, but I took a chance." She tapped a spoon against the side of one pot.

"Why have you gone to all this trouble? Is someone coming to dinner?"

"Just us. Hungry?"

"Yes, but—"

"Good. If you'll get Brianna up from her nap, we can eat soon."

His brow furrowed. "I thought her nap was earlier."

"It used to be," Amanda replied cheerfully. "But then by the time you got home she was sleepy and ready for bed. Now she can stay up with you for a while before bedtime."

Ryan had noticed that Brianna had been more alert the past few evenings, but he hadn't realized why. "Sounds like a good idea. But you don't have to cook dinner."

Amanda pushed the hair on her forehead back. "I think we've been through this routine before. I do what I want to. And I wanted to cook dinner."

"I could have made a sandwich," Ryan protested.

Amanda blew a puff of air upward at her unruly hair. "It's a novel but old tradition with my family. We put dishes on the table, cook food, sit down together and eat. We're hoping it'll catch on everywhere, but I don't think we'll be able to patent the process."

Ryan couldn't repress a quick grin. She was something, all right. A copper-topped original. "I don't know. Looks to me like you can do most anything you put your mind to."

"Right now I'm putting my mind to concocting the perfect sauce."

He was impressed. "Don't tell me you're creating your own recipe?"

"Of course. Cookbook recipes don't count."

"Like shells. I should have known." Ryan reached out at the same time to touch the bit of sauce decorating her cheek. Putting his finger to his lips, he tasted it. "Not bad. Needs salt, though."

She batted him with the clean wooden spoon she'd just taken from the drawer. "Philistine."

"And proud of it."

"So what do you know about sauce?"

"That it tastes better when it's on your cheek than it will on a plate."

He expected indignation. Instead, she leaned forward, rewarding him with a slow, toe-shaking kiss that threatened to curl his gut.

Clearing his throat when she finally released the kiss, he didn't move his gaze from her face. "I'll insult the rest of the dinner if it'll get me more of the same."

"You'll turn my head." Her smile flashed, like salsa and sunshine. "And I might consider it, but my perfectly seasoned and salted sauce would suffer."

Sparring with Amanda was like dueling with a dull blade while his opponent held the finest honed steel. "Maybe I'd better check on Brianna."

Amusement danced in her eyes. "Maybe you'd better."

Ryan went out through the side door that led to the dining room. He saw that the table had been set, including still unlit tapers atop shining crystal holders. It was neither fancy, nor casual. Instead, it looked inviting. The high chair was angled at the corner of the table between the two places set with china.

Ryan glanced at the high chair thoughtfully. This wasn't a romantic dinner Amanda had set up, but rather a family one. With a start he realized that he and Brianna had never shared a family dinner. He'd fed her oatmeal in the kitchen; on a few rare occasions he had come home during the day and taken over lunch duty. But they had never sat down together at their own dining room table.

Turning to glance at the living room, he saw the fireplace burning steadily. The smell of wood smoke drifted in, combining with the odors of freshly baked bread and the cooking dinner. Amanda had brought more than herself to the house. She had brought light and laughter.

Hearing lids rattle on one pot after another, he pulled himself from his musings and took the stairs two at a time. Entering the nursery quietly, he was pleased to see that Brianna was awake, playing with her floppy dog as she sat in the crib.

Spotting him, her face creased into a giant smile. Ryan's answering smile was equally open. With Brianna there was no reserve, no holding back. Anyone seeing him now would never label him lean and dangerous. For his daughter, Ryan shed his tough shield.

Holding out his arms, Ryan picked up her eagerly squirming body, then kissed her soft cheek. "How's Daddy's girl?"

Her little arms looped around his neck as she laid her face against his shoulder. Ryan felt the day's tensions ease. There were no complications with Brianna. He carried her over to tall, wide windows, pointing out the same things he always did: a favorite tree, flowering shrubs over a latticed fence, an elaborate stained glass window. Brianna responded as she always did, smiling at each one. Then they stood for a while, watching the traffic stream down the street, the pedestrians rushing home.

Knowing they couldn't stand there all night, Ryan ruffled her hair. "Amanda's made dinner, and we're going to eat together. She claims other people do it all the time, so I guess we'll give it a try. What do you think?"

"Man," Brianna responded.

Ryan blinked and stared down at his daughter. "Are you trying to say Amanda?"

"Man," she repeated.

Ryan let out a low whistle. He'd always thought a child this young didn't particularly care about the parade of people in her life other than parents. He hadn't noticed Brianna trying to say Mrs. Buchanan's name. Nor, now that he thought of it, did she seem to miss her long-time nanny. Her attention had shifted quickly and surely to Amanda. Warning bells clanged. He didn't want her to get too attached. After all, Amanda was only a temporary fixture in their lives.

"Man," Brianna insisted.

"You want to go see her? She's probably about ready for us. Let's check your diaper, then we'll head downstairs."

After a quick diaper change, they joined Amanda in the

dining room just as she was arranging bowls on the table. MacDougall darted between her feet, obviously hoping for a treat.

Amanda greeted Brianna with a smile and a tickle to her dimple-dented chin. "Hey, punkin. Bet you're glad Daddy's home."

"Daddy," Brianna replied, saying the word correctly for the first time.

Ryan stared at his daughter in astonishment, then growing pleasure.

Amanda clapped her hands. "I knew you could do it, sweetie."

Ryan turned his eyes toward Amanda. "You taught her to say Daddy?"

She nodded. "Seemed like the perfect choice for her first word."

Something deep inside him warmed even as he fought the feeling.

Amanda stroked the baby's hair as she leaned over to whisper in her ear. "Thanks for not calling him a dud." Her voice rose as she glanced up at Ryan. "If you want to put her in the high chair, I have her plate ready and I'll grab a bib."

Ryan settled his daughter in the chair, and in moments Amanda returned. She handed Ryan the bib before putting the compartmentalized plastic dish on the tray.

Ryan stared at the food in Brianna's dish. Mrs. Buchanan always served cereal. This didn't even vaguely resemble cereal. Although he'd given the reins of Brianna's care to Amanda, he wondered suddenly if she knew enough about babies. "Are you sure she can eat this?"

Amanda nodded. "I cooked Brianna's noodles longer so they're softer. The chicken and vegetables are minced, and the sauce doesn't have any salt or spices."

A light dawned. "The sauce I tasted?"

"Bingo."

No wonder it had tasted so bland. "And that's as good for her as cereal?"

Amanda passed Ryan the linguini. "The books I read said it's better. And that it's time to introduce more foods. Of course, I checked with her pediatrician first."

Ryan accepted the pasta and absently scooped some on his plate. She had been thorough. Not sure why he was worrying, he accepted another bowl and ladled some of the colorful sauce on his linguini, recognizing tomatoes, zucchini, golden and red peppers, asparagus and several types of mushrooms. Taking a tentative bite, he tasted wine, shallots and spices, realizing the sauce was delicious.

He glanced up to tell Amanda, and saw that she was busy feeding Brianna. "We could take turns doing that."

She shrugged. "Sure. I thought I'd get her started."

"You need to eat, too."

Amanda handed him the spoon. "I *am* anxious to try my perfectly seasoned sauce."

He took the spoon, feeling a smile tugging at his lips. "I don't know, maybe I should give Brianna's sauce another try."

Amanda speared a succulent piece of asparagus. "You could be right. The other might be too hot for you to handle." Her challenging gaze teased him as she popped the asparagus in her mouth.

Ryan spoke to Brianna, though he directed his words to Amanda as he dipped the spoon into the noodle mixture. "We can handle anything Amanda dishes out, right Bri?"

"Maybe you'd better check what's on the menu first."

Ryan nearly dropped the spoonful of noodles. Recovering, he met Amanda's eyes, hoping she planned to be dessert on the menu she mentioned.

Amanda laughed, a light carefree sound. Brianna caught the contagious laughter, her baby squeals reverberating between them.

Looking around the table, Ryan realized that Amanda had created a real family dinner. Music drifted in from the living room, scented candles perfumed the air, and the tasty, colorful food begged to be eaten. But it was the laughter that brought them all together.

Lifting his glass to hers, he saluted her silently, wishing he could believe that this was the real Amanda.

LATER, THE DISHES STACKED in the dishwasher and Brianna settled in for the night, Amanda approached Ryan as he worked in his study. "Hi."

He glanced up, his brow furrowed in concentration. "Yes?"

Clearly he was in his business mode, but Amanda had stalled as long as she could. "Ryan, a woman came by today."

His eyes had already returned to the report on his desk. "And?"

"She said she had a message for you."

That caught his attention. "A message?"

Amanda cleared her throat. "Yes. She...she said to tell you that your time was running out."

In that instant Amanda realized she'd never seen just how forbidding Ryan could be. "Did she say anything else?"

"Well, yes. She said that she might have to...repossess her security."

The veins in Ryan's neck throbbed with repressed anger as he listened.

"And I know this doesn't make sense, but I had the strangest feeling that she was referring to Brianna."

"When was she here?"

"When? I'm not sure, exactly. Before Brianna's nap, I think."

"Why didn't you call me immediately?" Ryan demanded in a tightly controlled voice.

"I didn't want to interrupt you at work." Amanda smoothed the skirt of the dress she had changed into before Ryan had come home. "I also thought she might be a...woman friend. Someone you wouldn't want to discuss at the office."

Ryan took a deep breath, obviously hanging on to his temper. "If she ever comes back, I want to know immediately." He reached for the phone. "I'm going to put a security detail on the house. I don't want you bothered again."

Even though she had a sudden, sinking feeling that she already knew, Amanda had to ask. "Who is she?"

"My ex-wife, Danielle. And you were right. She was referring to Brianna."

"But she barely glanced at Brianna. She didn't act like a mother who..." Amanda's hands flew to her mouth in horror. "What about her talk of repossessing?"

"Nothing you have to worry about."

"And you're sure—"

"If there's one thing I'm sure about, it's that Danielle doesn't *want* Brianna." He gestured toward the telephone, indicating the call he wanted to make. "Why don't you have a cup of tea? I'll be down shortly."

Ryan waited until he was sure Amanda had headed downstairs, then he quickly punched in Barry's number. Danielle was deadly serious. And it was up to him to make sure she didn't have the chance to steal his child.

Chapter Seventeen

Mrs. Buchanan's sister had come through her surgery fairly well, but now faced long-term recovery and needed Mrs. Buchanan's help. Although the nanny was torn by her sense of responsibility to Brianna, she felt compelled to nurse her sister.

Amanda insisted on continuing to care for the baby, and Ryan could tell from the pile of faxes on the desk that she was still keeping active control over her shop. Knowing the terms of their original agreement, and unable to shake the suspicions his investigators had turned up about her, Ryan didn't feel right about accepting Amanda's help with Brianna. At the same time, he didn't want a stranger in the house—one who might allow Danielle access to Brianna.

Amanda was still overprotective, worrying over Brianna as though she were a breakable doll. Even now, Amanda had gone to check on her again, though the child had been asleep for more than three hours.

Hearing Amanda descend the stairs, he enjoyed the journey as her slim body traveled toward him. He could tell by her face that her mind wasn't on him, though. "I still think she feels warm," Amanda fretted.

Ryan withheld a sigh. After all, he'd had a head start on the parent business. And Amanda, for all of her attachment to Brianna, wasn't her parent. "She's probably cutting a tooth. It makes them a little feverish."

Amanda shook her head. "I don't think so. She was cranky all day, and that's not like her."

"Cutting teeth makes them cranky."

"Maybe... But I think I'll go take her temperature."

Ryan stopped her. "She's fine. Stop being such a worrywart."

Amanda rested uneasily, flipping through magazines, then tossing them aside. She also resisted his efforts at conversation. To all appearances, she was the picture of concern.

Ryan remembered how convincing Danielle had been when she wanted him to believe that, she too, was a sweet, caring person. While he hated the comparison, he couldn't shake the memory of how stupid he'd felt, allowing himself to be duped.

A cry startled them both. It had come from the intercom, a clear sound of distress. Both of them jumped from the couch, running up the stairs, with MacDougall at their heels barking madly.

Ryan reached the nursery first. Brianna was sobbing as he reached down to pick her up, cradling her in his arms. Shock and a deep-seated fear gripped him. She was burning up!

Amanda laid the top of her hand against Brianna's cheek. "I'm worried, Ryan."

Seeing that he'd misjudged both his daughter's condition and Amanda's observations, he silently cursed himself. "Can you grab her blankets and bag?"

Amanda rushed to gather them. "Are we taking her to the hospital?"

"Right. We can call her pediatrician on the way." He silently thanked the fates for cellular phones as he strode down the stairs.

Amanda ran to keep up with him. "Shouldn't we take her temperature? So we can tell the doctor what it is?"

Ryan continued out the door. "He'll have a thermometer."

Not wanting to argue, Amanda closed the door behind them, after ordering MacDougall to stay inside. Reaching the car, she saw the indecision on Ryan's face as he handed her the baby to buckle into the car seat, obviously not wanting to release his daughter. But he chose to drive the car himself, and she suspected it was because he would speed to the hospital in record time.

He floored the car in reverse, getting them quickly into the traffic that never completely emptied the streets. Picking up the cell phone, he pushed the preset automatic dialing button programmed for the pediatrician. Although he reached an answering service, his commanding manner had him connected to the doctor in moments. He explained the situation, then clicked off the phone.

His glance cut toward Amanda, then at the baby in her arms. "He'll meet us at the hospital."

Amanda released a deep breath she hadn't realized she was holding. Brianna's sobs had slowed down to intermittent wails, punctuated by hiccupping sighs. Tucking her blanket closer, Amanda stroked the baby's damp curls. Not knowing how sick she was, Amanda was struck by guilt. If she were more experienced, she might have seen this coming, kept her from getting so sick. What had she been thinking, volunteering to take care of a baby when she didn't have the proper training?

Ryan sped through the streets, the long, low-slung car hanging curves, the powerful motor thrusting them through the dark city. Screeching into the parking lot, Ryan stopped the car sideways in the emergency entrance before leaping out, crossing in front of the car and ripping open the passenger door.

Amanda held Brianna up to him. "Take her in. I'll park the car." She paused, swallowing a knot of fear that was laced with the disheartening knowledge that she had no claim to the baby who'd come to mean so much to her. "You should be the one with her."

Nodding, he loped inside. The motor was still running,

and it didn't take long for her to park the car, then run inside the hospital.

Hearing Ryan's authoritative voice, she easily found them in one of the curtained partitions, where Brianna was stretched out on the examining table flanked by her father and a white-coated man she assumed was the pediatrician.

The doctor didn't appear intimidated by Ryan's forcefulness. "You can stay, Ryan, but keep out of my way."

Ryan muttered, and the doctor shot him a reproving look. "You want what's best for your daughter, don't you?"

Clenching his teeth, Ryan nodded.

Amanda slipped her hand in his, and he accepted the gesture automatically. "She'll be all right, Ryan. I just know it."

The doctor glanced up for a moment. "Listen to her, Ryan. She makes sense."

The doctor's examination seemed to take forever as he thoroughly checked over the little body. When the lab assistant took blood, Brianna renewed her sobs, clinging both to her father and Amanda.

The doctor glanced between Amanda and Ryan. "I'd like for you two to step into the waiting room. It's just outside this area. I know you want to be with her, but it will be easier for Brianna if you leave."

Ryan gripped Amanda's hand, then nodded reluctantly. He hated to leave, but wanted what was best for Brianna. Counting the dragging minutes, they sat together in the sterile waiting room.

"I should have listened to you." Ryan still held her hand, absently drawing circles over each finger, pausing on the one that held his ring. "If I had, she wouldn't have woken up screaming. She could have been treated by now."

"You don't know that," Amanda soothed. Her anxious eyes focused on him. "If I knew more about babies, maybe I'd have seen more signs, known what to do—"

"You told me. I've been parenting a lot longer, and I'm

the one who said not to worry. You saw the signs, recognized something was wrong, and I didn't listen."

"Just woman's intuition," Amanda explained.

Ryan's gaze met and held hers. "Don't ever lose that."

Hearing the doors whoosh open, they jumped up as the doctor strode toward them, lowering his stethoscope as he addressed Ryan. "Brianna has a severe ear infection. Her white count is elevated and the inflammation is extensive. She also shows signs of early dehydration. I don't see any sign of secondary infection. She's on an IV—"

"IV?" Amanda echoed in a horrified voice.

"I want to rehydrate her and run some antibiotics."

"Then she'll be all right?" Ryan asked.

"Yes. You were right to bring her in, though. The same symptoms can indicate something far more serious. I've written scripts for antibiotics and something for the pain when you go home. No aspirin, of course."

"You said she was dehydrated?" Amanda asked shakily.

"As she felt worse, her liquid consumption no doubt dropped. Coupled with such a high fever, it didn't take long to become dehydrated."

"She didn't seem to want her juice today. I didn't think too much of it," Amanda replied, guilt coating the words.

The doctor patted her shoulder. "The signs were probably very slight, her liquid consumption no doubt gradually tapering off over the last few days. Children are resilient, often more resilient than parents. As I said, now that we're bringing her fever down, it's not serious. I'd like to keep her in the hospital for the remainder of the night. The IV will jump start her in the right direction. But you'll be able to take her home in the morning."

"I want to stay with her," Ryan stated without a shred of questioning in his tone.

"No problem," the doctor agreed. "Most parents want to stay. There's a full-size bed in the room next to the crib. Don't make yourselves sicker than Brianna by worrying. She'll be fine."

The overhead speakers announced a page for him, and the doctor hurried away.

Ryan turned back to Amanda. "You'd better go home and get some sleep."

But she was shaking her head. "I couldn't sleep. I'd be too worried. I'd rather stay here, if you don't mind."

Something deep inside him splintered, then thawed. But he kept his voice emotionless, knowing he couldn't let himself become attached. Knowing what had happened the last time his guard had been down. "No, I don't mind."

Chapter Eighteen

Amanda offered coffee to Suzy, then glanced at Brianna, who sat in her walker contentedly gumming a cracker. Amanda could scarcely believe she'd been so sick only a week earlier. Apparently the doctor had been right. Brianna acted as though she'd never been ill.

Danielle had reappeared twice since her first visit, leaving cryptic messages, and both times Amanda had wanted to hide Brianna away, uncertain just how far the woman would go in her threats. Fortunately, and also sadly, Danielle had shown no interest in the baby. Ryan continued to assure her that Danielle had no intention of taking Brianna—something that was relatively easy to believe since the woman scarcely spared the baby a glance. Still, each visit made her uneasy. Suspecting that Danielle might be asking for more money, Amanda wondered if she was behind the importance of Ryan's deal.

"I'm so glad Brianna's all right," Suzy declared meaningfully as she accepted the coffee. "I still feel bad about not stopping by sooner, but my doctor said I shouldn't be near anyone who could be contagious."

Ryan couldn't quite keep his grin tucked away. "You sent enough flowers, toys and stuffed animals to fill the house. I don't think Brianna felt neglected."

"But I didn't want to neglect you or Amanda," Suzy continued, turning her huge eyes on Amanda.

"I don't think that's possible," Amanda told her friend gently.

"I guess I can be kind of overwhelming," Suzy admitted.

"Only to those who don't love you," Amanda responded loyally.

"Well, you're a peach," Suzy declared, reaching into her purse and pulling out a folded piece of paper. "I've double-checked my whole list of collectibles from your shop, and I've decided on everything except the grandfather clock."

"Just as well. It doesn't work. Has enough value to make it worth getting repaired, but finding someone qualified to work on that kind of clock can be a pain."

"Thank goodness you're honest," Suzy replied, not retrieving her list as she reached for a cookie, hopping up to offer it to Brianna. "It's a jungle out there with so many people selling fakes."

Frowning, Ryan wondered why he'd never heard of the Meriweathers' plan to buy merchandise from Amanda. What if after John's sizable investment, Amanda planned to fob off impressive-looking forgeries? He hated that the thought plagued him, but the last set of documents his investigators turned up had shown clear discrepancies. He feared that Amanda was playing fast and loose with her import-export license—something that could send her to prison.

Brow furrowed, Ryan reached over and picked up the list, tucking it out of sight as Suzy cooed over the baby. Perhaps he could check these items out, prevent anything that might happen. It was hard to believe that Amanda would cheat her friends, but then it was difficult to understand why she'd ever felt compelled to lead this double life. Amanda glanced up, sending him a smile. The paper weighed heavily in his pocket as he watched her, knowing his suspicions were still alive. And bothering him for more reasons than he wanted to admit.

"You're lucky to have an expert in the house, Ryan," Suzy said as she sat back at the table. "That way you can be sure everything you have is genuine."

Amanda's expression was thoughtful. "That's very comforting, isn't it Ryan?"

It took great effort, but he kept his face unreadable. "Very."

BARRY SAT ACROSS from the desk, using its edge to prop up his feet. Ryan wondered what had brought his friend into the executive offices. These days, the security division was in overdrive, keeping Barry constantly busy. And the rest of his time was spent with Karen.

"To what do I owe the honor?" Ryan asked, pouring them both coffee from the carafe his secretary always kept filled.

Barry hesitated.

Instantly alert, Ryan abandoned the coffee. "Problem?"

Tossing a folder into the middle of the desk, Barry sighed. "Depends on your point of view."

Ryan picked up the folder, flipping it open and quickly seeing that it was an update on Thorne's Treasures and the list he'd given to Barry. "Something I should know about?"

Barry ran his hands through rumpled hair. "How long are you going to keep this going?"

Slowly Ryan lowered the folder. "What?"

"You heard me." Barry rose and abandoned the chair. "Hell, the woman's living in your home, spending more time with Brianna than you are, caring about her every bit as much as you do."

"Your point?" Ryan asked tersely.

"When are you going to drop the investigation? Amanda's one step from being removed from your bank records. And neither the bank or my whole division could prove that she was the one who put her name there."

"I suppose you believe in computer imps and tooth fairies now?"

"I *do* believe mix-ups can happen. Why can't you let this rest? The list from the Meriweather woman checked out—everything's been authenticated."

Ryan passed a weary hand across his face. "I know I owe Amanda a lot—without Meriweather I'd still be scrabbling for investors. But I don't open my life to dishonest women." Then he gazed at his longtime friend, hating to voice his doubts about Karen, but knowing he had to. "Is Amanda still acting on her own?"

Barry met his gaze steadily, apparently not taking offense. "All of the papers are signed only by Amanda. But so many of them are still obscure. Isn't it time to put a stop to this?"

Ryan's fingers whitened as he clutched the folder. "Is there something in here that clears her completely?"

Barry exhaled, then met Ryan's eyes. "No. But we don't have anything conclusive, either."

"Then, keep digging."

"Why can't you just let it go, Ryan? Tell Amanda what you want from a relationship—and what you don't want. She's been good for you. It's obvious you're crazy about her. Why don't you try trusting her?"

Ryan sucked in an unexpected breath. No one but Barry would dare test his resolve, much less tell him to toss away that resolve. "And that worked real well last time, didn't it, Barry? I thought I was on to all the gold-digger tricks. Remember? I told Danielle I didn't want marriage, and she didn't argue. No, she was sweet, thoughtful, understanding. She said she agreed—that she wasn't looking for marriage, either. Then she purposely got pregnant."

"And if she hadn't, you wouldn't have Brianna."

"And if I hadn't believed Danielle, she wouldn't be holding me up for another fortune right now, threatening to take Brianna back!"

"Amanda isn't Danielle," Barry reminded him quietly.

"You have to take another chance and trust her." He met Ryan's eyes. "Or you'll lose her, my friend."

Ryan held Barry's gaze, then dropped his eyes to the folder as he remembered Danielle's cold message. "Then, bring me proof, Barry. 'Cause I'm fresh out of trust."

RYAN CLIMBED THE STAIRS, pausing at the doorway, watching as Amanda grappled with the garment bag hanging over the closet door. Her overflowing suitcase was propped haphazardly only a few feet away on a chair, looking precariously close to tumbling over. Beside it rested her weekend bag and makeup case.

Dropping the papers in his hand on the dresser, Ryan reached over Amanda's head, pulling the hook loose, then laying the garment bag on the bed. "I've told you to use the closet. There's no need for you to be living out of suitcases."

Amanda blew at the wayward curls tumbling over her forehead, then yanked at one of the hangers in the overcrowded bag, succeeding only in pulling out the hanger, minus the dress. "I told you. It's no—" she reached again for the dress, wrestling it from among the other clothes "—trouble."

"I can see that," he replied wryly. "I know there aren't any extra bedrooms, but the rooms are huge. Why don't you let me have another chest of drawers moved in here? Or one of those antique wardrobes from your store?"

She met his gaze, a trace of pain flashing in her eyes before she shuttered them. "There's not much point, is there? That's a lot of trouble for a temporary situation."

Guilt attacked him. "But I want you to be comfortable." He waved toward the small, overcrowded desk in the corner of the room. "You don't even have enough room to do your paperwork. We can get a bigger desk—"

Her voice, though quiet, was firm. "It's fine." She gestured toward the garment bag. "Did you need something? I'm a little busy."

Ryan remembered the papers he'd been bringing her. Turning, he retrieved them, handing her the stack of faxes. "I'm afraid this will only make you busier. Quite a few faxes came in this afternoon."

She pushed at her hair again. "Nothing seemed to go right today. Brianna had quite a time with her new tooth, the phone never stopped ringing, just one of those days." She glanced down at the faxes a bit wearily. "And one of those nights, it seems."

Ryan could see her fatigue. Caring for Brianna, running her business and trying to live like a gypsy without her own camp was taking its toll. Even though the cleaning woman now came in five days a week, the rest of the load was all falling on Amanda's shoulders. "We should look harder for someone to help with Brianna."

Amanda's head shot up sharply. "No! I mean, that's not necessary. She and I are doing just fine. She doesn't cut a tooth every day."

"But you're still taking the brunt of all this." He thought again of Danielle's threat, knowing he couldn't lose Meriweather's investment since it was crucial to the success of the deal. Still, Amanda had taken on more than her share. While her machinations had been the cause of their elaborate charade, he doubted she ever counted on the resulting upheaval in her life.

Amanda's voice quieted. "As you've pointed out, I'm the one who got you into this."

Ryan flinched, regretting his candid words. But he'd never expected her to take an active role in his child's care. "Look—"

The strident ringing of the doorbell interrupted his words. Issuing a muffled curse, he met Amanda's gaze. "I'll get rid of whoever that is and then we'll talk."

Slumping against the bed, Amanda closed her eyes in relief at the reprieve. She didn't want to talk about finding someone else to sit with Brianna. Knowing their days were numbered, she cherished each one. Whether the baby was teething or not.

True, it was difficult keeping up with everything, but her busy schedule could be handled if her emotions weren't in a constant state of turmoil. And, as Ryan continued to shut his mind to sharing any possible future, that turmoil only increased. Aware of his inability to trust, she knew even her faint seeds of hope were foolish. But despite that logic, she couldn't squelch them.

Voices were drifting up the stairwell, and it didn't take long to recognize Suzy's bubbly laugh. Amanda's face slumped into steepled hands. Why tonight of all times? Knowing her relentless friend, Amanda suspected it would do no good to hide out. Suzy would simply come looking for her.

A distracted look in the mirror had her finger combing her curls, then tucking the flyaway tail of her shirt into her jeans before dashing on some lipstick. Still feeling untidy, she walked downstairs, seeing that Ryan was making an incredible effort to disguise his irritation at the Meriweathers' unexpected appearance.

Glancing up, he turned to meet Amanda's gaze, conveying his annoyance with a glance. "Look who dropped in."

Forcing brightness into her tone, Amanda smiled. "What a nice surprise. Why don't we go into the living room and have some coffee? I picked up a new blend the other day—hazelnut chocolate. The best part is it doesn't have any calories—unless you add cream, which I plan to pour in by the tablespoon. And there's fresh biscotti. Some croissants, too, I think. Raspberry, maybe cream cheese, almost certainly at least one chocolate."

"Whew!" Suzy whistled under her breath. "You trying to steal my act? I'm the one who talks nonstop, remember?" She laughed, then looked between Amanda and Ryan. "Are we interrupting something?" She turned to John. "We're interrupting them."

"Don't be silly," Amanda replied. "Let me grab the

coffee and biscotti...or scones...oh, I said croissants. Well, I'll bring in something. If we get desperate, we've got tons of teething biscuits. Brianna really seems to like them." Knowing how feeble she sounded, Amanda fled to the kitchen. Although grateful for the respite from the talk she knew Ryan intended to continue, it was unnerving to be on display just then. Still, she took some comfort in the normality of preparing the coffee and arranging an inviting-looking tray.

Feeling back under control, she returned to the living room, if not with a flourish, at least with her calm restored.

"Ryan told us that the baby was teething all day," Suzy began sympathetically as she accepted the fragrant cup of coffee. Inhaling the rich aroma, she sighed in appreciation. "This does smell wonderful, but I want lots of that cream you promised." Spying the tray, she picked up a croissant, as well. "I wasn't even hungry until you brought this in, but I *am* eating for two now."

John chose biscotti, one edge of his mouth curving upward. "I don't have that excuse." He glanced at his domineering wife. "Or do I, Suzy?"

Mouth full, she made a muffled sound.

John reached for a napkin. "After all, from what you tell me, we're sharing this pregnancy."

Choking on her croissant, Suzy could only cough. Solicitously, John patted her back, unable to disguise his full-scale smile.

Ryan picked up the heavy coffee tray, intending to move it out of the way. Suzy and John's behavior eased the tension, and Ryan even managed a smile as the doorbell rang. "Excuse me. It seems we have more company."

John rose, waving him back. "You have your hands full. Let me get it."

Between Suzy's miffed gasps and their attempts not to laugh as they comforted her, no one heard the conversation at the door.

Amanda glanced up first, her mouth nearly falling open before she closed it in a tight line.

"Someone here to see you, Ryan," John announced.

Ryan looked toward the arched doorway and his face closed immediately. Abruptly abandoning the coffee tray, he walked toward the woman who stood next to John.

"Ryan, I haven't heard from you. If I didn't know better, I'd think you were avoiding me." Danielle's cool beauty was reflected in her voice. To a stranger, she sounded intriguing. Ryan, however, could hear the hidden malice.

John looked between them and moved away, rejoining Suzy on the couch.

Having recovered, Suzy gazed curiously at the unexpected visitor. "Hello. I don't believe we've met."

Danielle looked briefly amused. "Yes, Ryan. Aren't you going to introduce us?"

His lips tightened. "John and Suzy Meriweather, Danielle Parker." He didn't add West, since she'd dropped his name immediately after the divorce.

She awarded them a faint smile, something that wouldn't wrinkle her exquisite face. "How do you do?"

Suzy and John murmured responses, their usual enthusiasm slightly dampened by Danielle's cool manner. But she didn't waste any more time with them, instead dismissing them along with Amanda, after a brief inspection, as unworthy of her interest.

"Ryan, did you receive my last message?"

"I'd rather not to discuss that right now."

Danielle's frosty laugh was scarcely a ripple in the quiet room. "I'm sure you wouldn't." A cry from the nursery poured from the intercom. Startled only briefly, Danielle's smile widened. "Just remember the terms of the agreement. I'd hate for anything to happen to my...security."

Ryan's hands fisted at his sides as Amanda jumped up, glaring at Danielle before she headed toward the stairs to check on the baby.

"My, she does seem to be quite efficient," Danielle

commented. "So glad to know she's taking care of... things."

John and Suzy looked uneasily back and forth between Ryan and Danielle, obviously wondering about their odd exchange.

"I must be going," Danielle purred, turning toward the entryway. "It's so tiring tidying up loose ends." Her gaze drifted purposely over John and Suzy. "We'll talk again, Ryan. Soon."

Ryan walked to the front door, barely restraining himself from slamming the door behind her. A few moments later, Amanda poked her head around the top of the stairwell, worry crowding her expression. Ryan signaled Danielle's departure, and Amanda descended the stairs, a sleepy Brianna held firmly in her arms.

Suzy and John, uncharacteristically quiet, remained on the couch looking distinctly ill at ease. Ryan, torn between his desire to choke his ex-wife and his need to smooth the incident over, took a deep breath. "I must apologize for—"

"No need," John interrupted. "Looks like you've had more than your share of unwelcome company this evening. The coffee and dessert was super, but we need to be heading home."

"You're always welcome," Amanda broke in, fearing a breakdown in their charade. "Admittedly, today has been hectic. And we weren't expecting...other company, but please don't feel you have to go."

Suzy reached out to pat Brianna, whose tiny head was tucked protectively against Amanda's shoulder. "I think we're all tired. It has been quite a day. I shouldn't have insisted on running over here to show you the decorator's sketches." She scrunched her face into a comical mask. "I gave in and hired him. On my own, I'm rather helpless. I still want all the pieces I picked out from your shop. The decorator says they're all perfect—that he'll probably want more things from you. But this can wait till later in the week. Why don't we plan on lunch Wednesday? Say at Calzones.''

"How about dinner here, instead?" Amanda asked. "That way Ryan can see the sketches, too. And by then, this little one's tooth should be in.''

Suzy clucked in sympathy. "The poor little thing. No wonder you're all exhausted. But we don't want to impose on you for dinner.''

"No imposition," Amanda insisted, firmly shoving her huge workload to the back burner. "We'd love to have you. And I've been dying to try a new scampi recipe. Are you game?''

"For your cooking, always," John replied.

Although tension lingered in the air, much of it had been dissipated with Amanda's dinner invitation. Ryan watched her, his admiration and guilt growing in direct proportion. What he'd told Barry the other day had been true. He was greatly indebted to Amanda. Rewarding her with his lack of trust was more than unfair. But it was reality, and he wasn't a man who believed in anything else.

Chapter Nineteen

Amanda packed the last of the silver away. The tea had been a success. The Spode had been bid on, and a competitive spirit had grasped her most serious collectors. That enthusiasm would up the profit margin for the quarter. Although she now only spent two to three days a week in her shop, each one was rewarding—especially with something like the Spode tea to relish. They had postponed the event longer than Amanda wanted, but her now-complicated life had thrown her quite a few curves.

Karen, despite the blinding stars in her eyes, had organized the event with meticulous care. And Barry had been an invited guest, Amanda had noted, first with surprise, then amusement.

Karen had initially appeared sheepish, then proud of her attentive date. The older women, many widowed, divorced or simply spinsters, were delighted with Karen's romance. At one point, it commanded as much attention as the Spode dinnerware.

It was all rather sweet, Amanda acknowledged. And no one deserved happiness more than her faithful assistant. It still seemed odd that they had both become entangled at the same time, even though Karen would be the only one with a happy ending. She wondered briefly if the Lone Ranger and Tonto had ever had the same dilemma.

Suspecting her giddiness was the product of sleep deprivation, Amanda decided to finish putting away the rest of the silver either the following day when the shop was closed, or early Monday morning. Too many evenings spent fencing with the Meriweathers, followed by nights where she thought of nothing but the man sleeping across the hall, had taken their toll.

Having allowed Karen to leave early with Barry, Amanda hadn't minded closing the shop, but one of the luxuries of being the boss was the right to slough off.

Hearing a jingle at the front of the shop, she realized with a groan that she'd forgotten to lock the door. Sighing, she prepared to face this last customer, planning to slide the bolt closed as soon as the person left.

Forcing a welcoming smile on her face, she left the back room and headed toward the front of the shop. Seeing Ryan leaning casually against a Victorian gramophone cabinet, her smile broadened. "Too late for tea, I'm afraid."

"Small blessings," he responded without malice.

Realizing he looked far too male, far too overpowering to sit in one of the fragile Queen Anne sidechairs, sipping from delicate china, she could only agree. "You're a Philistine, remember?"

"And proud of it. Have you finished for the day?"

"Not really, but I'd decided to leave anyway. Tomorrow *is* another day, and Monday's still another one."

"Good theory."

"I thought so. It's one of the reasons I like being self-employed. It's not hard to talk the boss into time off."

"Good. Then we'll have time to get to the wharf."

"Wharf?"

"I booked a cruise." His smile grazed her. "I told you about it one morning a few weeks ago—but a lot of things have gotten in the way since then."

She furrowed her brow together, trying to sort out the fuzzy mornings. "I thought I dreamed that."

"It's a dream cruise, but we still have to get on the ship."

She narrowed her eyes. "You wouldn't be trying to take advantage of the sleep-impaired, would you?"

"If it works."

She thought of the beautiful bay, the starlit night. "You're exploiting the unconscious, but as the victim, I'm in agreement."

"Victim?"

"Okay. Willing accomplice." She smiled, then widened her eyes. "Wait! We can't go on a cruise—the night air would be terrible for Brianna."

"There are such things as babysitters."

Amanda immediately bristled. "Not just *anybody* can take care of her."

Ryan looked properly concerned. "How about Karen and Barry? Think they're trustworthy?"

Deflated, she couldn't miss his wide grin. "Possibly." Her own grin was fighting to surface. "Good thing I let Karen leave early. But I'll still have to go home and change first."

He held up her weekend bag, a combination garment bag and tote. "Everything's right here."

Her brows lifted. "My, we are prepared."

Ryan handed her the suitcase, then leaned forward to remove the glasses she had absently perched on top of her head.

Seeing them, she blew out an exasperated sigh. "I've been looking for those all day. I'm probably the world's best living example of the phrase "It's a good thing my head's attached.""

"Just part of your charm."

Amanda sucked in a breath at the unexpected compliment. Feeling the winds of emotion shifting, she leaned against a sturdy highboy for support. "Flatterer."

"How's this for flattery? You had better get changed fast or we'll miss the boat."

Brought back to earth with the practical, she clutched the

suitcase closer. "Won't be a minute. Have some coffee while you wait."

Leaving him to grapple with the last cup of coffee in the pot, which she knew must have the consistency of sludge, Amanda dashed into the curtained-off back area that contained two rooms in addition to her office. One was a small bathroom, equipped with a claw-footed bathtub since the shop had once been a home. Some time ago, she had added a showerhead, and had been glad for it numerous times. Always busy, she'd often brought a change of clothes when she had an engagement after work.

Unzipping the suitcase, she lifted out the dress, then stared at it in surprise. This wasn't one of her dresses. The tags still pinned to the material confirmed she wasn't hallucinating from fatigue.

The golden material was soft, almost decadently so. Holding it up to her waist and shoulders, she surveyed the effect in the full-length cheval mirror. While it was skimpier than what she was used to, there was no denying the dress was a knockout.

Hanging the dress on a peg, she curiously investigated the remaining contents of the bag. She lifted out a brief, low-cut, strapless lace bra fashioned to flatter, perhaps incite. A matching wisp of panties followed along with a sheer bit of slip. Thigh-high hose so sheer they barely existed were next, then a tiny evening bag, and finally delicate shoes with heels high enough to flatter the plainest legs.

Oh, the man was smooth.

Still, she couldn't resist stroking the delicate, wickedly feminine things. She'd never had anyone purchase such intimate items for her before. And rather than being annoyed by his presumptuousness, she was curiously warmed by an insistent flame of desire that was licking through her.

She had two choices. Wear the slightly rumpled suit that had seen a day of work. Or...

Not taking time to examine her reasoning, she scooped

up the new lingerie, plucked the dress from the peg and entered the bathroom.

Shedding her tired suit and practical undies, she stepped under the shower, revived by the bracing water. After a liberal application of perfumed lotion, she slipped on the silky, almost fragile lingerie Ryan had purchased for her, feeling sinfully pampered. Applying new makeup from the supply she always kept at the shop, Amanda found herself humming. Then she reached for the dress and put it on.

Even prepared, it still stunned her.

Staring in the mirror, she saw instantly why he'd chosen the dress. Its simplicity was deceptive. The cut emphasized her narrow waist, and the material fell in graceful folds to swirl around her legs. But it was the bodice that drew the eye. The design nearly bared her shoulders and dipped to a provocative vee, but the cleverly tailored wisps of remaining fabric were more enticing than an expanse of bare skin.

And the color. Resembling spun gold, it was as though the dress sent a sunbeam through her already shiny curls, setting them on fire. Always trying to tame her wild hair, she'd never thought to flaunt it. Staring at her reflection, she liked the emphasis. The feeling would probably wear off soon, but for now her hair actually looked like an asset.

Only the shoes were left, and she eased her feet inside, marveling at their perfect fit. Ryan must have gone to a lot of trouble, she realized, to learn all her sizes from underwear to shoes. Smoothing her hands over her hips, she turned from side to side, unable to criticize any of his choices.

Except that the outfit was slinkier and sexier than anything she'd ever owned.

She would never have picked the same outfit, but had to admit that she loved it. Glancing in the mirror, she touched bare earlobes, realizing the silver earrings she'd worn with her suit wouldn't do. It was only a small flaw, but she never went without earrings.

Dabbing on a few drops of her favorite perfume, Amanda picked up the tiny evening purse and took a fortifying breath before leaving the back room.

When she reentered the store, Ryan was strolling down one of the aisles close by. He turned just as she was about to call out to him. The expression on his face reinforced the flow of feminine power that had been building since she'd stepped into the delicately sexy lingerie.

Still, she hesitated. But Ryan didn't, crossing the space between them in seconds.

He reached out and touched one hand to her hair. "You look like a flame."

She smiled, struck by the emotions journeying over his face. "I love the dress."

"And I..." He cleared his throat, then reached in his coat pocket, removing a small box and offering it to her.

Amanda managed not to tremble as she opened the jeweler's box. Inside were delicate gold drop earrings resembling sunbursts. She knew before trying them on that they would be perfect with the dress. But she didn't reach for them. Instead, she looked up at Ryan.

"Why are you doing all this?"

His expression didn't reveal his thoughts. "I have my reasons."

She set her chin at a belligerent angle.

But Ryan spoke before she could. "After Suzy and John left the other night, I thought about how much you're sacrificing so that I can make this deal go through." He inclined his head for a moment, knowing it was true, also knowing he'd been eaten alive with guilt since his confrontation with Barry. Also knowing he couldn't change, not because his friend demanded it. Not even because Amanda may have deserved it. And before they parted, she deserved this one special evening. No strings. Ryan picked up one of her hands. "It's a crucial situation for me, but not for you. It would be easier for you to come clean and walk away. But you haven't. And I don't think I've thanked you.''

She was still skeptical. As much as Amanda was enjoying the unexpected gifts, she was afraid of losing more of her heart. "So this is your way of saying thank you?"

He shrugged. "I could have said it with Hallmark or FTD, but I thought you'd enjoy this more."

Glancing down at the earrings, she realized he was right. The dress, lingerie...it had taken a lot of thought, planning and originality. As Ryan released her hand, she carefully lifted the earrings from the box and put them on. Light from the crystal chandelier glinted on the earrings as Amanda lifted her head for inspection.

Unable to resist, he reached out to touch the earrings. "Your ears should never be bare, Amanda." Ryan kept a grip on his control, but it was a tenuous grip. She looked so damned beautiful—like a column of pure fire. Even though he'd chosen every item with care, picturing her in each one, his imagination hadn't begun to compare with the reality. It would be difficult to remember the "no strings" part of this evening.

"What time do we have to be at the dock?" Amanda asked, interrupting his reverie.

"Soon." He walked with her to a cherrywood hall tree situated near the front of the store, where her black wool wrap hung.

Ryan held out the coat. As she slipped into the soft cashmere, he allowed his hands to linger on her shoulders. Unable to resist, he dropped a gentle kiss on the side of her neck. He felt the sudden tremble, imagined the look on her face as he buried his nose in the soft silk of her hair, inhaling her unique fragrance.

Then he pulled back, making his voice brisk as he took Amanda's arm. "The boat won't wait for us."

The dinner cruise was as exquisite as he'd been promised. White-jacketed waiters anticipated their every need, and the food was excellent. But neither he nor Amanda ate much. They spent most of their time on the dance floor, unable to resist the lure of being in each other's arms.

The sun disappeared, leaving a crimson trail across the sky. As the spectrum of colors changed into ebony, the lights strung across the bay came to life. It was a magical transformation. Sea and sky melded into one, and the lights competed with the stars for prominence.

Amanda's fingers curled trustingly within his hand, and he couldn't prevent an involuntary reaction. A surge of unexpected protectiveness assailed him, and he suddenly wished for the proof he'd asked Barry for.

"The cruise is everything you promised and more," Amanda said softly against his shoulder.

"We just passed Alcatraz," he murmured, his breath near her ear.

"All those prisoners locked away for so many years," she replied in a breathy voice. "It's so sad."

There were all sorts of prisons, Ryan realized. Ones without bars and locks. Emotional prisons were even more difficult than real ones to break out of. Even when the lure to leave was strong.

"The music has stopped," Ryan replied, realizing they were swaying to silence. But he didn't release her; instead, he smoothed his hands over her back, then the curve of her waist.

"I think the band's taking a break," Amanda said, not attempting to move away, either.

"Would you like to walk on the deck?" Ryan asked as their bodies swayed to a nonexistent beat.

"The night air might be nice," she replied, still not stopping the provocative motion, unresolved desire crackling between them. The tension had constantly escalated since the reunion weekend, and now it had built to sense-drugged proportions.

Dragging himself away, Ryan took her hand as they stepped through glass doors to the deck. The evening wasn't particularly cold, and luckily the wind was only a gentle breeze. The bay was susceptible to stiff winds that whipped off the water, but tonight was perfect, as though it had been specially ordered just for them.

"The sky looks big enough to swallow us," Amanda said, gripping the rail and looking upward.

Ryan watched the nervous gesture, wondering what Amanda was feeling, wondering if the romantic evening bothered her.

But it wasn't apprehension he saw in her eyes when she turned toward him. A gentleness at odds with her striking looks lingered in her expression. "This has been a very special evening."

Ryan eased his thumb over her cheek, so smooth and soft. Like her. Even though she looked like a golden goddess, there was so much more to Amanda Thorne. So much more than he had expected. So much he still wanted... needed...to know.

She turned just then to look out over the water. The moonlight washed over her, making Amanda look like an ethereal being, her hair and dress aglow, her face an ivory silhouette.

When she turned again to face him, Ryan thought she was the most beautiful woman he'd ever seen. All fire, no ice.

Danielle was an icy beauty, and he'd known his fair share of other beautiful women, but none had affected him like Amanda. None had thawed his frozen heart.

And, staring at Amanda, he realized that was exactly what she was doing.

Chapter Twenty

They arrived home to MacDougall's wagging tail and a distracted-looking Karen and Barry, who assured them that all was well. The baby-sitting duo appeared anxious to be alone and quickly departed. Intensely aware of their own tension, which still simmered between them, Ryan and Amanda quickly checked on Brianna and found her fast asleep, her lips curved in a contented smile.

Amanda pulled the miniature quilt up a bit, making sure she was completely covered. "She's probably dreaming happy baby dreams," Amanda whispered in the near darkness.

Ryan bent to kiss his daughter's velvety cheek, then took Amanda's hand as they walked into the hall. When he stopped abruptly, she looked at him questioningly.

His voice was quiet, mindful of the sleeping baby. "I didn't tell you the entire truth tonight."

She angled her head in question, and he touched her cheek briefly.

"I did want to thank you for all you've done, but I also wanted us to have a romantic evening." He reached for her hand. "Just the two of us. Without a bargain between us, without an audience to perform for."

Amanda's throat closed as she struggled against the emotions locked there.

Then she reached to touch his face, a face that had grown

so very dear. She longed for his complete trust and knew with sudden clarity that she'd never have it. Whatever had wounded him wasn't easily healed. But in that moment, it didn't matter. Though she knew their time together wouldn't last, she wanted him. All of him. So that she could preserve the memories forever. "And I want a magical interlude," she responded, the catch in her voice barely noticeable.

"I promised myself this was a 'no strings' evening."

"And when we first met, you promised me an interlude."

His eyes showed a light of hope that quickly darkened to passion. "One that lasts until sunrise?"

"You *did* promise a magical night."

In one motion, he picked her up, carrying her soundlessly over the thick rugs that carpeted the wood floor, stopping at the bed and then meeting her eyes. "Are you sure, Amanda?"

Her hands looped around his neck and tightened. "Could you stop talking and kiss me?"

He did, his lips saying for him the words locked inside his chest.

Then he lowered her to the bed, remaining on one knee in front of her. She reached to unfasten her shoes.

Ryan's hand on her arm stopped her. "Let me."

Amanda sat on the edge of the bed as Ryan unlaced the thin straps of her shoes. His hand cupped the arch of her foot, and she found the caress immeasurably provocative.

Then his fingers hooked beneath the band of the thigh-high hose on her right leg. He peeled the stocking off slowly, drawing out the motion, his hand caressing the curve of her calf, then tantalizing her as he drew those same sure fingers down the length of her inner thigh.

Knowing she was trembling, Amanda sat spellbound as Ryan repeated the actions with her left leg. Still fully clad, she was more aroused than if he'd stripped off her dress and lingerie.

His hands were infinitely patient as he reached toward her shoulders, gradually folding her dress down to allow it to slide at her feet. The slow, sensual journey revealed the sheer, undeniably sexy lingerie he'd chosen. He sucked in a deep breath, then leaned forward to kiss the bare flesh just above her bra.

Feeling as though he were worshiping her body, Amanda tilted her head back at the onslaught of sensation.

But Ryan was just beginning.

Her slip came off so slowly that she could feel every silky nuance of the fabric as it slid against her skin. The sheer bit of fluff joined the golden pool her dress formed against the pine-planked floor.

Every nerve in her body quivered as only her bra and panties remained. Ryan's hands stroked the length of her arms and torso, coming tantalizingly close to her breasts and the triangle of flesh her scant panties covered.

It was adoration. It was torture. And Amanda wondered if she could die from the pleasure of it.

She reached out to unbutton Ryan's shirt, but he gently moved her hands aside, concentrating only on her.

His fingers caressed her collarbones, and she felt the flutter of her pulse jump out of control.

Ryan's hands continued to stray toward her breasts until she thought they would burst from the bra on their own. When he finally eased the clasp open, her breasts tumbled free gratefully, begging for his touch.

But he didn't accommodate them. Instead, his fingers danced over her rib cage, around her waist, then up the sides of her torso.

Realizing that he wouldn't touch her breasts until all of her clothing was gone, she longed to rip off her panties, but he stretched out the pleasure, making each moment center on the sensation.

When his fingers skimmed over the lace panties, she bit her lip to keep from crying out; still, a moan echoed low in her throat. Ever so slowly he hooked his fingers in the waistband of the wisp of lace. Instead of removing them, he slid the silken fabric from side to side, further inciting every already-charged nerve.

Ready to beg him to hurry, she issued a moan instead as he slipped the lace and silk over her hips, letting the wisp join the pool of glowing fabric on the floor.

Thinking he would shed his clothes, her senses were assaulted as he began an identical journey over her body with his mouth. He kissed her aching breasts, circling them with his clever tongue.

Trailing nibbling, heat-filled kisses over her flushed skin, Ryan brought every nerve ending in her body to full alert. Electricity thrummed through her body. Disregarding his earlier protest, she pulled open his shirt, wanting the contact of his skin against hers. He cooperated this time, shrugging off the shirt as her hands closed around his belt buckle. Feeling his engorged flesh, she was gratified when he took over, finally shedding the remainder of his clothing.

She wondered that their heated flesh didn't burn each other. Expecting him to take her quickly, boldly, she was surprised when he continued pleasuring her body with his hands and mouth, drawing out each moment, forcing her to dwell on and enjoy each touch.

Moonlight poured in the huge wall of windows, bathing them in silver light. It was magical, it was wondrous, and Amanda felt each caress imprinting itself on her soul.

Every move Ryan made was incredibly tender. Impossibly giving. While she'd expected passion, she hadn't expected the tenderness. It was as though his hands voiced the words he wasn't able to speak. The words she longed to hear. No, this wasn't passion. This was better. This was more.

So much more that he took her breath away. Again and again.

When he finally entered her, she felt the tears slide from beneath her closed eyelids, and knew this was what love felt like. The exquisite moments further fractured her already wounded heart. How could she ever bid this man goodbye…ever walk away from him? Because now she knew with certainty what she'd denied all along.

She loved him.

Each impossibly puzzling aspect of him. And she knew with certainty that her heart and life would never be the same again.

Then she felt the overwhelming rightness as his strokes filled her, buoyed her, and sent her tumbling past reality. Her body bowed with the intensity of her climax and the whipcord struck, sending her helplessly over the edge.

Chapter Twenty-One

Clad only in a brief silk robe, Amanda rooted through the refrigerator, assembling sandwiches, then adding wine goblets to the tray for a rakish touch to their midnight picnic. Too drawn up in the enchantment of the cruise, she'd had no appetite. Now she was ravenous. Sated, impossibly satisfied, she hummed as she selected a bottle of wine and added a corkscrew to the tray. She might be crazy, but despite all the inherent problems in their relationship, after what they'd just shared, she felt hopeful. Hearing the phone ring, she reached for the cordless, saw the light blink on and realized Ryan had answered it.

She continued humming, finding elegant linen napkins to place the sandwiches on. It was a whimsical addition, but she was feeling such a mix of emotions. Whimsy, elegance, abandon and love were racing through her, each holding its own. Always optimistic, she wanted to believe that somehow Ryan would overcome the wounds of his past.

Amanda stilled her busy hands. Ryan must have planned this special evening for some time. Which meant that little by little he'd been abandoning his suspicions, realizing that their bank record mix-up had been just that. Her heart tightened as this realization dawned. Could it mean that he'd finally come to understand what kind of person she was?

That together they were building something special, something lasting?

Euphoria rushed through, leaving a sweet aftertaste. As the emotion filled her, she suddenly longed for a blazing fire to settle in front of, to share with Ryan as the night dwindled into day.

Impulsively deciding to ask him to build the fire, Amanda momentarily abandoned the tray and padded into the hall, but didn't see him in the living room. Smiling, she decided he must still be upstairs. Dancing up the stairs, she saw that the door of the study was ajar.

A giddy, satisfied smile on her face, Amanda reached toward the door. Ryan's voice stopped her. Realizing he was still on the phone, she moved to turn away when she heard her own name.

Curious, she remained in place, ready to tease him with whatever tidbit she overheard.

"Are you sure about the invoices for her shop, Barry? There can't be a mistake?"

Why would he be asking Barry about invoices if they were discussing her? Suddenly chilled, her reckless smile faded. Not now, not after...

Ryan's quiet voice drifted easily through the partially opened doorway. "I know I asked for proof, Barry." He was quiet, listening for a few moments. "Do they match the bills of lading?"

Amanda's heart sank. The bank records apparently weren't forgotten. And now he was investigating her business practices, as well.

There was another silence before Ryan sighed. "And the forged collectibles?"

Amanda didn't wait to hear any more. Fleeing down the hall to the bedroom, she grabbed her jeans and a shirt. Forcing herself not to look at the pool of exquisite lingerie that told its own tale, Amanda dressed rapidly, shutting her mind to anything other than escape. She grabbed her purse, then raced down the stairs, knowing that with Brianna asleep in the nursery, Ryan couldn't follow her.

And knowing that after tonight, there was only one thing left to say. Goodbye.

AMANDA AND KAREN BENT over an oversized crate, cataloguing the latest shipment—something unusual and sought after. Called architecturals, the crate contained columns, statuary, stained glass windows, shutters—all once part of homes from the Victorian era. They had become popular indoor decorating pieces, often displayed as fine art, always used to define the time period of the room. Even though it had been a wonderful find on her last buying trip, Amanda couldn't keep her attention on anything.

"Earth to Amanda," Karen said, waving her hands in front of Amanda's face.

"Sorry. I'm not much help, am I?"

"Actually, you've been great. I know it was cruel not telling you that you were on automatic pilot, but I couldn't bring myself to blow the whistle. You've been hauling all the pieces out of the crate. Tomorrow you're going to have some screaming muscles."

Amanda glanced inside the nearly empty crate. While she easily admitted being forgetful, she wasn't usually this absentminded. She didn't even remember removing the heavy pieces.

Leaning back into a wicker table holding a collection of treens, Amanda heard the fruit-shaped wooden collectibles slide forward in protest. Shifting to one side, Amanda sighed as she realized just how muddled her head was. Though absentminded, she always remembered the placement of her stock and was equally careful with its treatment. It wasn't like her to nearly topple a display. But then nothing about her was normal today. Even coming into the store today hadn't been planned, but for once Ryan would have to cope. Although it tore her heart out not to be there for Brianna, she couldn't face returning to Ryan's home.

Karen scooted her rolling stool closer, her face wreathed in concern. "You okay, Amanda? You've been acting so...preoccupied."

"I guess it shows."

"A little—like stripes on a zebra. I'm worried about you."

Amanda pushed the hair off her forehead. "You've got enough concerns of your own."

"If you mean Barry, I'm obsessed about him. I think I love him. But I'm not concerned."

Amanda stared slowly at her friend. "You're sure it's love...already?"

"I guess sometimes when it hits this hard, you know right away."

"You don't think it could be a sudden flash, something that might fade?"

Karen's smile was secure, knowing. "I realize you think I'm an incurable romantic.... You're probably right about that. But I don't have any doubts about Barry. He's the man I want to spend the rest of my life with."

The seriousness of her words sunk in. In less time than Amanda and Ryan had had together, their friends had formed a commitment. "And Barry feels the same?"

Karen nodded solemnly, but her eyes shone. "Neither of us expected this. Who knows? Maybe that's why it happened—when we were least expecting it."

Could it happen that easily? Amanda's smile was bitter. Only if you both believed in happily ever afters. And only if the man could muster some share of trust.

Karen reached out her hand, covering Amanda's. "Are you worried about you and Ryan? I couldn't help but notice—"

Amanda wasn't ready to share the pain, or the sleepless night she'd spent listening to the phone ring. "We're talking about you, not me. Do I get to be flower girl?"

"Nah. I had you pegged for matron-of-honor."

Trish poked her head into the backroom. "Phone, Amanda."

Both Karen and Trish watched Amanda's reaction, since she'd refused all earlier phone calls.

"It's Suzy," Trish added. "She's called several times— said she'd stop by later if you were too busy to talk on the phone now."

Not wanting to see Suzy, Amanda reluctantly picked up the extension phone. Suzy's voice effervesced through the wires. "Hi! I've been trying to reach you all day. I know we're supposed to see you at seven tonight...."

Amanda's stomach sank, knowing she couldn't face the Meriweathers or Ryan.

"But actually, that's not convenient," Suzy continued.

Relief whooshed through Amanda.

"But we'll be there at eight, instead. I'm sorry to change at the last minute, but John has some more papers for Ryan—says he won't have them ready in time for us to be there at seven."

"But—"

"I know. Men have the darnedest way of messing up plans, don't they?"

Amanda gripped the phone. "Suzy, I should have called you. Tonight won't work for us. I'm sorry to cancel at the last minute."

"Is Brianna all right?" Suzy asked in sudden concern. Then she laughed. "Of course she is. Silly me. If anything was wrong, you'd be there. No problem, Sunshine. We'll make it another time."

The buzzing of a disconnected line echoed in Amanda's ear. *If anything was wrong, you'd be there.* And in all her life, Amanda had never run from the truth. She'd had no intention of seeing Ryan that night. She wasn't certain she could ever face him again. But Suzy's words continued to haunt her. *If anything was wrong, you'd be there.*

Everything was terribly wrong. And that wouldn't change until she faced Ryan.

She also couldn't leave without bidding Brianna good-bye. So many loose ends to tie up—in her haste to escape the previous night, she'd completely forgotten Mackie. However she and Ryan ended this arrangement, she couldn't abandon her dog. MacDougall had always been faithful and loyal—something she couldn't say about Ryan. Suzy in her nonchalant way had been right. Men messed up everything.

STOMACH QUIVERING, her nerves shredded, Amanda quietly closed the front door of Ryan's house, laying her purse on the table in the entryway. From the living room she could hear the deep rumble of Ryan's voice, accompanied by Brianna's intermittent laughter.

Despite everything weighing on her mind, a melancholy smile tugged on her lips at the little girl's happy giggles. Shedding her silk windbreaker, Amanda stopped at the entrance into the living room, taking in the scene in one quick look, knowing no one had noticed her yet.

Brianna squealed as she pulled on MacDougall's ears. Despite the dog's patient, long-suffering look, he wouldn't stand still much longer. Ryan reached out to disengage the small fingers, looking as though he had repeated the action several times.

"Be nice to the dog," Ryan cautioned. "And he'll be your friend."

Responding to her father's words, Brianna patted MacDougall's muzzle clumsily and with a tad too much force.

"Better," Ryan muttered. "Now, let's work on not knocking him over with affection."

Brianna pulled again at Mackie's ears. Spotting Amanda, MacDougall's black button eyes pleaded for rescue. Knowing the dog was near the end of his patience, she walked inside, trying to look casual despite the turmoil assaulting her. She scooped Mackie up and carried him to the couch, ignoring Ryan's thundering look.

"Duh?" Brianna asked, pointing at the dog.

"MacDougall's tired, sweetie." Looking at anything except Ryan, Amanda spotted one of Brianna's favorite books lying between the cushions on the couch. She held the book up so that the baby could see it. "I can read you this."

Brianna bounced up and down on her Pampers-padded bottom.

"I think that means yes," Ryan interpreted tersely. "Are you going to tell me what's going on?"

Amanda deliberately chose an oblique answer, forcing her voice to sound emotionless. "We had a valuable shipment come in that we had to catalog. I had to stay until it was done so I could fax an inventory to the insurance company."

"And you took off in the middle of the night to get a head start?" He glared at her. "And you never heard the phone ringing off the hook?"

Ignoring him, Amanda picked up the child, whose stretched-out arms already reached toward her. "We like this story, don't we, sweetie?"

Brianna gurgled a reply, happily entrenched in Amanda's lap, not noticing her father's continual glare.

The sudden peal of the doorbell startled them all. MacDougall jumped down from the couch to challenge the visitor while Brianna tugged at the book, wanting Amanda to continue.

"I'll get it." Annoyed by the interruption, Ryan strode to the door, prepared to get rid of whoever was there. But once the door opened, he stood in silence.

"Hello, Ryan. Aren't you going to ask me in?" Danielle's sultry voice carried through the hallway.

Amanda stiffened as a chill penetrated. Instinctively, she clutched Brianna closer.

The door closed, and the tapping of high heels echoed on the marbled tile. Danielle's brows lifted slightly as she took in Amanda's appearance, from her possessive hold on Brianna to the expensively tailored business suit. But she dismissed both Amanda and Brianna, turning instead to Ryan. "I assume you've been working on our...arrangement."

Tightlipped, Ryan nodded. "Yes."

The cultured tone of Danielle's voice didn't change. "There's been a change in the timetable."

A dangerous edge of anger vibrated in Ryan's words. "What kind of change?"

"I want the money now—all of it. And if I don't get it, I'm afraid I'll have to take Brianna back."

Amanda leapt from the couch, holding Brianna defensively, no longer a silent observer. "You have no right to Brianna!" The heat of battle flushed her cheeks. "What kind of mother are you? Selling your own child!"

Danielle remained unperturbed, if anything a trace of deadly amusement flickered across her perfect features. "I fail to see where this concerns you." Dismissively, she started to turn away.

"It concerns me, all right," Amanda retorted, refusing to accept Danielle's dismissal this time. She had transformed into a magnificent mother bear, protecting her cub. "We're a family. Brianna, Ryan and I. And *you* don't have any claim on *our* child!"

"My, my, Ryan. Your little friend is quite a hellcat."

"Get out," he growled from between clenched teeth, scarcely containing his fury.

"We have terms to discuss, Ryan."

"You'll get your money, Danielle. All of it. Now, get out."

Danielle's gaze moved between Ryan's explosive anger and Amanda's thundering glare. But she wasn't intimidated. Instead, a curtain of steel entered her eyes and tightened lips. "Make no mistake, Ryan. You have forty-eight hours. If I don't get my money, I take Brianna. The courts won't waste any time granting final custody to a thoughtful, sensitive mother like me. I believe those are the qualities that attracted you to me initially." A cold smile curled her lips. "And the courts won't feel it's in Brianna's interest to be raised by a workaholic father who's never home. Not to mention that you come from a broken home yourself—hardly role model material."

Ryan looked as though he was one step away from strangling her. "I paid what you wanted, Danielle."

"At the time. But I'm not signing final papers until I have what I want. And of course, you can't prove we ever had the first agreement, since I haven't signed anything. You know how messy it would look in the courts." Her glance roved back toward Amanda. "It would be a pity if you couldn't come up with the money. I'm sure Brianna will miss her father and her...*nanny.*"

In a swirl of overpoweringly expensive perfume, Danielle turned back toward the entryway, leisurely exiting, leaving a trail of malice behind as well.

"She can't do that!" Amanda spluttered. But fear suffused the words as she looked anxiously at Ryan. "Can she?"

Ryan pushed one hand through already disheveled hair. "She didn't sign the final custody papers."

"Why not?"

"I thought she'd gotten what she wanted. The only thing she ever wanted from me was money. She'd hoped to get it by simply marrying me. When I wouldn't go along with that, she got pregnant and then held Brianna as ransom. I liquidated every cash asset I owned to pay her off in exchange for Brianna. I never expected to see Danielle again."

"Then why..."

"I underestimated her again. She knows how much I'm worth and she wants it all. I'd already begun putting together this deal and knew it was the only way I could come up with the new amount of money she was insisting on."

"Which is why it was so highly leveraged."

"Exactly. Only I didn't expect her to change her mind and demand the money *now.*"

"Is the deal ready to close?" Amanda asked, not relinquishing her hold on Brianna.

"No."

The word echoed between them.

"Then—"

"I'll sell my business," Ryan interrupted. "I've had plenty of offers. I won't get as much as I could in lengthy negotiations, but there's not time for that."

"You won't get anywhere near what it's worth, will you? Not with everything so leveraged."

Ryan's expression tightened. "Not even in the ballpark. But all I'm worried about is getting enough to satisfy Danielle so that she'll sign the papers. I won't let her take Brianna."

Amanda glanced down at the sweet child, tears already forming in her eyes, the words barely able to pass over the huge lump in her throat. "Oh, Ryan. We can't lose her."

Seeing her tears, Ryan reached out to them both, comforting her, taking comfort in her.

"I THINK SHE'S ASLEEP," Ryan murmured in a quiet voice. He and Amanda stood next to Brianna's crib, the glow of the night-light relieving the darkness. They had kept her up far too long, neither wishing to release a protective hold on the baby.

Amanda rewound the cuddly lamb crib toy that softly played lullabies. Placing it close enough that Brianna could hear the soothing tunes, Amanda whispered, "I know. I just keep thinking how vulnerable she is. How innocent. How I don't want that to change."

He watched as she patted Brianna's back one last time before straightening up. He bent to kiss his daughter, then took Amanda's hand. Reluctantly they left the nursery, fearing to let the baby out of their sight, even while knowing that Danielle wouldn't swoop in and steal Brianna. She was too smart for that. She would let the court do her work.

Amanda walked closely beside him down the hall, pillowing her head against his shoulder. Despite the tough core of strength he knew she possessed, now she was all softness, her own vulnerability exposed.

"It's late," she commented needlessly.

"I know."

He hesitated at the doorway of the bedroom, gently kissing her cheek before he turned. Amanda caught his hands before he could complete the movement. "I don't want to be alone."

Neither did he, but he could no longer take advantage of this woman of so many secrets. Secrets he wished he'd never tried to unravel. Because now, regardless of what Barry uncovered, Ryan no longer cared what she kept hidden. A woman with a heart large enough to encompass his child with such concern deserved better. Far better than he could offer. He thought again of how she'd fled the previous evening—how whatever had caused it still stood between them. "It's been an emotional evening."

Amanda clamped down on her lower lip, worry engulfing her. "I know you don't want to leave Brianna alone...but could you stay...for just a while?"

He couldn't refuse her now. Stepping inside the bedroom, he watched as she shook her head, her wild hair swaying with the movement, its fiery highlights picking up the glow from the bedside lamp, glinting like polished gold beneath a candle flame. Every precious moment they'd shared reached up to taunt him. He could remember every curve of her body, every nuance of emotion.

She moved forward, her body only inches from his. Unable to resist, Ryan traced the curve of her shoulders as he drew his hands forward, resting his fingers on the fragile collarbones, feeling their delicacy. His thumb eased over the hollow of her throat, and he felt her pulse jump.

Her eyes as he met them were clear, untainted by whatever had come between them. "I need you, Ryan. To hold me...to take me where we've been before."

Ryan knew that their emotions were skittering out of

control, intensified by Danielle's words. Still, he reached out—intending only to comfort.

But Amanda's kiss was soul shattering—an incredible combination of tenderness, compassion and undeniable hunger. All three pulled at him, drugged his already overstrung senses. Cupping the back of her head, he sank his fingers into the silky curls, wishing he could erase everything that stood between them. Foolishly wishing his past wasn't a permanent barrier.

But Amanda was tearing down the barriers, her fingers impossibly tender, endlessly giving as she wove them over his skin, rekindling the desire, then making it flame.

He wanted to be gentle and patient, but suddenly he needed all of her, to pretend even for a moment that she was his forever, that there were in fact happily ever afters.

The silk blouse and tailored skirt that she wore stood as impediments. As though she read his mind, Amanda pulled her shirt off, then reached forward to tug at his.

Ryan lowered her to the mattress, reveling in the feel of her naked skin against his. Skin that tasted of wild honey and summer rain. He ran his hands endlessly over her taut, porcelain body, over her sloping abdomen, the valley of her waist, up the tender skin of her inner thighs, each touch making him crave more.

As each touch entrenched a permanent place in his memory, her skin stroked his. Heated silk and satin inflamed him. Burying his fingers in the wealth of her soft hair, he let the strands caress his face as he sought her lips, relishing their eager response. He pulled back for a moment, studying her face, memorizing each feature. "Oh, Mandy."

Amanda heard the tenderness in the nickname and her throat thickened. She longed to voice her love for him, to shout it to the world, to offer him hope and a certain future. What had begun as an attempt to comfort him, now blazed far beyond solace. Then his lips covered hers again. She tasted need, desire and desperation. And understood them all.

Then his mouth lowered to suckle her breast. Arching off the bed, her body bowed in response. As she felt her bones turn liquid, her blood thrum restlessly, Amanda gripped his shoulders, praying he would never stop, knowing she would perish from pleasure if he didn't. His fingers sang promises over her body, promises she wanted to cherish. Promises she knew he could never voice.

Greedily, her hands roamed over his skin, its texture like velvet rippling beneath her fingers. Corded muscles bunched beneath the surface, his lean strength dangerously apparent. But it wasn't fear she felt. Instead, she hungered for each touch, each movement.

Using his mouth, he trailed kisses over her abdomen, up the line of skin between her breasts, to the fragile hollows of her throat. A telltale, betraying pulse fluttered, and he nibbled gently on the soft flesh beneath her chin, then her lips.

Amanda's fingers left a trail of fire as she touched him, nearly destroying his control. Drawing back, he gazed at her unadorned length and bit back a torrent of words. Words he knew he couldn't say. Then his mouth captured hers as his fingers sought her sensitive flesh, met her slick heat.

Amanda felt that whipcord of desire snaking through her, threatening to seize all feeling. She had been right that first time back in Stanton. What flowed between them *was* magic. Only magic could be releasing such a flood of feeling.

His hands skimmed over her, leaving a riot of sensation where he touched, a need for more when he stopped. She felt his hands beneath her hips, the pulsing heat and fullness as he poised to fill her. Then the certainty of their unity as he took them even further.

Moonbeams pushed past the lace curtains, bathing them in silver light. Amanda buried her cries in Ryan's shoulder as she clung to him fiercely, not wanting the moment to end, not wanting her time with him to ever end. And knowing it must.

Chapter Twenty-Two

As the door closed behind Ryan, Amanda raced upstairs and quickly changed her clothes, trading her jeans and T-shirt for a silk suit. No morning fog affected her today, for she'd not fallen into even an exhausted sleep the previous evening. Instead she'd lain awake, drawing comfort from Ryan's embrace, feeling foolish for not guessing Danielle's full intentions.

And plotting.

Now she wanted to spend as much time as possible with Brianna. Although that time was bittersweet, Amanda refused to sacrifice one minute. The nursery was bathed in bright sunshine, highlighting Brianna's silky hair as she bent over the oversized foam blocks in her playpen, chattering in her baby talk.

"Hey, sweetie."

Brianna lifted her head to chortle, her face creasing into a huge smile. "Man!"

Amanda swallowed the lump in her throat. Knowing the baby was trying to say her name, Amanda reached into the playpen, lifting Brianna into her arms. "You're the smartest girl, you know that?"

Brianna curled tiny fingers around Amanda's hair, but she didn't pull.

"See, you already learned not to pull my hair. I'm not

sure that'll matter much longer, unless Daddy's hair gets even longer.''

"Daddy," Brianna responded happily.

Amanda thought of all the time she'd spent coaching her, wanting to surprise Ryan as his daughter called him Daddy for the first time. It seemed difficult to believe that she wouldn't see Brianna again, that she would no longer be part of her life.

After changing Brianna's diaper, Amanda strolled with her to the wide bank of windows and they watched the city scurry by.

Reluctant to put her down, Amanda turned from the window. "How 'bout we rock for a while? I know it's not time yet for your nap, but I think we could cheat just this once."

Amanda settled them into the rocking chair, at first playing patty cake, peekaboo, itsy-bitsy spider, and every other baby game she could think of. Then, as Brianna's eyelids finally started to droop, Amanda sang quiet lullabies. She continued long after the child had fallen asleep.

Realizing that she had to leave soon, Amanda reluctantly settled Brianna in her crib. She reached for the crib toy. Bringing the stuffed lamb close, Amanda stroked the cuddly toy, remembering how she'd enjoyed buying little things for Brianna. She buried her face against the soft fleece and made one more wish. That she, Ryan and Brianna could be a real family. A forever family.

Nothing dropped from the shelves this time. No books, not even a speck of dust seemed to stir. It was foolishness, she knew. But if hope could make wishes come true, she knew she had hoped enough. Perhaps she'd simply run out of wishes.

Determinedly, she wound up the toy lamb so that it could play soft lullabies, knowing if she lingered much longer she would be in tears.

The doorbell rang and Amanda ran down the stairs, not wanting to waste a moment. Throwing open the door she pulled her friend inside before she had a chance to step into the hallway.

Karen took off her raincoat, then laid her purse on the entry table. "Reporting for duty, sir."

"Thanks for doing this, Karen. I know it's not part of your job and—"

"But it's part of being a friend," Karen gently reprimanded her, taking hold of Amanda's hands and giving them a gentle shake. "I just wish it was more. I wish I had millions to give you."

"At least you're not wasting your wishes," Amanda replied, her throat tight, touched by her friend's concern. "Right now, I'm just glad you're here. You know where everything is from the other time you sat with her. And I'll just be a phone call away." Amanda glanced at her watch. "I'd stay and drown you with instructions, but I don't have time."

Karen reached out to hug her. "Everything will work out—I know it will."

"Keep that good thought. I'm going to need every one I can find."

TEN HOURS LATER, Amanda sat amid the disarray of scattered papers and frantic faxes in her now disheveled office, exhausted but equally elated. She only hoped that Ryan would share her elation. She knew what an immensely proud man he was. He wouldn't like the thought of her tinkering with her business, but this was an emergency.

He was due to arrive any moment, and she absently sipped a cup of stone-cold coffee. It had to work. It just had to. Hearing the tinkle of the bell at the front of the shop, Amanda gathered her papers and stood just as Ryan entered her office.

Tension had taken its toll on him, evident in his scowl. "You shouldn't leave the front door unlocked. It's not safe."

"You couldn't have gotten in otherwise," she pointed out gently, mindful of the worry which consumed him. "But that's not important now."

Ryan met her gaze, his fatigue nearly overwhelming. He

had yet to finalize a sale of his business. Although prospective buyers were still interested, none were thrilled with the extensive leverage, the uncertainty of his current project without him at the helm. But he couldn't refuse Amanda's entreaty to meet her at the shop, knowing her concern for Brianna matched his. "You're right. And I only have a few minutes to spare. I still have a lot of figures to run, calls to make to international prospects."

"That might not be necessary."

Hearing the thread of excitement in her voice, Ryan gazed at her cautiously. "What do you mean?"

"I've spent the last ten hours selling the best of the best." She handed him several bills of sale for extremely valuable European pieces. Combined, they rivaled the value of nearly all the remaining inventory.

Ryan's gut tightened as he recognized most of the items from invoices Barry had collected. As much as he needed the money, he couldn't accept her illegal proceeds. Reluctantly, he met her eyes. "I can't take this money from...your...sales."

Amanda scarcely waited for him to refuse, almost as though she'd known he would. "This money is for Brianna." Her face was earnest, her voice persuasive as she continued. "It's not a matter of pride, Ryan. We simply can't lose her. We need this *now*. Not after it's too late. Sure, I could have made more money on the barter system, but that's not important—keeping Brianna is."

Ryan lifted his gaze from the papers in his hand. "Barter system?"

"It's kind of complicated, but basically since I specialize in American collectibles, when I find fine European pieces I register them with the exchange system. Then international dealers catalog them, and when they have American pieces of equal or near value..." She glanced up. "This is where it gets complicated. Sometimes you're trading one item for two or three, or vice versa. Sometimes if there's an impatient customer on the other end, you're sending a zero-value invoice, knowing you'll get one in return, along with an item of equal value when the dealer has one. But, in any event, we exchange items. Sometimes cash is involved, too, but not always. It saves a lot of taxes and charges. But of course the main reason for the exchange is that we can each sell the merchandise that we specialize in for far more than our counterparts.''

A light was slowly dawning. "How did you meet these dealers?"

She shrugged. "At the international trade shows. I work with some dealers more than others because their quality of merchandise is more dependable.''

Ryan thought of all the suspicious-looking transactions, ones that didn't tally, ones that couldn't be explained. Suddenly they all made sense.

Amanda pointed at the papers he still held. "Even though I don't generally sell my own European pieces, I have contacts with enough dealers who do. After they heard that it was a life-or-death emergency, I had full cooperation. And I put the squeeze on a few on my regulars—people who can well afford to collect the pieces—especially since I offered to take them back in the next six months if they decide they've been talked into something they don't really want. I figure by then, my cash flow will be able to stand it.''

Ryan looked again at the bills of sale, quickly tallying them in his mind, finally realizing how much they totaled. "There's a fortune here—and not a small one.''

She met his eyes, a wealth of compassion shining in her own. "Chump change in comparison to what you get to keep in exchange. That little girl's the one who's worth a fortune.''

Ryan felt his throat work as he dropped the papers on Amanda's desk and took her hands. "And so, Amanda, are you.''

Chapter Twenty-Three

Ryan watched with relief as Danielle reluctantly signed the final custody papers, the knot in his stomach not yet unwinding. Beside him, Amanda clenched his arm tightly, equally on edge. It had taken two days to complete the negotiations and the complicated set of documents his attorney insisted on preparing. They were precariously close to the forty-eight-hour deadline.

Danielle's perfectly manicured fingers accepted the check in exchange for the signed documents. She cooly verified the figure before dropping the check casually into her purse, apparently unconcerned about the lives she'd been willing to destroy to get what she wanted.

Danielle flicked back her perfectly groomed hair, making sure not one strand went astray. Then she took her time lighting a cigarette. "I suppose this concludes our business...for now."

Allen Sims, corporate attorney and brilliant legal strategist, chuckled. "Forever, Danielle. Paragraph four, subsection six—states that this is an irrevocable agreement. All of your rights to Brianna have been permanently signed away. In all effects, you're no longer her mother."

Danielle didn't flinch. "Ah, Mr. Sims, you take all the fun out of the posturing."

This time he didn't smile. "Perhaps. But I also concentrate on removing the cruelty and malice."

Danielle gathered her purse along with her dignity. "I believe this concludes our business." She glanced at Ryan. "Unless of course I choose to not cash the check."

Allen Sims's smile returned. "Paragraph seventeen, subsection five. This document is to remain in force, regardless of any monetary exchange, past, present or future."

Danielle's face started to tighten before she consciously relaxed each pampered muscle. Still remaining aloof, she turned toward the door.

Allen Sims drew out his words, a final parting shot. "So, if I were you, I'd beat it to the bank before Mr. West decides to cancel the check."

Refusing to answer, she pulled the door open and glided through. Only the overly loud noise of the door shutting revealed her anger.

"She's a cool one," the attorney commented. "Any bets on how fast she'll make it to the bank?"

Ryan, overcome with relief that it was finally over, draped his arm around Amanda's shoulders. "It's not worth betting over."

"Agreed." Allen's gaze moved between Ryan and Amanda. Wisely, he picked up his briefcase and diplomatically retreated to the outer office, closing the door behind him.

Ryan picked up Amanda's hand, meeting her gaze with a troubled one of his own. "I owe all of this to you."

"You'd have done it on your own. Selling the collection just speeded things up. Nothing would have stood between you and keeping Brianna."

Ryan absently caressed each knuckle, hesitating over her ring finger. "I don't deserve your help. You didn't even think twice about sacrificing your profits to save Brianna, giving up your own security." He hesitated, the pain creeping into his voice. "I have so much to make up to you. If you knew what I've thought...what I've done to—"

Amanda put her fingers to his lips, silencing him. "I don't want to hear. I don't want to know. It's in the past—where it belongs."

"I don't deserve you, Amanda."

She smiled shakily. "That depends. On how well you take care of...Brianna."

"She's not the only one I want to take care of, or the only one I want to make happy. I want to spend the rest of my life with you, Amanda."

"Sounds like you're signing on for a lengthy sentence," she managed to say shakily, afraid to hope, afraid not to.

Ryan drew Amanda close to him, his eyes filled with the love he had yet to voice. "That's one life sentence I'll never regret."

"There's no parole," Amanda warned him.

"How'd I get so lucky?" he asked gruffly, emotion crowding his voice.

Amanda gently ran her fingers over the angles of his dangerous-looking face. "It was predestined. I just didn't know I'd have to blackmail the man of my dreams into posing as my husband."

Ryan smiled, knowing she would always keep him smiling. "I guess we'll have to invite Allen to the wedding since we're in his office."

"He's a smart man," Amanda murmured. "Now we never have to worry about losing Brianna."

"I make a habit of choosing only the best people."

A smile flirted with the corners of Amanda's mouth, and her eyes danced. "I'm not sure I always do. My plan was to marry a quiet, gentle, patient man. Someone dependable, who I could totter into old age with, a companion."

"Sounds like MacDougall."

Amanda's fingers curled into the long hair at Ryan's neck. "Instead, I met this fierce, rugged man who lives on the edge of excitement."

Ryan's eyes darkened, his throat working, ready to give her up if it meant making her happy. "Regrets?"

"I also discovered that this man has a pure heart, and that he treats his daughter with gentle kindness, infinite patience."

Ryan's lip curved upward in relief. "I do sound like a great catch."

"That's what everyone at the reunion thought." She leaned forward to kiss him. Then, inches from his face, she stopped abruptly. "The reunion! They all think we're already married. What will they think when they get their invitations?"

Amanda spotted a definite twinkle in Ryan's eyes. "I'm sure you'll think of something. After all, you conjured up a husband once."

"No," she said softly. "That was a wish." A very special wish.

Humor now danced in his eyes. "Maybe you can wish for an explanation."

She shook her head. "Only the foolish waste their wishes."

"I'll have to remember that."

But she wasn't listening. Instead, her eyes held a new, excited gleam. "They all thought our elopement was so romantic...yes, with a little careful wording on the invitations...it'll work!" She grinned. "We'll tell them we're renewing our vows."

His expression softened. "In a way we are." He reached into his pocket removing a small jeweler's case.

With trembling hands, she opened the lid. Two perfect emerald earrings winked back at her. Reverently, she reached out to touch them, then glanced up at Ryan questioningly.

"So your ears will never be bare."

"Oh, Ryan," she breathed, remembering the exquisite evening of the cruise when he'd presented the first pair of earrings, the love that even then they'd shared, though neither dared express it.

"They're supposed to match your eyes." He angled his head critically. "But they'll never compare to the jewels nature gave you."

Amanda's lips trembled with the overflow of feeling.

He pointed gently to the jeweler's box. "There's something else in there."

Amanda shook away the mist of threatening tears and reached inside. Beneath the first layer of velvet she found a small, delicate chain. Suspended from the chain was a miniature pendant version of her emeralds.

Ryan met her questioning eyes. "Matching jewels for a mother...and her daughter."

Amanda stifled a cry.

Ryan eased his thumb over her lips. "Brianna's as much yours as mine." His eyes captured Amanda's. "I don't know how to tell you that I trust you...to tell you that I'd already decided to ask you to stay, before I knew the truth." He withdrew a single folded paper and handed it to her.

Shakily, Amanda unfolded it, her gaze skimming the contents—words that gave her custody of Brianna should anything happen to him. Her clouding eyes cleared as she read the date—the day after they'd made love the first time. The day she'd run away, before she'd joined in the fight for Brianna. Her eyes filled, realizing this was Ryan's ultimate gesture of trust. And one not born of gratitude.

Ryan gently brushed the tears from Amanda's eyes. "Brianna's one lucky little girl. Not everyone gets the chance to choose a mother like you—and she did that the minute she saw you." His fingers moved to caress her cheek. "And not every man gets a chance to marry a woman as incredible as you."

Closing her eyes, Amanda used her final wish. She wished they would remain as happy as they were now forever.

Ryan's words seemed to echo that wish. "I love you, Mandy."

Thanking the fates for her instant groom, her instant family and the joy they shared, she brought her lips to his, whispering her love for him.

And silently thanking the fates for not wasting those most valuable wishes.

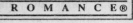

and

HARLEQUIN®

I N T R I G U E®

Double Dare ya!

Identical twin authors Patricia Ryan and
Pamela Burford bring you a dynamic duo of
books that just happen to feature identical twins.

Meet Emma, the shy one, and her diva double,
Zara. Be prepared for twice the pleasure and
twice the excitement as they give two
unsuspecting men trouble times two!

In April, the scorching **Harlequin Temptation** novel
#631 **Twice the Spice** by Patricia Ryan

In May, the suspenseful **Harlequin Intrigue** novel
#420 **Twice Burned** by Pamela Burford

Pick up both—if you dare....

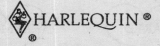